PRAISE FOR

THANKS A LOT, UNIVERSE

"*Thanks a Lot, Universe* demonstrates how you don't always know what your peers are going through, and how powerful kindness is. This honest portrayal of family trauma, changing friendships, and big emotions tugged at my heartstrings. Brian and Ezra will stick with me for a long time!"

—JANAE MARKS, author of *From the Desk of Zoe Washington*

"I loved this book. It's raw and heartfelt, and debut author Chad Lucas has a gift for detail: the way a shirt scrunches up beneath the arms, the dialogue that would fit right in any middle school hallway, the really poignant descriptions of anxiety and panic attacks . . . there is a distinctive honesty to the writing . . . This book is going to do a lot of good."

—WESLEY KING, Edgar Award winning author of *OCDaniel*

"A glorious ode to the beauty of pre-teen friendship and the beginnings of blurred lines and vital questions of identity. By far my favorite middle grade novel of 2021!"

—NIC STONE, *New York Times* bestselling author of *Clean Getaway*

☆ "Featuring snappy dialogue from earnest tween voices, skillful prose guides this engrossing story from start to finish. The themes and social commentary found here are gentle and organic—never heavy-handed—and the plot's antagonists are far from two dimensional, expertly reflecting real-life human complexity for a middle-grade audience . . . Tenderhearted and bold."

—*KIRKUS REVIEWS*, starred review

☆ "Lucas's prose is funny and deeply empathetic, respecting readers' ability to handle heavy topics but lightened with frequent laugh-out-loud moments . . . The book's hope and positivity are infectious."

—*SCHOOL LIBRARY JOURNAL*, starred review

☆☆☆ **A Junior Library Guild Selection** ☆☆☆

THANKS A LOT, UNIVERSE

CHAD LUCAS

AMULET BOOKS • NEW YORK

Library of Congress Control Number for the hardcover edition: 2021932549

Paperback ISBN 978-1-4197-5103-5

Text © 2021 Chad Lucas
Title page illustration © 2021 Nick Blanchard
Book design by Marcie Lawrence

Published in paperback in 2022 by Amulet Books, an imprint of ABRAMS.
Originally published in hardcover by Amulet Books in 2021. All rights reserved.
No portion of this book may be reproduced, stored in a retrieval system, or transmitted in any form or by any means, mechanical, electronic, photocopying, recording, or otherwise, without written permission from the publisher.

Printed and bound in U.S.A.
10 9 8 7 6 5 4 3 2 1

Amulet Books are available at special discounts when purchased in quantity for premiums and promotions as well as fundraising or educational use. Special editions can also be created to specification. For details, contact specialsales@abramsbooks.com or the address below.

Amulet Books® is a registered trademark of Harry N. Abrams, Inc.

ABRAMS The Art of Books
195 Broadway, New York, NY 10007
abramsbooks.com

For Team Lucas
And for Super Awkward Weirdos everywhere

1. SUPER AWKWARD WEIRDO SYNDROME

BRIAN

Shoot. Don't overthink. Just shoot.

The command flashed in my brain as I caught the pass. I was coiled and ready with a clean view of the hoop. Still, I hesitated a half second too long. By the time I let fly, Ezra Komizarek was running toward me with hands outstretched, and I launched the ball too high. The shot fell short, grazing the rim just enough to spare me the humiliation of an air ball.

No big deal. Everybody misses sometimes.

I didn't shoot again all game.

My miss still haunted me as the bell rang.

Everyone drifted into school in groups except me. I walked two steps behind Ezra and Ty, listening to them joke around and quote movies they'd watched over the weekend at Ezra's birthday sleepover. I tried to figure out how to join in without triggering a social catastrophe.

Brian versus Brian, Round 4,222
Me: I could say, "Hey, your birthday was last weekend?
Mine's tomorrow." That's an easy conversation starter,
right?
Also Me: Are you kidding? That's a guaranteed train wreck.
Me: . . .
Also Me: Think about it. They'll ask what you're doing
for your birthday. You'll mumble, "Not much," reminding
everyone you're a friendless loser.

So I stayed quiet. As usual.

As we filed inside, Ty slowed to fist-bump another kid
and Ezra noticed me trailing behind them.

"Hey, Brian. Good game, huh?"

I froze.

I was still flushed from playing basketball, which
helped disguise the instant layer of fresh sweat covering my
face as my brain raced for a reply.

Yeah, good game.

You played good defense.

Can't believe I missed that shot.

None of that came out of my mouth, though.

"Uh . . . fine?" I squeaked.

Fine? That didn't even make sense. Ezra tilted his head,
and everyone in earshot paused to bask in my awkwardness.

"See you later," I blurted, and veered toward the
bathroom. I didn't have to pee; I just needed an excuse to
change direction.

I splashed water on my face to cool down before French class. As I dried off, Victor MacLennan walked in. *Perfect.*

He smirked. "What's the matter, Ghost? Having a lunchtime cry?"

I hurried out without answering. Just another great lunch hour at Halifax North Junior High.

After school, Dad was waiting in the driveway in shorts and his ratty sleeveless Los Angeles Lakers T-shirt. He threw me a one-handed pass. I caught the basketball as I walked toward him.

"Hey, B-Man," he said. "Go change. Let's shoot hoops before dinner."

"Can I get a snack first?" I said.

Dad tossed me the banana in his other hand. I tucked the ball under my arm and snagged the banana before it hit the pavement.

Dad grinned. "Nice catch. Now, hurry up."

I ditched my backpack inside, called a quick "Hi" to Mom, then headed out with Dad, scarfing down the banana as I walked. A couple of kids were kicking a soccer ball on the field, but the basketball court was empty when we arrived at the park.

Shooting around with Dad was fun when we just played, but sometimes he liked to sneak in a father-son talk. I had a suspicion it was one of those days.

"So, the big thirteen tomorrow," Dad said all casually as we warmed up.

I hoisted a shot that banked off the backboard and dropped through the net. "Yeah."

"Nice shot." Dad tossed the ball back. "Want to have anyone over for your birthday dinner?"

My shoulders tensed, and my next shot bounced off the rim. "Not really."

Dad dribbled out and swished a jump shot. "You talk to Ezra much these days?"

Sure, one awkward word at a time. "Sometimes."

He collected the ball and tossed up a fadeaway. "I know social stuff stresses you out, B-Man. But you should make it a goal to hang out with Ezra at least once before the end of the year. He's not a werewolf. He won't bite if you talk to him. Just try."

Dad grinned. He was trying to be funny, and it didn't help.

I knew he was probably right. Ezra and I were both benchwarmers on the basketball team in the winter, and Ezra always joked around with me, even if I didn't say much back. He was one of the only kids who talked to me. Most didn't bother once they realized I was so quiet.

The thing was, I did try. Sometimes I spent all morning psyching myself up, rehearsing three simple sentences: *Hey, Ezra. You busy after school? Want to play ball?* But when I found him in the hall, he was always with his friends, so I'd bail. Every time.

My problem was social anxiety. I secretly called it Super Awkward Weirdo Syndrome, or SAWS for short. In crowds I got sweaty, my mind raced out of control, and the Brian Day who'd earned a 97 in English Language Arts last semester regressed into a tongue-tied caveman.

Me fine.

Mom told me social anxiety was common and nothing to be ashamed of, but that didn't make junior high easier. It didn't make talks with Dad easier either.

"Maybe," I said.

"Just put yourself out there, B-Man. You have to take chances sometimes." Dad bounced me the ball. "Ready to play Twenty-one?"

When we came home after Dad beat me 21–16, the kitchen smelled like tacos. They were cauliflower tacos, since Mom was on an eat-less-meat kick, but they'd probably still taste good.

"Mmm," Dad said. "Smells great." He walked up behind Mom as she washed dishes and wrapped his arms around her. She squirmed away, laughing.

"Yuck. You're so sweaty." She glanced at me. "You worked the old man hard today, huh Brian?"

"*Old man?* Please." Dad flexed his biceps. "Brian gets better every week, though. Once he has a growth spurt, I'm doomed." He peeled off his sweaty shirt. "Going to grab a quick shower. I have to go out tonight."

Mom's smile disappeared. "Tonight? Everett, you know tomorrow is—"

"Of course I know. Wouldn't miss it." Dad tossed

his shirt at me. I sidestepped, and it landed on the garbage bin.

"If you leave that there, I'm finally throwing it out," Mom hollered after him. Dad whistled as he disappeared into the bathroom. Mom rolled her eyes.

"Tell Richie dinner's almost ready," she said to me. She made an exaggerated stink face as I passed. "You should wash up too. You're starting to smell like a teenager."

I pulled off my T-shirt and lobbed it at her. With a squeal, she threw the dishcloth and nailed me square in the chest, splashing soapy water all the way into my shorts. We both laughed, and Mom gasped when I grabbed the cloth and made like I was going to scrub my armpit with it.

"Don't you dare!" She yanked the cloth away, then she brushed a soap bubble from my belly. "We'll order your favorites from the Hungry Chili tomorrow. And ice-cream cake for dessert. Anything else you want?"

Mom wasn't asking the same question Dad asked at the park. She understood my SAWS, and she didn't push me like Dad did. Still, I wished I could tell her: *Order extra food. I'm inviting Ezra over for my birthday.*

Like that would ever happen.

I shrugged. "Not really. Thanks, Mom."

She squeezed my shoulder. "I bet thirteen's going to be great. The universe owes you a good year."

I hoped Mom was right.

2. THE JUICY FOUR

EZRA

Here's a tip for making it through junior high: Find a group of friends who will randomly text you ridiculous things. Colby Newcombe, Kevan Sidhu, Ty Marsman, and I had a group chat that cracked me up at least once a day. We called it "the Juice." One day, Ty started a text with **what's the juice, lads?** and the name stuck.

On Tuesday night, Kevan got things rolling.

Kevan: I've been thinking
Ty: Always dangerous bruh
Kevan: If you could have a pointless superpower, what would it be?
Like it can't help anyone and can only make your life a tiny bit better.
You can't use it to get rich or powerful
Ty: Hmm . . . I want invincible toes so it doesn't hurt when I stub them
Me: Do you forget how to walk sometimes haha

Ty: It's not my fault! My feet grew three sizes this year!

Kevan: True, they're enormous

Me: My power would be an invincible mouth so I could eat infinite sour candy and never cut my tongue

Ty: If you ate infinite sour candy you'd go into a sugar coma

Me: Then I also want an invincible pancreas

Kevan: Invincible pancreas sounds extremely metal

Me: Adding it to my list of potential band names

Kevan: What about you, Colby? Where you at? Studying or something???

Colby: ya

Kevan: lol really?

Colby: if I do bad on the math test tomorrow i'm grounded

Me: That sucks. Your superpower should be math skills

Kevan: That doesn't count. Math skills can help you get rich

Ty: Colby was born with two superpowers: rich parents and white privilege

Kevan: hello 911 I'm reporting a third-degree burn

Colby: Not funny bro

Kevan: I lol'd tho

Ty: Just messing with you Co

Me: Do you need help studying?

Colby: nah gotta go

Kevan: I never told you my power yet.

Stealth farts

Silent and odorless

I could rip one anywhere and no one would

ever know

Ty: That's poetry Kev. I feel it in my soul

We messed around a little longer, dreaming up more tiny powers, like automatic minty breath and instantly evaporating sweat. It turned out Kevan was hung up on smelling fresh.

Kevan: Smell is connected to memory. It's science! If you're ripe all the time, people will remember you as the stinky guy forever

Colby never came back to the chat. I sent him a private message. Hey, hope studying's going OK. I could come help if you want

Colby and I lived one street apart in the Hydrostone district of the North End. We'd been friends since we were little and were practically inseparable. The summer between fifth and sixth grade, we hung out so much that Colby's mom started automatically making extra lunch for me.

Ty made us a trio on the first day of sixth grade. I always dreaded attendance on the first day, because two things happened. First, teachers reached my name on the class list and did a long inhale before they took a guess at my last name. A lot of people got it wrong and said Ko-MIZ-a-rek, instead of Ko-mi-ZA-rek.

That was bad enough, but when I raised my hand, sometimes there was an awkward pause while they stared at me, thinking: *Are you sure you're you?*

Because when people hear *Ezra Komizarek*, they expect a pale European kid. My dad immigrated to Canada from Poland, but my mom was from Trinidad. Growing up, when I had to pick a crayon for self-portraits, I usually chose gold fusion.

On the first day of sixth grade, I answered to my name and our teacher actually said "oh." She quickly cleared her throat and moved on, so most kids didn't even notice, but the tall Black kid next to me leaned over and whispered, "She thought you'd be white." He'd giggled. And just like that, Ty and I were friends.

Ty introduced us to Kevan, and then we were four. Four was perfect. With three, someone could feel left out. But four was even and not too complicated. There were four Ghostbusters, four Beatles, four Teenage Mutant Ninja Turtles. I was friendly with most people at school, but the Juicy Four felt like home base.

I had a recital coming up, so I grabbed my guitar and practiced while I waited for Colby to write me back. My phone stayed quiet.

Maybe he was in Do Not Disturb mode. His parents hounded him about his grades, and it must have been serious if they were threatening to ground him over a math test. We'd ended up in different homerooms this year, Ty and me in one class and Kevan and Colby in the other. I never asked Colby how he was doing in class, because I knew he hated school. Asking about his grades would be like asking, *Have you flossed lately? How's the plaque situation around your gums?* Nobody wants their friends to grill them on that stuff. Maybe he could have used my help, though.

As I wondered whether to send another message, I scrolled through old texts and noticed he'd been quieter lately, in the Juice and our private thread. I had to go back three weeks to find the last time he actually started a conversation.

I put my phone down, but I couldn't focus on anything else as I waited for the *ding* of a new text message. But Colby didn't answer me at all.

3. SITUATIONS LIKE THIS

BRIAN

My first day being thirteen started with a nightmare. I had to give an oral presentation in class, but I blanked on my topic. I dropped my notes, and everyone laughed, and Victor called me loser and freak and Ghost.

Happy birthday to me.

I lurched awake five minutes before my alarm and decided to read a scene from *The Voyage of the Dawn Treader* to wipe the dream from my mind. When I sat up, I noticed a card on my dresser, with my name written in Dad's slanted handwriting. A card probably meant he wouldn't be home before school. I swallowed my disappointment as I climbed out of bed. I had the card in my hands when my door burst open.

"Happy birthday!" my brother, Richie, yelled. "Nice underwear!"

"What did I tell you about knocking?" I said.

He rushed me and pummeled my ribs. I wrapped him in a headlock, and we scuffled until I sat on him.

He wriggled beneath me, half laughing and half groaning. "Get off! Your butt is so bony."

When I let him up, he yelled, "Happy birthday, Bony-Butt Brian!" and ran off giggling like he'd made the funniest joke ever. Richie was a goof, but he was decent as nine-year-old brothers go.

By the time I dressed and reached the kitchen, he was already plowing into a bowl of cereal.

"Slow down," I told him as I started rooting around in the fridge. "Where's Mom?"

Before Richie could answer, I heard a wail from her bedroom. It was the worst sound I'd ever heard.

I froze, carton of orange juice in one hand, fridge door propped against my hip. Richie's mouth hung open, and milk dribbled down his chin.

He swallowed. "Was that Mom?"

"Wait here."

In the six-second walk down the hall of our little bungalow, I considered the grand unfairness of the universe. Dad was out doing The Thing, and now it sounded like Mom was having a Bad Day.

I knocked on my parents' door. When Mom didn't answer, I slipped inside. She sat on her bed with her back to me.

"Mom?" I asked, taking a step closer.

Still nothing. Usually there were signs if she wasn't doing well. She'd seemed fine last night, but now it was straight to Zombie Mode. *Thanks a lot, universe.*

"Can I get you anything?" I said. "Juice? Tea?"

She drew a deep breath. "He's gone."

My intestines tied themselves in a triple knot. "He'll be back soon though, right? He said—"

"He's GONE." Mom's rising voice made me flinch. "See."

She held up a crumpled sheet of paper. A torn envelope lay at her feet.

An envelope. Like the one on my dresser. Mom had one too.

It wasn't about my birthday. It was bad.

This couldn't be happening. Not today.

My hand shook as I took Mom's letter.

Julia,

I had to go. Don't panic. We knew it might happen, and we planned for it. Here's what I want you to do . . .

There was more, but my eyes went blurry and it was hard to breathe. Dad was gone. A worst-case scenario was happening. He'd left in a hurry, which meant someone was after him. Maybe the police. Maybe someone worse.

My chest hurt. I wanted Mom to tell me everything would be OK, but she was so pale.

"I need to lie down," she mumbled. She curled into a ball on the bed.

I couldn't leave her alone. *OK, OK, think.* I'd send Richie to school, then read Mom's letter and whatever Dad left in my room and figure out what to do next. I'd miss a math test, but that was the least of my problems.

This couldn't happen today. Dad promised he'd be here.

Wouldn't miss it.

I closed my eyes and willed them to stop burning. I was officially a teenager now. I wasn't going to start by crying.

"Brian?" Richie called from the doorway. "What's going on? What's wrong with Mom?"

I turned back toward her. That's when I noticed her pill bottles on the floor by her dresser.

Lids off. Empty.

I scrambled to scoop them up. Mom had two blue bottles labeled with four-syllable names, pills that were supposed to help keep her from going zombie on my birthday.

One beige pill rested on the floor. The others were gone.

I checked the garbage can. Under the dresser and the bed. Nothing.

My stomach took a roller-coaster plunge. I found the phone and called 911.

"We need an ambulance, fast," I blurted. "My mom, she . . . she took too much medication. It's not good."

Richie burst into tears.

The 911 operator was calm and businesslike. "OK, where are you? Can you tell me your address?"

My mind was racing so fast I had trouble answering, but eventually I fumbled it out.

"Can you tell me what she took?"

"Um . . ." I picked up the bottles and read the labels.

"Do you know how many pills she took? And how long ago she took them?"

"I . . . I don't know."

"It's all right. An ambulance is on the way."

My head went dizzy. Mom must have done it before I heard her moan. Maybe when I was lying in bed rereading one of my favorite books, or wrestling with Richie.

We'd thought everything was fine. We hadn't known the world was ending.

Time broke. The clock in my parents' room said six minutes passed before the paramedics arrived, but as I tried to keep Mom awake and Richie calm, I swear it took an hour. Then our house filled with strangers in uniforms and everything went into hyperspeed. Heavy boots clomped on the floor and radios crackled and people kept asking me questions. I felt faint and had to sit down. Next thing I knew, the paramedics were wheeling Mom out on a stretcher. Space and time twisted, like in a nightmare where you're never sure where you are or how you got there. I ended up in the kitchen making sandwiches, the kind with fake peanut butter that you're allowed to take to school. I didn't know what else to do. Nothing made sense, so I packed Richie a lunch. I figured we might end up at the hospital for a while.

"Hi there."

I turned. A police officer leaned against the wall with his hat in his hands. He had a curly beard and a head shaved so bald his brown scalp gleamed. I wondered how long he'd been standing there. If he thought packing a lunch was weird, he didn't mention it.

"It's Brian, right?" he said softly. "I'm Sergeant States. Is there anyone I can call for you? Do you know where your father is this morning?"

My whole body clenched, and I shook my head. I felt guilty about it, even though it was the truth. Even if I knew where Dad was, I wouldn't have told him. A police officer asking about my dad was bad news.

My stomach turned and I ran to the bathroom. I stayed in there a long time, trying to calm down. When I came out, I found Richie sitting on his bed, staring at nothing.

"Hey." I sat and put an arm around him. "Mom's in good hands. The paramedics have everything under control."

This seemed like it was true when they'd left. I hoped it was still true.

Richie's chin trembled. "Where's Dad? I want Dad."

Me too, I thought. I wanted to say something comforting, but I wasn't going to lie and tell him everything would be OK. "Pack some comics and your Switch. We might have to wait at the hospital."

He wiped his eyes. "Do we get to ride in a police car?"

"Yeah, I guess."

This seemed to cheer him up—or distract him, anyway. He started packing. I filled my backpack with our lunches, my book, and Dad's letters. I was still light-headed as Sergeant States led us to his car. I kept my eyes closed as he drove. Richie asked a hundred questions. My chest was buzzing too badly to stop him. Sergeant States didn't seem to mind, though.

"Nope, never been in a high-speed chase," he said, like he was used to answering this question from nine-year-old boys.

At the hospital, he helped us find the right waiting room and sat down with us. I wasn't sure why he stayed. Maybe it was illegal to abandon kids in a hospital. Maybe he felt sorry for us.

When Richie got restless, Sergeant States offered to take him for a walk.

"Want to come?" he asked me. I shook my head.

I sat there alone, sort of. Nurses glanced my way as they hurried past. Other people in the waiting room spied on me in a regular cycle. They looked at the fish tank, then the TV, then the skinny ginger seventh grader in the corner.

One lady offered me a Werther's caramel and attempted to start a conversation. My SAWS was raging after my terrible morning and I silently sank deeper into my seat. Eventually, she left me alone and retreated to her spot across the room. Every so often she tried to mother me with her eyes.

Other people talked. They watched TV. Maybe they

weren't here for emergencies. None of them looked how I felt: close to crying or barfing or both.

I wanted to read Dad's letter, but I didn't dare dig it out yet. Instead, I opened my book to ward off any more terrifying intrusions of kindness from strangers.

But I couldn't focus on the words. My thoughts kept drifting to Mom.

We talked about books all the time. We both agreed *The Voyage of the Dawn Treader* was our favorite Narnia book, but she made me tell her why. She never let me get away with mumbling that I liked something because it was fun.

"You're smarter than that," she said. *"Don't be embarrassed about what you love. Words are powerful, Brian. Sometimes they're all you have."*

Why am I thinking about her like this? Snap out of it. She isn't dead.

I looked up to see a nurse bearing toward me. My heart started thumping.

"You're Julia Day's son?"

I nodded. Words were impossible.

"Your mom will be all right. She's sleeping now. We'll move her into a room soon."

She was alive. I bit my lip. No bawling in the waiting room with people watching.

The nurse said she'd come back soon and take me to see the doctor. After she left, I found a bathroom. I needed to read my letter.

I locked myself in a stall and tore open the envelope.

Brian,

If you're reading this, I had to go in a hurry. If things work out, I'll see you soon. If something goes wrong, well, I hope you'll understand someday. I did a lot of things wrong, but I tried the best I could for you and Richie and your mom.

This is when you step up, B-Man. Your mom needs you. She has a letter and I told her to see my friend that Richie thinks is funny. She might need your help, so I want you to go too. I also want you to talk with him on your own. He has something for you. Keep it secret.

Listen. You're smart, and you're tougher than you think. I wish this wasn't happening, but you'll be all right. I'm proud of you.

Dad

PS I'm <u>SO</u> sorry this happened today. I got you something. You know where it is. Happy birthday, B-Man.

I pressed my elbows into my knees to distract me so I wouldn't cry. With his letter in my hand, Dad's voice filled my head.

Tears won't help you, B-Man. Put on some armor and get things done.

Something else twitched in my chest, something ugly and alien.

They left me. Both of them. And they lied.

Dad said he'd be here for my birthday.

Mom said thirteen would be great.

They couldn't have been more wrong.

I bit my lip. I had to focus, for Richie. Dad wanted me to call his friend Hank, who worked at the bank. Richie always thought this rhyme was funny. I knew where my birthday present was hidden too: at home in the basement. Despite everything, I appreciated that Dad trusted me to figure things out.

But I needed a phone. I didn't have a cell phone. I thought about finding a pay phone, but when I stepped out of the bathroom, the nurse was waiting with Sergeant States and Richie. She led us to a conference room.

"Why don't you come with me, love, so the others can talk," she said to Richie.

Richie folded his arms. "I'm not leaving. Where's Mom? When do we get to see her?"

The nurse squatted at his eye level. "She's all right, but she needs her rest. You'll have to be patient, dear."

Richie looked to me. I knew I should say something to make him feel better, but my throat was so dry.

"Go with the nurse, Richie," I choked out.

He huffed, but I guess he decided it would be less boring than sitting in a room full of adults. "Fine," he relented.

For a second, I wished I could go too. Stepping into that conference room felt as scary as anything else so far. Inside, a man in scrubs and a woman with a government ID tag around her neck sat at a table. Sergeant States closed the door and joined them. My SAWS ramped up, and my stomach ached.

"I'm Dr. Heyward," the man said. "This is Ms. Evans.

She's a social worker. In a situation like this, we have a duty to contact Children's Services to make sure you and your brother get the care you need."

A situation like this. He made it sound so routine, like families regularly self-destructed on Wednesdays before breakfast.

Ms. Evans opened a blue folder. *She has a folder on us already? What's in there?*

"Hi, Brian, you can call me Kate. I want to confirm I have the right info here. Your date of birth is June seventh?" Her eyes widened. "Oh. That's . . . today."

Sergeant States exhaled. Everyone's faces said, *You poor kid.* I clenched my fists under the table. Kate was a nightmare come to life. She kept talking, and soon she said the words I'd been dreading most: "We have a nice couple for you and Richie to stay with, at least in the short term."

An acid wave sloshed in my stomach. She'd already stuffed us in a box.

What to Do with the Day Brothers
~~*A. Let them take care of themselves*~~
~~*B. Hard labor in the coal mines*~~
~~*C. Eccentric haunted boarding school*~~
D. Lend them to total strangers

I wanted to protest, but I didn't have any better options. I couldn't mention Hank without messing up Dad's plan, whatever that was. And we had no relatives nearby. Dad was an only child, his father had died when I was a baby, and he hadn't seen his mother in years. Mom's family lived in Ontario and she hated talking about them, let alone visiting them. My family was kind of a mess, even before we fell apart.

The adults waited for my reaction. Sweat broke out on my forehead as I forced out a shaky response.

"Can we"—*Breathe*—"ask Mom? When she wakes up?"

Kate and Dr. Heyward gave each other a look that sent me falling down a well.

"I don't want to build up false hopes here," Kate said. "It might be a while before your mother is ready to make decisions about your care."

What did that mean? Was Mom in a coma? Did she have brain damage? Had Kate put a big red stamp on her folder? UNSTABLE. UNFIT.

We were going into foster care. Even thinking the words made me dizzy.

"I have to ask you a few questions," Kate continued. "Have you ever felt unsafe at home, Brian?"

What? I shook my head.

"Have you and Richie ever been left on your own for any length of time?"

A social worker was asking horrible questions in front of a doctor and a police officer. I knew what was happening. She thought our parents neglected us. Or worse.

I was alone in an asteroid belt. One wrong move and my family was doomed.

"Stop it," I blurted. "My family's not . . . just stop."

My voice wavered. I was a half-step from collapsing into a puddle of waterworks and snot. I wasn't going to let Kate see me cry.

"Hey, listen," Sergeant States said calmly. "It's all right if you're scared and angry. Today's been a nightmare."

Kate frowned. "I don't know if this is helpful."

He ignored her. So did I.

"Can I give you one piece of advice?" he said. "Try thinking about ten minutes at a time. What will help you through the next ten minutes? And if that's too long, try five minutes."

Ten minutes. I tried to harness the tornado in my head.

"Need a minute to process everything?" Sergeant States suggested. I nodded.

He rose. Kate hesitated, but she went along when Dr. Heyward followed his lead. Sergeant States waited until the others left and slid a business card in front of me.

"I'll leave you in Ms. Evans's capable hands now. But if you need anything . . ." He tapped the card. "I know this is rough. Hang in there, Brian."

He seemed sincere—he was more helpful than Kate, anyway. Still, I only nodded and waited for him to go. I felt like my world had been blasted into a million pieces and I was about to be shipped off to some alien planet. What I needed most was five minutes alone.

4. SUPERHERO THEORY

EZRA

Before school, Colby finally texted back one line with a bunch of thoughts strung together, in typical Colby style. Sorry mom was a pain last nite she's driving me today see you at school

I didn't see him until the end of the day. I couldn't find him at the morning break, and Ty pulled me into the basketball game outside at lunch. It wasn't completely unusual for us to miss each other now that we had different schedules, but I was relieved when he showed up at my locker after the final bell.

He bumped me with his shoulder. "Let's get out of here."

Colby practically skipped out the back door like he was having the juiciest day ever.

"I guess you did OK on the test," I said as we crossed the schoolyard toward home.

"It was all right." He grinned. "I had help. From Jemma."

I straightened my glasses. "Jemma Hart?"

"Yeah. She *loves* helping me. Turns out Jackson's super-hero theory actually works."

"Jackson's what?" Jackson was Colby's older brother. He was a two-faced creep who acted charming around adults and treated Colby like trash when there were no witnesses. "Why are you listening to *Jackson?*"

Colby shrugged. "I know, he's the worst. But he's had three girlfriends already. He must be doing something right."

I was ready to change the subject, but Colby waited for me to ask. I sighed. "What's the superhero theory?"

Colby flipped his blond hair to one side. "Girls want a guy who's like a superhero. Strong and confident, but with one weakness. Because they want something they can fix."

I couldn't help it. I snorted. "Jackson found that in some chat room, right?"

Colby shook his head. "I know it sounds corny, but it works. I figured Jemma liked me, but after I admitted I suck at math she was all, *ooh, Colby, let me help you.*" He stopped and faced me. "She helped me study this week. Whenever I got something right, she'd touch my arm, like, *you're doing so great.*"

He batted his eyelashes and rubbed my arm in his best Jemma impression. My breath caught in my throat, and I straightened my glasses again, hoping he didn't notice.

"We did some last-minute studying at break before the test and she kept squeezing my arm. She was checking out my muscles." Colby's grin grew wider. "I'm going to ask her out. Not right away. I have to let things chill for a bit. But soon."

He started walking again. None of this was totally surprising. It was obvious that girls liked Colby. I saw the looks in the cafeteria and the halls, and I understood why. He moved with a confidence that made you think anything was possible. He'd talked me into lots of things over the years—scary movies, midnight snack runs, jumping off a bridge into a river—and I liked that he pushed me to be more adventurous. But it felt strange watching him focus all his coolness powers on convincing a girl to go out with him.

"Let things chill? Was that Jackson's advice too?"

"Nah. I just don't want her to think I'm asking her out because of the math test. Like I'm using her."

I tucked my hands in my pockets. "OK, but . . . *are* you using her?"

Colby scowled. "Bro, of course not. I like her." He kicked a pebble off the sidewalk. "Look, we don't have to talk about this if it's weird or whatever."

My face went warm. "No, it's cool. I'm happy for you. Just . . . don't pick up Jackson's bad vibes."

"Gross. Never."

We walked half a block in silence. I scrambled to come up with a joke.

"Hey, I know Jackson's real secret to getting girls," I said finally. "You know your mom's fridge magnets? He gives those out all over school."

Colby moaned. "Ugh, don't remind me about the magnets."

When we were eleven, Colby's mom ordered a million fridge magnets to advertise her interior design business. She enlisted us to stick them on mailboxes and give them to other kids at school. Colby nearly died of embarrassment.

I put on my best YouTuber voice. "Cindy Newcombe laminated magnets are *the* hot accessory this year. Everyone wants them for their lockers."

"Dude, shut *up*." Colby snorted. I knew we were imagining the same thing: Jackson strutting around his high school, handing out magnets with his mom's picture to girls.

We laughed all the way home.

I came home to an empty house, as usual. My parents worked long hours and they'd decided a while ago that I was old enough to stay home alone.

I snacked on a banana-Nutella wrap, then I videochatted with Natalie, my half sister from Dad's first marriage. She used to look after me a lot until she graduated from college last spring and moved to Toronto to study for her master's. We talked about music and school, and she dished the latest on her roommates and their neurotic cat. I liked that she let me into her adult-ish life.

"What's new in the thrilling world of seventh grade?" she asked.

"Not much. Oh, Colby's using his bad math grade to get a girlfriend."

I told her about Jackson's superhero theory, and Nat literally screamed in horror.

"Ezra, that's the most lizard-brained nonsense I've heard all week." She leaned so close to her camera that her nose nearly filled my phone screen. "Promise me you'll never take relationship advice from anyone in the Newcombe family."

"I'm ninety percent sure Jackson found it online."

"*Definitely* don't take advice from men online. The internet is a digital bathroom stall." She put a hand over her heart. "When you're thinking about dating, promise me you'll come to your big sister first."

I blushed. "I'm not thinking about dating."

"OK, but promise."

"I promise."

"Good. I have to run. Love you, Ezzy. Don't do drugs."

Nat always ended our calls that way. I groaned. "You know I hate that."

She smiled. "I know. But I have to bug you sometimes. Those are the big-sister rules."

"I thought you were against rules and systems."

"I'm against our patriarchal capitalist system, because it's built to benefit the worst people. But the big-sister rules are woven into the fabric of the universe. Bye, Ezzy."

She blew me a kiss and hung up.

While I was on my phone, I checked the Juice. Kevan had asked if anyone wanted to play video games online. Ty said he was busy, and Colby hadn't answered.

I wondered if he was texting Jemma instead.

I played with Kevan for a while. He was a more serious gamer than I was, so three rounds of him barking commands in my headset was all I could take for one day. After I logged off, I got curious and checked Colby's Instagram to see if he and Jemma had started following each other recently. Colby's page was mostly selfies and skateboarding videos. As I scrolled, I noticed he'd been tagged in a video I'd never seen. Alicia Smith had posted it with the caption **boys are so weird lol.**

I clicked Play. Colby, Victor MacLennan, and Scott Lund stood at the top of a muddy hill. Colby had his shirt off and they were all barefoot, each holding a sheet of cardboard. Colby shouted "Go!" and they sprinted downhill. After a few steps, Scott tripped and wiped out in the mud. The video shook as Alicia giggled. Another girl off-camera laughed too. Colby and Victor leaped onto their cardboard and surfed into an enormous mud puddle. Colby hit first, spraying a wave of brown slop, and Victor splashed in a second later. The girls cheered. Scott stumbled down the hill and flopped in the puddle. Then the three boys wrestled.

"What a bunch of goofs," said a voice I recognized as Jemma's.

The boys stood up, totally caked in mud. They struck muscle poses that made the girls giggle again. Colby said something to Victor, and the whites of his teeth showed through the mud as he grinned. Then the boys yelled and charged at the girls.

"Don't you dare!" Alicia screamed, and that's where the video ended.

I noticed the date. **Posted 4 days ago.**

That was Saturday. My birthday.

I had invited Ty, Kevan, and Colby over for dinner and a sleepover. Colby told me at the last minute that he'd be late, and he didn't show up until eight, with wet hair like he'd just showered. The rest of the night, he kept checking his phone.

It had bugged me at the time, but I'd let it go. Because at least he'd shown up. But now it bugged me more. He could have told me the truth about why he was late.

I closed Instagram and thought about texting Colby to ask about Saturday, but I chickened out. Instead, I picked up my guitar and plugged it into my amp. I needed to play something loud.

5. ENEMY TERRITORY

BRIAN

Our house felt haunted. As I approached my room, I swore I heard echoes of the paramedics' radios coming from my parents' room. Goose bumps prickled my arms.

Kate had let us stop by to pack, but she hovered in the hall between our rooms, like she was too suspicious to leave us unsupervised.

"Hey, Richie," I whispered. "Distract her while I do something for Dad." He gave me a thumbs-up.

"How strong are you?" he called to Kate. "Can you carry my dresser to your car?"

Kate rushed into his room. "Wait, *what*? You can't bring your whole dresser."

"But I need my clothes!" He folded his arms. "All of them. And my most favorite LEGO sets: the ninja temple and the rescue helicopter and the Batmobile . . ."

Kate sighed. While she tried to reason with him, I snuck to the basement to find a suitcase and retrieve my present from Dad's hiding spot. *Presents*, it turned out. Two boxes, wrapped in black paper dotted with basketballs. My eyes grew watery. I shoved both boxes in the suitcase.

As I lugged the suitcase upstairs, my chest tightened. I didn't want to go with Kate, but I didn't want to stay either. Our house felt all wrong.

Kate had told us our temporary guardians were grandparents, but it still surprised me to see the gray-haired couple waving from the front steps of their two-story house. Gordon and Emma Wentzell were way older than my parents. Mom had me when she was nineteen. Dad was eighteen. They were barely in their thirties now. Dad played *Overwatch* and cranked Jay-Z in the car, and when Mom was doing well, she sang in the kitchen and climbed trees with Richie. One night when I was awake late, I heard them laughing their faces off in their room. In the good times, they were full of energy. They were fun.

Dad would never in a million years wear the dull brown blazer Gordon Wentzell had on. I bet he'd owned that jacket longer than my dad had been alive. Dude belonged on an oatmeal box.

As we approached, Emma descended on us. She called us "dear" and patted Richie's messy brown hair and said, "Aren't you the most handsome thing."

Richie caught my eye and gagged.

She reached toward me as she ushered us inside, but I squirmed away.

Ten minutes later, Gordon went back to work, Kate left, and Richie and I were alone with Emma in her living room. Photos lined every wall and ceramic cat figurines stared at us from the bookshelves, the coffee table, the top of the upright piano. There had to be fifty, at least.

There was an entire life jammed into that room, a life that had nothing to do with me. And I wanted nothing to do with it.

"Should we put your things in your rooms?" Emma said. "Maybe you'd like to relax first. Can I bring you some cookies? Would you like milk? Or apple juice? You're not allergic to milk, are you? Do you have any allergies I should know about?"

Emma was a verbal avalanche. I could barely breathe. My face tingled. I caught Richie's eye and he read my expression: *Get me away from this lady.*

"We'll go to our room now," he said.

Emma clucked in sympathy. "Of course. You probably want to rest. You've been through a lot today, haven't you? Poor dears."

She led us upstairs. Thankfully, my temporary bedroom was simpler than the rest of the house. The sky-blue walls were mostly bare, and there were no cats in sight.

"Brian, we'll put you in here," Emma said. "Richie, you're next door."

Richie didn't move. "I'm staying with Brian."

I stared at him in surprise. We hadn't shared a room

since we'd moved out of a dingy apartment when I was seven.

Emma frowned. "Are you sure, dear? I thought you'd be more comfortable in your own space."

"No." Richie folded his arms. He blinked fast, suddenly fighting tears. Seeing him upset helped me find my voice. I rested my hands on his shoulders.

"It's OK. We can share the bed."

Emma wavered. "Well, if you're sure."

"We are." Richie straightened, satisfied that he'd gotten his way. "Can I have a cookie now? And can I watch TV? Mom lets me watch after school, and it's after school now."

"I suppose so," Emma said.

I didn't follow them back downstairs. I curled into a ball on the bed, trying to ignore that the mattress was too squishy and smelled old. I tried to imagine I was in my own room.

"Would you like more gravy? Some peas? What's your favorite class in school?"

Emma never stopped. Richie had woken me ten minutes earlier, and I was still so groggy that nothing felt real. A giant ceramic Siamese cat watched me from a hutch across the room.

"For heaven's sake, Emma, give him a minute." Gordon winked at me. "You look like you could have slept for a week."

What did that mean? Was it code for *I suspect you are sleep-deprived due to your terrible home life?* Even sympathy was a trap.

I never shared much about Mom and Dad, because they weren't exactly cover models for *Today's Parent*. But now that a Worst-Case Scenario was unfolding, we couldn't afford to slip up and provide evidence for Kate's blue folder. I'd already warned Richie.

"Pretend we're spies in enemy territory. We have to figure out who's trustworthy and who's not," I'd whispered as we made our way downstairs.

He'd nodded. *"Got it."*

At dinner, Richie fished out intel on the Wentzells and told rambling stories about his best friend, Leo Sidhu. Honestly, I was jealous of how Richie could captivate a room with his breezy confidence. He'd inherited Mom's good looks and Dad's swagger. I got Dad's freckles and Mom's tendency to find the world overwhelming. It was a raw deal.

I chewed slowly so I had an excuse not to talk. I tried not to look at that dang fake cat, but my eyes kept drifting to it. By the time I finished, Gordon had already cleared the table.

"I hope you saved room for dessert," Emma said.

She retreated to the kitchen. As she clanged around, I caught a metallic whiff of something igniting, followed by a sizzle. I realized what was happening as she rounded the corner carrying a tray. Sparks jumped. I swear she was about to break into song until she saw my face and thought better of it. Instead, she set the tray before me and backed away.

A birthday cake, with chocolate frosting and *Happy Birthday Brian* scripted in yellow icing. And sparklers. Three of them.

Nobody spoke until the sparklers fizzled out, leaving a bitter curl of smoke wafting toward the ceiling.

"Ms. Evans told me it was your birthday," Emma said. "I hope it's all right. I didn't know if you liked chocolate."

I stared at the cake. I was wide awake now. It was June 7, my thirteenth birthday, and I should have a belly full of Hot Numbing Chicken and the cake should be made of ice cream and I should be at home with Mom and Dad.

This was wrong. Everything was wrong.

"Brian?" Gordon said. "You OK, fella?"

"I told you he'd hate it," Richie said.

Emma waved her hands. "I thought you'd want—but if it's too hard we can save it for later—oh, I don't know. What do you want, Brian?"

Wasn't it obvious? I wanted a time machine. Or a wormhole to an alternate universe. I wanted to be any-where but here.

I stood up and left the room.

A few minutes later, Richie followed me upstairs and entered the bedroom, closing the door behind him. He sat beside me on the bed.

"I told her cake was a bad idea. She didn't listen."

We were quiet.

"Are you OK?" Richie asked. "You won't end up in the hospital like Mom, will you?"

I swallowed hard and squeezed his shoulder. "I'm not going anywhere, Rich. We're a team."

He pulled his knees to his chest. "Emma talks so much. It's annoying. She's a good cook, though."

"Yeah."

"You don't like her, do you?"

I shrugged. "I guess not. This is all so weird. And the cats creep me out."

Richie's eyes bugged. "She has *so many cats*. It's freaky."

I stretched on the bed. Richie flopped next to me and poked me in the ribs. I pulled him close. We stayed there a while.

"Brian?"

"Yeah?"

"I ate a piece of cake."

"I know, Rich. You have icing on your face."

He wiped his mouth. "It was really good."

"I'm glad you liked it. Honestly."

"You should open your presents now."

"I don't feel like it."

"Please?"

I sighed. "Oh, all right."

He hopped off the bed and dug a small box out of his suitcase. "Mine first."

I pulled off the wrapping paper and opened the box. It

held a cord necklace with a silver dog tag inscribed with two Japanese characters.

"It means 'ninja,'" Richie said. "'Cause you're quiet like a ninja. Mom helped me order it."

I traced the characters with my finger. "This is super cool. Thank you."

After I put on the necklace, Richie made me open Dad's presents. The bigger box held a Russell Westbrook basketball jersey. He's my favorite player because he's aggressive and fearless, two things I'm not. I slipped the jersey over my T-shirt. It was long and loose, but I imagined Dad telling me I'd grow into it.

I unwrapped the second present and stared.

"No way!" Richie said. "Dad got you a phone?"

I hadn't mentioned how much I wanted one, but Dad knew. When I lifted the sleek black phone from its packaging, I found a handwritten note underneath.

Sorry I didn't have time for a proper card. I recorded a message for you.

I fiddled with the screen until I found Dad's recording. I popped in the phone's earbuds.

"Hey," Richie protested. "I want to hear too."

I waved him off and hit Play. Dad's voice filled my ears. He sounded tired.

"*Hey, B-Man. I was looking forward to giving this to you. It took me forever to convince your mom. I told her, 'Come on, he's the most responsible kid in the world. He'll be fine.'"* He sighed. *"Anyway. I put some music and pictures on here for you. Hank's in your contacts. He's expecting your call. I'm using a burner and can't give you the number, but I'll call as soon as I can. Hang in there, buddy. Look after Richie and your mom. Love you."*

I couldn't hold out any longer. Tears came and I couldn't stop them. I pulled the front of my new jersey over my face.

"What's wrong?" Richie said. "What did Dad say?"

Emma knocked on the door. "Boys?"

"We're fine," Richie said. "Leave us alone."

She opened the door. "Just wanted to say good night—oh dear. Brian—"

Richie hopped up. "I told you to leave us alone! Why don't you ever listen?"

"Hey now," Gordon said. "Watch your tone there, fella."

I pulled the jersey all the way over my head. Richie argued with Gordon and Emma, but she kept talking, and I hated her seeing me cry, and blood thumped in my ears. She put a hand on my knee, and I rocketed forward, nearly knocking her over. I ran out and locked myself in the bathroom.

"Brian, are you OK?" Emma called, but I ignored her.

I tried to avoid the mirror, but I caught a glimpse of my face—all blotchy and tear-stained, like a little kid's.

Emma paced in the hall. "Oh dear. Should I talk to him? One of us should talk to him. Gordon, you should talk to him."

"Do your ears not work?" Richie said. "Leave. Him. Alone."

"Young man. Don't be rude—"

"Seriously, shut up for once and listen!"

Silence.

"Brian hates strangers asking him a million questions," Richie continued after a moment. "You're bothering him and making it worse. Just leave us alone."

The bedroom door slammed. Emma sighed.

"Let them be," Gordon said. "Tomorrow is another day."

Their footsteps moved away. I sat on the toilet lid and fiddled with my phone until I found the photos Dad had saved for me. The first showed a freckled teenager with a huge grin, holding an infant. Me. I'd never seen that picture of Dad before. He looked so young, and so happy.

He'd loaded pictures of trips to the beach, poses on playgrounds and by the lighthouse at Peggy's Cove. One from Richie's sixth birthday, four Augusts ago, where Richie's shirt bunched around his armpits as Dad dangled him upside down. I hung on to Dad's back with my eyes closed and my mouth open in mid-yell. Dad was laughing.

We were so happy.

Houses are never completely quiet. I was used to the sounds of my own house at night, but at the Wentzells', a clock ticked too loudly and Gordon or Emma snored and something went *thunk* downstairs—probably the ceramic cats coming to life and forming an army to murder me. Richie slept through it all with his butt jutting onto my half of the bed. I couldn't sleep, so I picked up my phone for the tenth time.

How to Drive Yourself Bonkers in a Strange House at Night
1. Open cell phone contacts.
2. Stare at Hank Ferris's number.
3. Reach for Call button.
4. Fall paralyzed with anxiety.
5. Convince yourself it's too late to call at ~~10:12~~, ~~10:26~~, ~~10:46~~, ~~11:03~~, *11:17 P.M.*
6. Set phone down.
7. Repeat.

Hank was practically my uncle. He played video games with Dad and horsed around with Richie. We never had deep life conversations or anything, but I knew him well enough that calling should have been easy. I was a coward.

I'll call in the morning, I decided. For the tenth time.

Who was I kidding? I'd never sleep if I didn't call. I'd lie awake, hating myself.

Finally, in a spasm of bravery or panic or both, I pressed the green button. My head tingled and my mouth went dry as the phone rang.

Hank answered on the second ring. He sounded wide awake.

"Brian? Thank goodness. I'm so glad you called."

My shoulders unclenched. "I didn't wake you up?" I kept my voice low, even though Richie could have slept through Godzilla laying an egg in the backyard.

"No, no. How's everything? How's your mom? I called, but no one answered."

He didn't know.

"Brian?" Hank said at my stunned silence. "Is everything all right?"

"Mom's in the hospital," I blurted out.

"She's *what?* What happened? Where are you?"

I forced out as much as I could without falling apart. Hank cursed.

"Oh, Brian. Sorry, I shouldn't swear. But this isn't good."

Hearing Hank so upset was oddly comforting. All day I'd dealt with strangers who followed rules and gave orders and tried to fix things, when all I wanted was to curl up and disappear.

"Are you and Richie all right?" he asked.

"I guess."

"OK, good. Can you come to the bank tomorrow? You know where I am, right?"

"I'll come after school."

"You're going to school? You could take another day off."

I hadn't even considered that. But school seemed better than Emma pestering me all day.

I said good night and hung up. With a glance at Richie, I slipped out of the room. I was still wearing a T-shirt and basketball shorts. At home I slept in my underwear, but I didn't trust Emma not to barge in again. Obviously she had trouble with boundaries.

In the kitchen, I tested the cake, because why not. It was way too sweet. I carried the leftovers outside and dropped the whole thing into the compost bin.

I looked up at the hazy night sky. I was a ten-minute drive from my house in the North End and an entire universe removed from my actual life.

"Ten minutes," Sergeant States had said. *"Five if that's too hard."*

But at night in a strange house, every minute was its own infinity.

6. PRIORITIES

EZRA

Staying up past midnight on a Wednesday wasn't my choice. Ty said it was a sacred duty of our friendship. It was Game 3 of the NBA Finals, LeBron James and the Cleveland Cavaliers versus the Golden State Warriors. The Warriors were supervillains with a 2–0 series lead, and LeBron needed my support. This was Ty's pitch. He could be very convincing.

Ty lived for basketball. He'd made the provincial under-fourteen team that trained all summer. He and Jayden Grouse, an eighth grader, regularly argued about LeBron versus Kevin Durant like two old men in a barbershop. I was just good enough to be the guy on our school's team who played garbage-time minutes when the game was practically over. I mostly sat on the bench cheering for my teammates, but I didn't mind.

I watched in bed with the sound off and probably would have fallen asleep if Ty hadn't kept texting me. Colby didn't care about basketball and Kevan's parents made him put his phone away at 9:30 every night, so it was just Ty and me.

When the Cavaliers took the lead in the third quarter, he called me.

"You're still watching, right?"

I yawned. "Yeah."

"This is their night. You believe, right?"

"I believe, Ty."

Ty's play-by-play was better than any announcer's. He let out a "WOO!" when LeBron dunked, and I heard his dad say, "Shush. If you wake up your mother, we'll both get it."

During the commercial break before the fourth quarter, Ty blew out a long breath.

"This is stressful. Let's talk about something else. What's your take on the Colby-Jemma situation?"

"You know about that? Did Colby tell you?" I asked.

"Nah, I was talking to Jemma and Madi, and Madi was teasing Jemma about liking Colby, and Jemma was all, *cut it out, Madi,* but she was also like, *but seriously, Ty, do you think he likes me?* And I said yeah, because it's obvious."

Ty's play-by-play of school gossip was as detailed as his basketball commentary. "I didn't know you talked like that with Jemma and Madi."

"I talk to everybody."

"True story," his dad said. "You came out of the womb talking and haven't stopped yet."

"Dad, shush. You'll wake up Mom."

"Don't you shush me on my own couch."

"So? What do you think?" Ty said to me.

I didn't want to start any rumors, but I wasn't telling Ty anything he didn't already know. "Colby told me he likes her," I admitted.

"Of course he does. Colby likes every pretty girl who looks at him."

I swallowed. "You think Jemma's pretty?"

"For sure. I mean, I'm not into her like Colby is, but I get why he likes her." Before I could respond, Ty said, "Enough girl-talk. The game's back."

His dad chuckled. "That's good, son. Keep your priorities straight."

Basketball was the last thing on my mind, but I hung in till the bitter end as Cleveland's lead disappeared. When Kevin Durant hit a three-pointer with forty-five seconds left and put the Warriors ahead, Ty wailed like someone had set his best sneakers on fire. The Cavaliers didn't score again, and the Warriors won.

"I hate Kevin Durant with my whole heart," Ty moaned. "Thanks for the support, Ezra. You're a good friend."

"No problem. Good night."

I put my phone away and settled into bed. Even though I was tired, I didn't fall asleep right away. I was still thinking about Colby and Jemma. I thought about how everyone gossiped now about who *liked* who. Kevan did that now too. Whatever *Hey look, girls!* hormone had swept through my friends, it hadn't hit me. I never said that out loud, though.

Sometimes junior high is the most ridiculous place.

Nat had warned me about this, before she moved. "Hang in there," she'd told me. "You'll find your people, Ezra. It might take time, but it'll happen."

I hadn't understood what she meant. I told her I had lots of friends. She gave me a Knowing Big Sister look. "There are people we hang around because it's comfortable or convenient or safe, then there are our *people*. When you find them, you'll know the difference."

The Juicy Four are my people, I thought. *Especially Colby.* Sure, lots had changed this year—new school, different classes, other kids in the mix. But it was almost summer break, and everything would go back to normal then. We'd be inseparable, like last summer.

But I kept seeing Colby's mud-caked grin as he chased Jemma instead of eating jerk chicken with me on my birthday. It still stung that he didn't even tell me.

Maybe he wanted to, but he didn't know how?

"Don't be so dramatic," I told myself, only I yawned so it came out as "draaaahck."

When I was younger, Mom told me that tonight's problems will seem smaller tomorrow after a good sleep. *Maybe she's still right*, I thought as I closed my eyes.

7. SIZZLE SAUCE

BRIAN

Visiting the bank wasn't so simple with Emma and her cat army on my case. She even had a bobblehead kitty stuck to the dash of her car. On the drive to school, I sat in the back and ignored Emma's chatter as I looked up bus routes on my phone. I needed a plan.

School seemed less suffocating than the Wentzells' house, but as other kids joked and hollered in the hall before the bell, like it was just another day and nothing terrible was unfolding, I felt even more invisible than usual. Until a hand touched my shoulder.

"Hey, Brian."

I turned. Ezra drew his hand back and cleared his throat. "Sorry. You, uh, looked kind of bummed. You running low on sizzle sauce today?"

This was a joke from basketball season. Our coach loved acronyms and made us recite at every practice that TEAM stood for Together Everyone Achieves More. Back in January after we lost a game, Ezra declared in a dead-on Coach voice that every LOSS was because we were Low On

Sizzle Sauce. The joke stuck. If anyone hit a three-pointer or did something cool in a game, they'd yell, "Sizzle sauce!" Once, when a kid on the other team airballed a free throw, Ezra leaned into my shoulder and whispered, "Tragically unsizzilicious." I laughed so hard I got the hiccups.

Basketball was practically the only time I laughed in school. Usually because of Ezra.

He was also the only person who'd notice me enough to stop me in the hall. I almost blurted out the truth: *No, Ezra. I am completely out of sizzle.* Instead, I faked a yawn.

"I'm just tired." It wasn't a lie. I'd barely slept.

"Yeah? Me too. Did you stay up watching the game? I wasn't going to, but Ty made me. Are you a Cavs fan too? Ty looks as bummed as you do today." Ezra turned to open his locker as he talked. Before I could answer, two other guys approached, Colby and Kevan. They were both in my homeroom. Kevan lived on my street and Richie was best friends with his brother, Leo.

They brushed past like I wasn't there.

"Hey, Ezra. Did Ty make you stay up for the whole game?" Kevan asked.

While they were still talking, I slipped away and hurried to homeroom. Kevan wasn't so bad, but Colby was cocky and he hung out with Victor a lot. My SAWS always acted up around him. Especially on a day like today.

So much for flying under the radar. At the end of homeroom, Mrs. Clelland softly asked me to hang back as the other kids filed out. She was my favorite teacher, the one I found easiest to talk to, but when our principal, Ms. Floriman, and the guidance counselor, Mrs. Barton, stepped into the classroom, my heart clanged.

"Hi, Brian," Ms. Floriman said. "Ms. Evans called me. She didn't go into details, but she explained you had a difficult day yesterday. We're so sorry."

A high-pitched ringing filled my ears.

"I'm happy to talk with you at any time, if you'd like," Mrs. Barton said.

"Your teachers will be understanding with assignments," Ms. Floriman said. "Your school community is here for you."

I stayed quiet, wishing I could disappear through the floor.

"You can head to your next class now," Mrs. Clelland said gently. I gathered my things and left without a word.

I tried to be invisible for the rest of the day. When school ended, I made it to the foyer and stopped cold. Emma stood by the front doors, scanning the herd of students like she'd lost a toddler in a pool. She might as well have held up a poster that said LET ME TELL YOU ABOUT BRIAN DAY'S TRAGIC LIFE.

That settled it. I'd felt slightly guilty about my plan to ditch her, but not anymore. I engaged Stealth Mode, backtracked, and slipped out the back door.

My pulse thumped as I walked away. Catching the bus downtown in the middle of the day was no biggie for a normal junior high kid, but I was Captain Anxious of the Order of SAWS, Boy Who Preferred Not to Leave His House, and this was treacherous territory.

I had to get over it. Step up, like Dad said. I had a mission: make it to the TD Bank on Spring Garden Road and rendezvous with Hank. Become a character in a book, some brave kid who outwits world-conquering villains, or fearless Reepicheep from *The Voyage of the Dawn Treader*. What would they do in my shoes?

They would catch the #7 bus pulling up across the street.

8. THE HISTORY OF BEEKEEPING

EZRA

On Thursdays I catch a city bus to my guitar lesson after school. I felt silly at first, carrying my guitar in public, like *look at me, a wannabe rock star*, but I got used to it.

I'd just settled in the back row of the bus when Brian came down the aisle. He looked around cautiously, like he wasn't sure he was in the right place. I turned off the music on my phone and waved at him. He made his way to the back beside me.

"Hey," I said. "You disappeared on me earlier. I hope your day got better. Where are you headed?"

"Um . . . the library," Brian answered slowly, like he stopped to think before each word. That was typical. He didn't say much at school and always looked like he was deep in thought. He was different from most guys, but in a good way. I liked talking to him.

"How about you?" he asked.

I patted my guitar case. "On Thursdays I ride around

Halifax Transit playing 'Wonderwall' until the driver gets mad and kicks me off. My record is thirty-seven seconds."

Brian smiled and went "Heh." This was a good start. He was so serious most of the time, so I liked trying to make him laugh.

"I have a lesson," I told him. "Last one before my recital on Saturday."

Brian scanned the bus. We had the back half to ourselves. I was used to filling the silence, so I started to say something else when he surprised me by asking another question.

"What are you playing at your recital?"

"Oh, 'Blackbird' by the Beatles. It's a great practice song for guitar. It's tricky, but really pretty."

I instantly wished I'd picked a different word. Colby and Kevan would have teased me forever if they heard me call a song *pretty*. But Brian didn't react.

"Cool," he said.

"You know it?" I asked.

He shook his head.

I offered him an earbud. "You want to . . . ?"

"Sure."

I stuck in the other earbud and started the song on my phone. Near the end, I noticed Brian smiling.

"What?" I said.

He pointed at my left hand sliding along the neck of my guitar case. "You're playing it right now, aren't you? And you were humming along."

I laughed. "Yeah, I guess. Habit."

He took out the earbud. "You're right, that is pretty. It sounds complicated. You must be really good."

I adjusted my glasses. "Nah, I just practice for a million hours. So, what's at the library?"

He gave me a puzzled look, like this was a trick question. "Books?"

I couldn't help it. I cracked up. Brian laughed too. I elbowed him. "I know the library has *books*, dingus. What are you going for? What do you like to read?"

He shrugged. "Anything, really."

"Come on. Fantasy? Horror? The history of beekeeping? Ooh, that would make a good band name."

He grinned again and started to answer, but I realized the bus was whizzing past Chebucto Road. My stop was four seconds away.

"Shoot!" I dove and yanked the stop cord. We lurched forward as the driver slowed to a quick halt, just past the bus shelter. She shot me a look in the mirror.

"Sorry! Thanks!" I called. I gathered my backpack and guitar. "Maybe I could come with you to this mysterious *library* place sometime," I told Brian. "You could introduce me to these alleged *books*."

As I hopped out the back doors, I looked back and waved. He smiled one more time.

9. TERRIBLE QUESTIONS

BRIAN

As the bus pulled away, I watched Ezra turn up Chebucto Road with his guitar in hand. Finding him on the bus was surprising enough, but the strangest part was how we just *talked*. The bus was half empty, no one was watching, and my SAWS left me alone. I wish he hadn't gotten off. Hanging out with Ezra was the first time I'd felt not-terrible in days. I hadn't laughed like that since . . .

Since Tuesday night. In the kitchen. With Mom.

Reality came flooding back. I wasn't going to the library. It was just the easiest lie that popped into my head. But I wished it were true.

I got off the bus at the top of Spring Garden Road and walked past the Halifax Public Gardens to the shopping district. I was sweating by the time I entered the bank. I scanned the room, trying not to look helpless. A receptionist smiled at me, so I told her I was looking for Hank Ferris. She picked up her phone.

I had barely settled into a leather seat when Hank rounded the corner. It was weird seeing him in a suit.

"How are you holding up?" he asked as I followed him into his office.

I shrugged.

"I'm sorry, Brian. This has all gone sideways."

For a moment I thought he was going to hug me. Instead, he awkwardly patted my shoulder. "Have a seat."

"Have you talked to Dad?" I asked. "Are the police after him? Or—"

Hank sat and fidgeted with his computer mouse. "Uh, yeah. Cops." He glanced at me. "You know, right?"

I nodded. I was eleven when Dad filled me in on what he really did. *"You're a smart kid,"* he started. *"I'm going to be honest with you."*

He told me he was in the cannabis production and distribution business. He said it wasn't as bad as it sounded, and he stayed away from the dangerous stuff. *"It'll be legal next year, and the government will make a killing in taxes. That's why they go after guys like me. The system's rigged, kiddo."*

Hank exhaled. "Your dad planned ahead so you guys would be fine financially for a while if anything happened. Of course, he wasn't expecting your mom . . ." He shook his head. "He set up an account for her. And one for you."

I blinked. "I already have a bank account."

"Now you have two. We, uh, had to be creative in stashing assets. But your dad specifically wanted you to have a contingency fund." Hank slid a sheet of paper in front of me.

My chest went hollow. There were more zeroes than I expected. I searched Hank's face for signs he was messing with me.

"I know, it's nuts," he said. "Who gives this much money to a kid? I wanted to put it in an education account, but your dad insisted I give it to you straight."

Dad left me ten thousand dollars. Thinking about it made me sweaty.

Hank grinned. "You know how he talks about you, right?"

Of course I knew.

"It's great that he reads so much, but we can't let him hide at home all the time. He'll never get over this thing if he doesn't try."

Hank reached across the desk. "Everett never shuts up about how smart you are. He thinks the world of you."

A dozen questions filled my head, starting with *Then why did he leave?* Just then my phone buzzed, making me jump.

"Speak of the devil," Hank said.

My hand shook as I answered. "Hello?"

"Brian."

"Dad." So many feelings overwhelmed me that I froze, which was good, since it stopped me from bursting into tears.

"Where are you?" Dad said.

"Hank's office." I looked at Hank. With a nod, he rose and stepped out, leaving me alone.

"Good. So. Hank gave me the rundown. But tell me what happened."

Dad was in Ice Mode. It was like he had a switch: He goofed around like an overgrown kid sometimes, but if things got shaky—usually when Mom wasn't doing well— he turned into a stone-cold boss. Dad's the guy who takes charge and leads everyone to safety in a disaster movie. It could be intimidating. But his *I got this, just give me the facts* tone helped calm me down.

I wished he was closer than a voice on the phone.

"You did great," he said after I fumbled out my recap. "None of this is your fault. Understand?"

I bounced my knees to keep from losing it.

"Brian? You understand?"

"Yeah," I whispered.

"Good. Your mother is alive because of you. You stayed cool, and you did the right thing. If you can do yesterday, you can handle anything. I'm trying to sort things out, and I need you to buckle down and hold tight for a while."

I glanced toward the door. "Can't we stay with Hank?"

"I wish, B-Man, but it's too risky. Hank can explain. We can get through this, though. You just need to be strong." *Just like he always said.*

Dad kept talking. "I need you to do one other thing, OK? Go see your mom. I need to know what shape she's in. Can you do that?"

I swallowed hard. "Yeah."

"Good man. I'll call tomorrow night. Tell Richie I miss him. Miss you both. I have to go."

The line went dead. If I sat there too long I'd crumble, so I opened the door.

"You good?" Hank asked.

I nodded. I didn't trust myself to speak.

Hank gave me a new debit card. He scratched his neck. "Look, I wish I could take you and Richie. Your dad's like my big brother. He ever talk about when were kids?"

I shook my head. Dad barely mentioned his childhood.

"My situation was rough to start with, but when I was twelve, my mom fell for the worst guy. I mean the *worst*. Whatever you're imagining, he was worse." Hank looked away. "Your dad figured out what was up and made me move in with him. This was after his mom left and his dad was in rough shape, so he had his own hands full. But he looked after both of us." Hank smoothed his tie. "Your dad knows how to survive, Brian."

"I get it. You can't take us because of the money." I'd figured it out. If Dad's best friend who happened to be his banker took us in, the police might get suspicious.

"Yeah. He thinks it's for the best, long term."

Hank didn't sound so sure. I wasn't either. Here's what else I figured out: You don't leave your kid a ten-grand emergency fund if you expect to be home next week. What if Dad wasn't coming home at all?

60

My SAWS hit hard after I left the bank. I spent ten minutes in a Starbucks bathroom. After I washed my hands, I touched Richie's dog tag and tucked it under the collar of my shirt. The cool metal felt comforting against my skin. On the walk to the hospital, I tried to summon some Ninja Energy. I found Mom's floor and approached the nurses' station, where two nurses were talking.

"Excuse me, um."

They turned to me. My face went hot.

"I'm here to visit Julia Day," I squeezed out. "My mom."

The older nurse gave a sympathetic smile. "She's resting, hon. It might not be a good time."

I swallowed. "That's OK. I won't stay long. I . . . I brought her a book. For later. So she won't be bored."

I held up the book I'd bought at Bookmark, a collection of short stories from a writer she liked. The nurses exchanged a look that made me nervous, but the older one nodded and the younger one led me to Mom's room. I paused outside, caught in the thrum of my nerves.

Just rip off the bandage, already.

I walked to Mom's bed. Her eyes were closed. She was paler than normal, and the IV snaking from her hand to a beeping, whirring machine was not comforting. But she wasn't a zombie or a corpse, so that was something.

I pulled a chair to the edge of the bed. "Mom," I said softly. Nothing.

I held her IV-less right hand and struggled to ignore

the machines, the clatter in the hall, the antiseptic hospital smell that made me think of disease.

"I took the bus downtown, Mom. I saw Hank. And I talked to Dad. He asked me to come see you. I wanted to see you too. But—"

I couldn't finish my sentence. Something rose up in me, something I couldn't stop.

"Mom, why? I wish you'd given me a chance. If we could have talked." I was squeezing her hand too hard, but I didn't let go. "It was my birthday. You never gave me a chance."

Mom moaned. I looked up, into her open eyes. My heart locked up.

She shook her head slightly. Her eyes darted away from me.

"I can't," she whispered. "Not here. No no no."

She pulled her hand from mine and covered her face.

I jumped up. "Mom, it's OK. I'm sorry. I just wanted to see you."

She buried her face in her hands. "You shouldn't . . . I don't want you . . . I can't."

Her shoulders shook. The nurses showed up and the older one attended to Mom while the younger one led me from the room. She said Mom was still disoriented. I should give her a few days. It all washed over me as I stared through the door until she pulled it shut.

"Are you alone?" she asked. "Do you have a way home?"

The probability that I could make my brain and mouth work together was zero percent.

"I'm his ride."

I turned. Sergeant States stood in the hallway.

"Oh. I'll leave you two, then." The nurse walked away slowly, glancing back at us.

"Need a minute?" Sergeant States asked.

I needed out immediately. I started for the elevators and he followed. I wasn't surprised someone found me at the hospital, though I figured it would have been Kate. Thank goodness it wasn't.

He didn't ask questions or lecture me about disappearing. As we passed through the sliding doors and back into the hot sunshine, I spoke first, to stop my brain from replaying Mom's hospital room scene on a terrible loop.

"Sergeant is a high rank, right?" I asked.

"It's up there," he said.

"I bet you don't usually pick up stray kids." Something clicked. Anger swelled in my chest. "You're following me because you're after my dad. If you think you can act all nice and convince me to help you, forget it."

"Brian—"

"You're the jerk who ruined my family. Stay away from me."

We slowed at an intersection and I dashed across the crosswalk. I weaved through a gaggle of tourists outside the Museum of Natural History and tried to ignore how they stared at me, a rude young delinquent fleeing a cop. I sprinted, backpack thumping against my spine. If I kept going north, past the Common, I could run all the way home. To my house.

But then what?

I pulled up in front of Citadel High and slumped on a bench. Dad was gone, Mom was sick, and Hank could barely help. I had nowhere to go. I was alone. The Void was winning.

Heavy footsteps plodded along the sidewalk. Sergeant States caught up and sat beside me. "You're fast," he panted. "Barely winded too. You play sports?"

"Basketball," I mumbled.

"Me too. Master's league, though. None of us move that quick anymore." He wiped his forehead. "You're right about one thing. I guess you know why I'm interested in your father."

I didn't answer.

"That's not why I showed up, though. I don't want anything from you, Brian. I just don't like seeing kids like you get hurt."

Kids like me? What did that mean? The poor, unfortunate children of criminals?

"You're just like Kate," I blurted. "You think you know us, but you're wrong. Mom takes me to the library and Dad plays basketball with me. They're not bad parents. There are worse people than Dad."

My face grew hot. Even this was too much.

"I'm not judging," Sergeant States said. "Life's complicated. But I know going into foster care isn't easy. I was eleven when it happened to me." His voice went soft. "You're a thinker, aren't you? You like quiet. Living with strangers is stressing you out."

I nodded, avoiding his eyes.

"Is that why you're barely talking to anyone?"

Kate must have told him. I don't know why I answered. But his deep, relaxed voice made me feel less SAWS-prone than usual. He wasn't even mad that I'd tried to ditch him. He seemed like he understood. If his family had problems when he was a kid too, maybe he did understand.

"They baked me a birthday cake," I said.

He frowned in confusion, then it clicked. He whistled. "Aw, man. I'm sure that felt pretty clueless, huh? I get it." He stretched, grimacing as his knees creaked. "Sounds like they're trying, though. Even good people get it wrong sometimes."

That didn't make me feel any better.

"How about that ride now?" he said gently. He led me to his car, and we drove in silence.

As he turned onto the Wentzells' street, I said, "Sorry I called you a jerk."

He laughed. "I've been called worse."

Kate's car was in the Wentzells' driveway, so he parked at the curb. "Want me to come in with you?" he asked.

I didn't want to go in at all. Exhaustion hit me, and I just wanted to lie down in the back seat and sleep. But I couldn't do that, and I couldn't get too friendly with the officer chasing my father. I hopped out to face the music alone.

Things went as I expected. When I ignored Kate's questions, she lectured me and said that she was trying to help, and I was only hurting myself, blah blah blah. Emma repeated "I was so worried" a dozen times. Gordon wore a disappointed-grandpa frown.

Eventually, Kate left and we ate dinner in silence. Even Richie was quiet, until we retreated to our room and he punched me in the stomach.

"Ow!" I doubled over until I caught my breath. "What was that for?"

"You lied." Richie glared at me. "You said we were a team and you wouldn't leave, then you ditched me."

I rubbed my stomach. "Sorry, Rich. I had a secret mission. From Dad."

"I can keep a secret! Kate asked a million questions and I didn't say anything."

I cursed myself for giving Kate a chance to interrogate Richie alone. "What did she say?"

"She said she's trying to help. I didn't fall for it. I told her I have rights and I wasn't going to talk without a lawyer. Was that OK?"

I grinned. "You did great." I told him about the bank.

His eyes bugged. "WHAT? We're rich!"

"Shh!" I covered his mouth. "We can't tell anyone.

But I got you something." I dug a graphic novel and bag of M&M's from my backpack. "Don't eat them all at once."

He tore into the candy. "Did you see Mom?" he asked through a mouthful of chocolate.

I shoved away my memory of the hospital. "She's still resting. We can't go back for a while."

His face fell. "Oh."

"And I talked to Dad. He misses you."

"Can we call him?"

"No, but he said he'd call tomorrow." I pointed at the candy. "That's enough for tonight."

Richie rolled his eyes, but he put the M&M's away. "Could we get Emma to take us to buy a LEGO set tomorrow? It's so boring here."

"We'll see," I told him.

Four hours later, Richie was snoring while I stared at the ceiling. The hospital scene haunted me.

"*I don't want you.*"

That's what my mom said.

It was only a half-sentence. *To see me like this.* That's what she meant, right?

But I couldn't stop seeing the panic in her eyes.

"*I can't.*"

I couldn't stop my brain from asking terrible questions.

What if Dad never comes back?

What if Mom never gets better?

What if she doesn't want to get better?

What if she's mad that I saved her?

What if she doesn't want to be our mom anymore?

Dad told me not to blame myself, but I'd trade the world for a ten-minute do-over.

Somewhere in a better universe, Alternate Brian woke on his birthday, sensed trouble, and headed straight for his mother's room. He took her hand before she touched her pills and said, "It's OK. We can do this together." Maybe they both cried, but they kept going. Maybe in that universe, Dad figured out his plan and made it back. Maybe those Days ran away together and were chilling on a beach in Cuba right now. Maybe it was real, somewhere. But here, it sped farther away every minute. I was stuck in a broken universe where even good people got it wrong.

10. SECRET LANGUAGE

EZRA

My fingers drummed on my knee as my turn to play approached in the church hall beside the music studio. Even though I'd been taking lessons since I was nine, I still got nervous at recitals. Mom noticed my fidgeting and offered me a piece of gum. I popped it in my mouth, but that didn't slow my fingers down.

I checked my phone. Ty and Kevan said they would have come if they hadn't been busy, but they did text me.

> **Ty:** You're going to kill it
> Remember, the crowd will be 57% grandparents. Old people get emotional at concerts and cheer for everyone and cry and stuff
> **Kevan:** omg imagine if someone booed a small child at their recital???
> **Ty:** Not helping Kev
> **Kev:** No one's going to boo you Ezra
> You'll do awesome

Besides if you're playing after the little kids
you'll sound like a genius
Ty: Break a leg E. Make grandmas cry

The girl onstage finished her violin performance. Everyone clapped. I put my phone away and scanned the program again. Two more people to go.

I'd only skimmed the list of people after me, but now a name three down from mine caught my eye. *"Let It Go"* — *Madelyn Jacobs—Voice.* Madelyn Jacobs? Madi in my class? I tried to search the crowd, but I couldn't see past the two large men behind me.

A boy started his piano piece and it was almost my turn. I headed to the side of the stage to strap on my guitar and check my tuning. Then the boy was bowing, his mom snapped some pictures, and my teacher, Morgan, stepped to the microphone.

"Next, playing the Beatles classic 'Blackbird,' please welcome Ezra Komizarek." Morgan beckoned me onstage.

"Knock 'em dead," he said to me.

I plugged in my guitar, sat on the stool at center stage, and looked up. Four rows behind my parents, I spotted Madi, with her parents on her right and her friends on her left. Alicia and Victor. And Jemma and Colby.

Colby grinned at me, like *surprise!* I froze. Playing to a room full of parents and grandmothers was one thing. Performing for kids from school was a whole new level of nerve-racking. Even Colby hardly ever saw me play.

I took a breath and tried to forget he was there. I set my fingers, tapped a steady tempo with my foot, and began.

"Blackbird" is constant motion on the guitar, picking with the right hand and changing chords with the left. Your fingers never stay still for long. I hummed the melody as I played. I hit one wrong note, but I kept going. Morgan told me most people hardly notice mistakes if you just keep playing.

I nailed the ending and tried not to make my sigh of relief too obvious. People clapped. Morgan gave me a fist bump as I walked offstage.

"You have pleased the rock gods, my young apprentice." He was always saying cheesy stuff like that. It made me smile.

"That was excellent, honey," Mom said when I sat down. Dad gave me a nod of approval.

"Sir Paul himself would be proud," he said.

Soon after, Madi took the stage. Her hands shook as she waited for her backing music to start, and I felt a tug of sympathy. She closed her eyes and launched into the song. She was too quiet at first compared to the music, but the sound guy fixed it before she got to the chorus. Madi could definitely sing. When she finished, Jemma and Alicia burst into wild cheering.

After the recital ended, they all approached as I packed up my guitar. Colby slapped my shoulder. "Nice job, bro."

Madi beamed at me. "Ezra, you were *amazing*. I didn't know you could play like that!"

"Thanks," I said. "You were really great."

"You two could perform together," Alicia said. "You'd make a great duo."

Madi's cheeks went pink. Colby and Jemma smirked.

"Are we still going for pizza?" Jemma said. "You should come, Ezra."

"Yeah, come with us," Colby echoed.

My eyes drifted around the group. Madi gave me a shy half-smile. Colby had his arm around Jemma, and his chest puffed out with *I have a girlfriend* confidence. Victor and Alicia were holding hands. I didn't know them well, but it looked like they were a couple too.

The whole vibe felt funny, but I tried to shrug it off. Colby wanted me to come. Maybe I'd been in my feelings lately for no reason.

"Sure," I said. "Let me check with my parents."

Mom said it was fine, even though we'd planned to go eat together. "Have fun with your friends," she told me. Madi's parents' van was full, so Dad dropped me off at the pizza place. When I arrived, the others had pulled two tables together. I took the only empty seat, between Madi and her dad. Her mom was across from me. Colby, Jemma, Victor, and Alicia sat at the other end.

"It's the guitar player," Madi's father greeted me. "I respect a guy who knows the classics."

Madi sighed. "*Dad.* Don't start."

"What? Just admiring Ezra's taste." He leaned closer, like he was telling me a secret. "The Beatles were before my time, of course. I'm not *that* old. My British rock growing up was Radiohead and Blur."

"My teacher loves Radiohead," I said. "He taught me a few riffs."

His face lit up. "Yeah? What songs?"

Colby cut off my answer with a fake-sounding cough. I turned. Everyone at his end of the table looked like they were enjoying some joke I'd missed. Colby rolled his eyes at me and jerked his head toward Madi, who was still scowling at her dad. It took a second, but I figured out what he was trying to say. My face heated up.

I shrugged Colby off and turned to Madi. "What kind of music do you like?"

Her expression changed instantly. "Carly Rae Jepsen is my favorite."

"She's great," I agreed.

Madi's eyes widened. "You listen to Carly Rae?"

"Yeah. Why wouldn't I?"

"*Some* people are too insecure to listen to 'girly music.'" Madi made angry air quotes and glared at Colby.

He laughed. "I like what I like. Sorry I'm not a massive music geek like Ezra."

I knew he was only teasing. He did that sometimes, and I didn't mind if we were alone, or with Ty and Kevan. But it felt different here. Sharper. Like it got stuck in my skin.

"It's good to have eclectic tastes," Madi's dad weighed in. Colby's smirk got bigger.

Madi and I continued to talk music as we ate. I liked talking with her. I liked talking about music with just about anybody. I didn't mind when her dad jumped in either, though Madi always looked annoyed.

At the other table, Colby teased Alicia, whispered to Jemma, joked with Victor. He hardly looked at me. I felt as if I were sitting three seats away from a clone. He was still Colby: same flawless smile, same scar on his left elbow from a skateboarding wipeout. But this Colby knew a different secret language than the one we'd written together over years of sleepovers and lazy afternoons. This Colby traded looks with Victor and snorted so hard that root beer dribbled down his chin.

"Gross!" Alicia squealed. Jemma swatted his arm and left her hand on his bicep. All four of them collapsed in laughter.

"What's so funny down there?" Madi's mom asked.

Colby shrugged. "Nothing." They bit back more laughter.

I set down my pizza crust. I wasn't hungry anymore.

Madi's parents offered to squeeze me into their van on the ride home, but I said I'd walk. I didn't want to jam myself in somewhere I didn't fit.

"Thanks for inviting me," I said.

"Thanks for coming," Madi said. "This was fun."

"Nice meeting you," her dad said. "Keep rocking."

Madi sighed. *"Dad."*

"For real, you were great," Victor said.

This was the first thing he'd said to me directly all day. "Uh, thanks," I said.

Colby waved. "Later, bro."

I didn't expect that he'd detach from Jemma and walk with me. It would have been nice, though.

It would have been nice if he said more than "Later, bro."

As I walked, I shielded my eyes against the sun and turned on a playlist to distract me from thinking about Clone Colby. The song came on that had been playing when I boarded the bus on Thursday, and it reminded me of riding with Brian.

He didn't think it was weird when I called a song *pretty* or shared my earbuds.

What if Brian had showed up at my recital? He would have sat quietly in the back by himself, I bet. I would've talked him into going out for fish and chips with Mom and Dad, like we'd planned. Brian would have smiled when Mom pulled out the hot sauce she always kept in her purse. He'd have been shy at first, but maybe after a while, he would have told me about his favorite books. Maybe I would have made him laugh again.

I was so wrapped up in the daydream that I made it home and halfway up the front steps before I noticed Mom in the garden, waving. I turned off my music.

"Earth to Ezra," she said. "How was pizza with your friends? That looked like a different bunch than your usual crew, other than Colby."

I shrugged. "Yeah. They're Colby's friends, mostly. It was fine."

Mom tugged off a gardening glove and pushed back her hair. "Fine, huh? How's Colby these days?"

I didn't know where to start. "Fine," I repeated.

Mom watched me. "Well, if everything's fine, be a sweetie and keep me company. Your guitar's in the front hall. You know I love hearing you play."

She made her *pretty please* face, so I didn't have much choice. I brought my guitar outside and played on the front steps. I played the one Bob Marley song I knew, "No Woman No Cry." I knew Mom liked that one. She hummed as she hunched over her flower bed, and I drifted back into my daydream.

"That sounds so good, Ezra." Mom was at the foot of the steps, pulling off her gloves. "I like when you sing too."

"What? Oh." My cheeks went warm. "I did it without thinking."

Mom smiled. "I know. You do that sometimes, until you get self-conscious and stop. But you don't need to hide the things that make you happy."

She lightly brushed her fingertips over my curls as she walked up the steps. I stayed outside a while longer, playing as the sun slanted through the trees and the street turned golden.

11. ICE MODE

BRIAN

"Brian? Brian."

I lifted my head from my arms. The classroom was empty except for Mrs. Clelland and me. I didn't remember hearing the bell.

I struggled to orient myself: It was Friday afternoon. A whole hazy week had passed, a week where I'd avoided everyone. At the Wentzells', I barely left my room. At school, I hid in the library on breaks and stopped playing basketball at lunch. When I saw Ezra with his friends, my chest ached, and I ducked away. He'd joked about hanging out with me sometime, and I would have loved that more than ever. But talking in school felt harder than ever, so I avoided him.

Now it was almost the weekend, and I'd have to spend two days with the Wentzells. Yay.

Mrs. Clelland straightened books on the bookshelf. She was pretending to look busy as she kept an eye on me. Suddenly she turned. "I don't mean to pry, but are you all right? Is there anything I can do for you?"

How pathetic did I look? I hadn't slept well or eaten much all week, and the dark rings under my eyes practically shouted *Please, ma'am, take pity on me*.

I rose without looking at her. "I'm OK. See you next week."

As I stepped out of the classroom, Victor nearly ran me over. I flattened against the wall to avoid him, but he stopped. His two usual sidekicks, Scott and Colby, hovered on either side of him.

"Heads up, Ghost." Victor grinned. "Taking some special time with Mrs. Clelland, huh? You have a thing for her, don't you?"

Scott snickered. I put my head down and tried to move, but Victor blocked my path.

"Do you talk at all anymore? I swear you're getting weirder. You going psycho on us?"

I focused on breathing. This was our pattern. Victor had twenty pounds on me, and no conscience.

He leaned in with a grin that said *I could crush you if I wanted*. I just had to stay quiet until he grew bored.

Finally, he backed off.

Normally I would have fled in the opposite direction, but I stood frozen as Victor and his buddies walked away. A few kids gave me sideways glances. Others moved past as if I were invisible. At the far end of the hall, I saw Ezra watching me, wide-eyed. I knew from his eyes that he'd seen everything.

But he looked away.

No one was coming to rescue me. Not from school bullies or social workers or the Void. I was on my own.

Dad's voice filled my head.

Listen, B-Man. We could go to your principal, get this kid's parents involved, but some things you need to handle yourself. Bullies are sharks, kiddo. You act all quiet and fragile, they smell it on you. Want this goon off your back? Deck him. Send a message, to Victor and every jerk like him. I know this is the opposite of what teachers tell you, but trust me, B-Man.

I touched my ninja tag. My feet moved before I knew what I was doing. An unsettled calm gripped me, the way the air goes still before a nor'easter strikes and suddenly the wind is so fierce the rain hits you sideways. My hands didn't shake and my heart didn't race as I walked toward Victor, who'd stopped to flirt with Alicia by her locker.

"Victor," I said.

He turned, scowling.

I punched him in the face.

I wasn't that strong. One normal Skinny Brian Punch wouldn't have done much. But a one-in-a-million coincidence of physics happened. Alicia's locker door was half-open and Victor's nose crashed into it—hard.

The *crunch* made every kid near us stop cold. Blood geysered out of Victor's nose and splashed across Alicia's shirt. He pressed his hands to his face, but a crimson waterfall gushed through his fingers and splattered on the floor. I'd never seen anyone bleed so much. Alicia covered her mouth and stared at me. Everyone stared.

Victor slumped to the floor, swearing into his cupped hands. Teachers came running. Mrs. Clelland arrived first.

"What on earth?" She gasped, looking around. "Who did this?"

Everyone pointed at me.

The adults sat without speaking. I wasn't sure if they were trying to make me squirm or holding a silent turf war. Ms. Floriman, Mr. Hartland—the vice principal—and Mrs. Clelland sat on one side of the table, across from Kate, Gordon, and Emma. I sat at the head, unusually calm. Let them figure it out. I could wait in silence forever.

Finally, Ms. Floriman started. "This isn't like you at all, Brian. I know you've had a rough time lately. Can you tell us what you're feeling?"

Feelings After Punching Victor, in Order
1. Holy smokes, that's a lot of blood. (Dizziness)
2. What if it doesn't stop? What if I pushed a bone into his brain? What if I accidentally killed him? (Panic)
3. Ah, he's cursing. He'll live. (Relief)
4. Look at his nose. I wrecked him good. (Satisfaction)
5. I wish Mrs. Clelland didn't look so worried. (Guilt)
6. People are talking about me. "Holy crap. Can you believe Brian did that?" (Embarrassment)
7. Yeah, I did it. Quiet, invisible Brian who never does anything, never says anything. Not this time. Not anymore. (Determination)

A reaction began in the chemistry lab of my brain. Two beakers crashed to the floor and mixed for the first time, unleashing something new and bubbly and purple.

But I said none of this out loud.

"Victor's nose is likely broken, Brian." Mr. Hartland jumped in. "Alicia said you blindsided him. Now would be a good time to explain yourself."

Six adults watched me, but for once, I didn't care. As Mr. Hartland talked, I pictured the purple ooze burning through the floor, opening a secret passage.

I pointed at Kate and the Wentzells. "I don't want them here."

Kate bristled. "I'm your social worker, and the Wentzells are your legal guardians. We need to be here."

I made eye contact with Mrs. Clelland, then Ms. Floriman. I made myself look 25 percent sadder. "They don't know me. I don't like it."

"I'm sorry, Brian, but this is how it works," Kate said.

Ms. Floriman and Mrs. Clelland stiffened. I had a chance. *Set sadness to 50 percent.*

"Let's consider what's best for Brian," Ms. Floriman said. "This happened on school grounds—"

"And you know you have to involve his caregivers in a situation like this," Kate interrupted.

Hearing someone say "situation" again pushed me over the edge.

"I'm not a baby. I'm right here."

Everyone watched me, but I wasn't nervous. I followed

the secret passage in my mind until I reached a set of cob-webbed doors. I pushed them open.

"You know what works for *you*, not me," I continued. "I'm just a folder with a number to you."

The doors opened on a gleaming room, a superhero's hidden fortress. I approached a control panel.

Kate faltered. "Brian, I understand you're upset, but—"

Now. Press the red button and finish her.

"But you have all the answers, right? You're always like, 'Hey, I know your dad left and your mom nearly died, but suck it up and do as you're told.'"

This was the first time I'd said any of that out loud. But my throat didn't go lumpy. I was in control. I could do this.

"I'll talk," I said. "After. They. Leave."

Ms. Floriman stared across the table. After six long seconds, Kate sighed. She rose. Emma watched me in confusion as Gordon ushered her toward the door.

After they left, I turned to Ms. Floriman. "I don't trust Kate. If I need a social worker, can I get a different one? Maybe I'm being unreasonable, but I don't care."

"Oh, Brian," Mrs. Clelland said. "You're allowed to feel whatever you want."

This was the first thing she'd said this whole meeting. She looked sad, and I didn't want her to throw me off, so I stared down at the table.

"I'm not sure what we can do there, but I'll look into it," Ms. Floriman said. "How about you tell us what happened with Victor?"

"He ganged up on me with his buddies and called me Ghost and psycho. Same stuff he's done all year. This time I'd had enough."

The adults paused.

"Does he pick on you often?" Mr. Hartland asked.

I almost laughed. *How could anyone not know?* "Victor's the meanest kid in our class. I should have hit him months ago."

Saying this out loud felt amazing. More lights and switches flipped on on my control panel. Gravity felt lighter, as if I were floating in space. I could see more clearly in the cool and quiet a thousand miles from everyone. I didn't have to feel anything at all.

"I'm sorry you felt you had to take matters into your own hands," Ms. Floriman said. "I don't think you meant to hurt Victor like that."

I didn't mean to split his face open, but I had still punched him. I almost apologized, like always. But a message flashed on the monitor in my bunker.

Activate Defense System? Y/N. I pressed *Y*.

"I'm not sorry. I honestly don't give a crap."

Only I didn't say "crap." I said a word no sensible kid would say in the school office. The adults recoiled in shock. I sat there, not caring about Victor or Kate or swearing in front of my principal. I officially Did Not Care anymore. This had to be what Dad had been trying to teach me: how to stop caring, so I didn't get hurt. I had found my fortress and unlocked Ice Mode. And it ruled.

"You don't mean that, Brian. That's not who you are."

Mrs. Clelland's voice was barely a whisper. I didn't dare look at her. Ice Mode was too fresh, and I didn't want to lose it.

I slouched. "There's only so much crap a guy can take." (I did say "crap" this time.)

Dad's voice returned.

Life is probably going to kick you right in the junk someday, B-Man. This is all the fatherly wisdom I've got: Brace yourself and kick right back.

Mrs. Clelland sighed. "You're right, Brian. You've taken too much crap."

The room went silent.

Ms. Floriman cleared her throat. "It's true we probably could have—and should have—done more for you lately. So how about this: We'll give you an in-school suspension. Punching a classmate is serious, but it's completely out of character. And I gather you might feel more comfortable here than in your foster home."

The words *foster home* made my forehead wrinkle. "I guess so," I said.

Ms. Floriman nodded. "I don't know if you know this, but we have a mental health clinician here at school twice a week. We'll make you an appointment for Monday. We should have done that sooner too. I'm sorry."

My ears grew warm. "Wait. I'm not . . ." *Easy. Don't falter. Maintain Ice Mode.* "Just because of my mom, that doesn't mean there's something wrong with me."

Everyone looked at Mrs. Clelland.

"Brian, that's not what anyone's saying," she said. "It's OK to feel whatever you're feeling. But you can't carry it all on your own. I understand if you don't want to talk to your social worker, but you should talk to someone."

A thought wiggled into my fortress, a thought that had simmered in my brain all week. Saying it would shut down Ice Mode, and I didn't know if I could keep surviving without it. So I didn't say it.

I focused on the table. "What I need is for everyone to leave me alone. Suspend me if you want. Make me write Victor a letter telling him I'm sorry he's such a monster—I don't care. But forget the mental health nurse or whatever. The last thing I need is another stranger telling me what I need." I folded my arms. "Can we be done now? I'm done."

Silence. I could sense Mrs. Clelland trying to meet my eyes, but I didn't dare look. Ice Mode depended on it. Ice Mode was all I had left.

I remembered what Hank said: *"Your dad knows how to survive."* Maybe Dad had been fragile like me once. Maybe he hadn't unlocked Ice Mode until his parents let him down.

I had to learn how to survive too. And I had to do it on my own.

12. INVISIBLE KID

EZRA

"Look out, Ezra!" Kevan took a running leap off the deck, soaring over my head toward the basketball net at the edge of Ty's pool. He flapped his arms before he dunked the ball and hit the water face-first with a *splat*. Ty and Colby erupted in laughter.

"Nice belly flop, bro," Colby gasped as Kevan surfaced, spluttering. "If you weren't brown, you'd be so pink right now."

"Two-point-five," Ty declared. "That was *turrrrible*."

"What? Come on. I made the dunk." Kevan looked to me for sympathy.

"Eight," I said.

"*Eight?* Put your glasses on," Colby howled in protest.

"I'm serious," I said. "One point for the dunk, two for comic flailing, five for maximum horizontal spreadage."

Everyone cracked up.

"Horizontal spreadage?" Ty repeated. "All right, I support that."

"Thank you!" Kevan threw his arms up, victorious. Colby slapped his sore belly. As they scuffled, I climbed up to the deck and cannonballed, drenching them both.

This was our first swim of the almost-summer, and the cool water gave me goose bumps, but it was perfect. The four of us were together, like old times. Along with maximum horizontal spreadage, we were having maximum funnage.

When the battle died down, Ty relaxed with his arms draped along the edge of the pool. "That reminds me. Did you guys hear what Brian did to Victor yesterday?"

"Oh *man*." Kevan bounced with excitement. "I saw it. Brian smoked him. No warning, nothing. Just 'Hey Victor,' and *bam!* Right in the grill."

I shivered.

"I wish I'd recorded it on my phone," Kevan continued. "*So* much blood came out of Victor's face. It's the coolest thing that's happened all year."

"I'm not surprised someone popped that dude," Ty said.

"No kidding," Kevan said. "Victor's the worst."

Colby scoffed. "He is not."

"Not to you," Kevan shot back. "He thinks you're cool, so he's friendly with you. He's a jerk to me. I brought samosas for lunch *one time* and he started calling me Captain Curry. Sometimes he even uses a gross accent."

"He's just messing around, Kev," Colby said.

"It's not funny. It's racist."

Colby rolled his eyes.

"Your samosas are the most-ah," I joked, to lighten the mood. Kevan groaned, so I kept going. "You should put them on a postah."

"Ezra—"

I broke into song. *"You could heat them in the toastah. Eat them on a rollah coastah."*

Everyone finally cracked up. "All right, Dr. Seuss," Ty said.

"That's Supreme Overlord Seuss to you," I replied.

Cue a three-minute riff where we imagined an evil dictator who spoke in rhymes. (*I will hunt you, rebel scum. I will stab you in the bum.*)

I thought we were done with the fight, but Ty jumped back in. "I can't believe it was Brian. He's so quiet." He looked at me. "You're like the only person he talked to all season."

My stomach tightened. I'd barely seen Brian since the bus. I passed him in the hall a couple times and thought about trying to talk to him, but he always rushed off like he had somewhere else to be. And then on Friday . . .

I didn't say anything to my friends.

"Ghost has been weird all year," Colby said. "Maybe he has mental issues. Like he snapped or something."

I winced. "Don't say stuff like that. And please tell me you don't call him *Ghost*."

"For real," Ty said. "That's not cool."

Colby rolled his eyes. "I didn't make it up. It's not like I mess with the guy."

"But Victor did, right?" I said. "And nobody did anything about it."

Colby scowled. "Why are you taking this so personal?"

I looked away. "Brian wouldn't punch someone for no reason."

We fell into an awkward silence until Ty's mom stepped onto the deck and reminded him he had a fundraiser for his provincial team.

Kevan shook his head. "Being a superstar is going to eat up your social life."

Ty splashed him. "The pursuit of excellence requires sacrifice. That's what my dad says, anyway."

Kevan's eyes lit up. "Speaking of excellence, my uncle tried my cardamom coconut cream pie today and it sold out. He wants two more for tomorrow. I'm making them tonight."

"That's awesome, Kev," I said. Kevan's desserts were amazing. He'd been pestering his uncle to sell them in his café for months.

"You should be on *Kitchen Stars Junior*," Colby said. "You could be famous."

Kevan sniffed. "I'm not going on TV so a bunch of rich dudes can use me to get richer."

"Whatever, bro." Colby grinned. "While you chumps are working tonight, I'll be at the movies with Jemma."

"So are you two 'official' now?" Kevan made smoochy faces.

Colby's grin grew wider. "Yeah. We are. I should probably go get ready."

We climbed out of Ty's pool and dried off.

Colby and I walked home together. He draped his shirt around his neck instead of putting it on, which was a very Colby thing to do. He already had a tan in mid-June. As we walked, he held his arm up to mine.

"I'm darker than you now," he joked. "You gotta put your guitar away and get some sun, bro."

I bit my lip. I didn't like jokes about how dark I was or wasn't. They made me feel self-conscious. I didn't say that, though. I knew how Colby would respond: *Relax. I'm just kidding.*

"I can't help it, my Polish genes are strong," I joked back. Colby laughed, but I didn't feel good about it.

He shook out his still-damp hair. "You could come tonight. Madi'll be there. You know she likes you, right? And this time her dad won't be around to distract you by talking about old-people music."

My cheeks tingled. Madi and I had talked at school a few times since the recital, and I'd had a suspicion she liked me. I wasn't totally clueless. But I hadn't mentioned it to Colby. I hadn't talked to him about last Saturday at all.

"Is Victor going too?" I asked.

"No. His face is pretty messed up." Colby glanced at

me. "He's not a bad guy, Ezra. He just jokes around some-times. He liked hanging out with you last weekend."

I didn't know what to make of Victor. He'd been fine to me, I guess. But Brian obviously didn't think his jokes were funny. Neither did Kevan.

But I didn't mention that to Colby either. I was doing a lot of not-talking with Colby lately.

I pictured two awkward hours in a dark theater with him and Jemma being all boyfriendy-girlfriendy, and Madi maybe wanting to do the same things. I liked talking music with her, but I didn't like her like *that*.

Being friends with girls was less complicated before junior high.

"I'll pass," I said. "But good luck."

"Suit yourself." Colby grinned. "And I don't need luck."

At home, Dad sat at the kitchen island in his Saturday-night best, watching golf on his tablet while Mom rushed around looking for earrings to match her shoes or vice versa. I grabbed an Italian soda and slid up beside Dad. On one of her passes through the kitchen, Mom noticed me and deliv-ered the rundown without breaking stride.

"Ezra? You're home already? Have you eaten? We have that charity gala at Saint Matthew's and we're meeting the Maxwells first. Paul, leave him money for takeout. You can start the car. I'll be thirty seconds."

My parents were big on arts and culture. They usually brought me if they were going somewhere fun, like the symphony. And sometimes they dragged me to art galleries and museums, which could either be great or boring. I'd gone to one fancy gala a year ago and fell asleep in the coat closet, so we'd all learned our lesson about galas.

Dad gave me twenty bucks, along with a salute and a wry grin. Mom swept through once more with a brisk peck on my cheek, and then I had the house to myself. I did the usual: ordered jerk chicken and rice, video-chatted with Nat, watched anime on Netflix, and played guitar. Somewhere in there I wondered how Colby's date went.

I almost texted to ask, but I decided that would sound pathetic.

When I eventually went to bed, my thoughts turned to Brian. I could still hardly believe he'd punched Victor. It made me realize how little I actually knew about him. He was so quiet. I knew he was secretly the second-best seventh grader on the team, after Ty. He was too timid to shoot much, but he was a great passer.

And I liked being around him. He seemed like a guy you could tell stuff and he wouldn't make fun of you. He seemed like he wouldn't turn into a clone.

I grabbed my phone and searched for him online. I couldn't find him anywhere. I scrolled my friends' friends and followers. Nothing. He didn't even show up in the background of other people's photos.

I hated the nickname "Ghost," but Brian really did seem like the most invisible kid in school.

A wave of guilt sloshed in my belly.

Here's another thing I didn't tell my friends: I saw the punch too.

I saw Victor corner Brian as he left Mrs. Clelland's room. I was too far away to hear what Victor said, but it was obvious Brian hated every second of it.

I saw Colby standing with Victor. I should have stopped them. I should have confronted Colby. But I didn't.

After they walked away, Brian looked right at me.

The look in his eyes haunted me. Like he was totally alone.

I should have gone to him, told him I was sorry, tried to help somehow. But I didn't. I did nothing.

Everybody knew what happened next. If I hadn't been such a coward, maybe it wouldn't have happened at all. I owed it to Brian to do something now.

13. GETAWAY

BRIAN

Emma kept trying to talk to me about punching Victor. The tender knuckles on my right hand and the nagging voice in my head reminded me what I'd done, but no way was I talking to her about it. I mostly ignored her. But on Sunday, she and Gordon wanted to drag us to the Common for a Father's Day outing with their family. I thought about refusing, but I wanted out of their house.

"I need a basketball," I said.

Emma blinked in surprise. I hadn't said a full sentence to her in days. "You need what?"

"A basketball," I repeated. "I'll go if I can buy a ball on the way."

They agreed. Gordon tried to pay at the store, but I insisted on using my debit card. When we reached the Common, Richie and I shot around on the basketball court while Gordon and Emma played with their grandkids on the nearby playground.

Handling a ball felt good. My body followed a familiar

pattern and I could forget everything else, including that it was Father's Day and I had no clue where Dad was.

Launch. Rebound. Dribble. Repeat.

As I settled into a rhythm, an idea bubbled in my mind: *I have to get away.*

Regular Brian would have dismissed this as ludicrous, impossible, terrifying. But I needed to strengthen Ice Mode. I needed control of my life.

"If you could go anywhere tomorrow, where would you go?" I asked Richie.

He thought for five seconds. "I'd ride a waterslide."

That night, when everyone was asleep, I used the Wentzells' computer to book a hotel room, then I deleted the browser history to cover my tracks. I wasn't sure my plan would work. It might be a disaster. But I had to do something.

Ditching school on Monday was easy enough. After Emma dropped me off, I looped around back and just walked away. If anyone asked, I'd say I'd forgotten my homework and I'd be right back. But no one asked.

Richie waited outside the corner store we'd chosen as our rendezvous. I hadn't been sure he could be stealthy enough to sneak away without getting caught, but there he was, grinning like he'd won the lottery.

"That was fun," he said once we were on a bus. "Have you skipped before?"

I shook my head. I never missed school, not even when I dreaded facing Victor so much my stomach hurt. Regular Brian didn't break the rules. But Ice-Mode Brian did not give a crap.

We transferred buses and crossed the bridge to Dartmouth. Neither of us had packed swim trunks after the Incident, so we hit Walmart for supplies, and then we ate lunch and headed to the theater for an afternoon showing of the newest Marvel movie. Every time an adult looked at me, I assumed they were considering calling the cops on two kids who should have been in school, but it was mid-June, close enough to the end of the year that nobody questioned us.

After the movie, we followed a woman through the back door of the hotel near the theater and slipped into the bathroom. I splashed water in my hair and ran my new swimsuit under the faucet before I changed in a stall. I left Richie with my backpack and padded down the hall, barefoot. I was dizzy with nerves as I approached the front desk. To summon Ice Mode, I thought about arguing with Kate in the school conference room.

I'd handled worse. I could do this.

The woman behind the counter smiled at me. Her name tag said her name was Lisa.

"Uh, hi," I said. "This is embarrassing, but I got out of the pool and remembered my mom took the room key. She went to pick up dinner, so I'm stuck."

Lisa smiled again. "No problem. What's the room number?"

"Um . . . shoot. It's the family suite? My mom booked it. Emma Wentzell." Booking online required a credit card, so I'd slipped Emma's Visa from her purse.

"Right." Lisa checked her computer. "That's odd. I see the reservation, but it says you haven't checked in yet."

"Weird. We got here an hour ago." I stepped back so she could see my wet shorts. "I've been swimming already."

She looked from me to the computer and back again. My heart sped up. I could feel Ice Mode dissolving. Lisa was going to figure out I was a runaway and call the police. Kate would say I was turning Richie into a delinquent. She'd separate us, and I'd be charged with fraud and thrown in jail and everything would be ruined forever.

What was I thinking? This was *a terrible idea.*

Should I run? I should run.

Lisa clicked her mouse. "Must be a glitch. This system has a mind of its own sometimes. We can't leave you stranded in your swim trunks. Here you go, Mr. Wentzell." She slid a key card across the counter.

"Thanks." I resisted the urge to sprint back to the bathroom. *Be cool.*

Half an hour later, Richie was making endless trips down the waterslide in the hotel pool. I rode a few times before I watched from the hot tub. Every time his giddy laugh echoed through the room, I grinned too. I was happier than I'd been in weeks. We were free.

I took a selfie with my phone, just because.

"This is the best night ever," Richie declared. He lounged on the queen-size bed in his underwear, propped up on four pillows like a Roman emperor, watching TV and eating chicken and fries with his fingers. Takeout from Swiss Chalet tasted extra delicious in your own hotel room, free from the oppression of foster parents and pants.

"Can we stay all week?" Richie asked.

I shook my head. "Too risky."

Obviously the Wentzells knew we were missing, and we'd be caught in a flash if Emma checked her account. I gambled that she wouldn't think of it right away, if she thought of it at all. Regular, quiet Brian wasn't the type to jack a credit card. Like he wasn't the type to punch a guy. But we still couldn't stay too long.

When Richie finally fell asleep, I made an account on an online rental site. I fudged some of the details, like my birth date, and booked a secluded cabin that would leave a key and take online payment from my bank account, so I never had to meet the owner face-to-face.

When that was done, I scanned local media for stories of two missing brothers. We weren't breaking news yet.

Before I could change my mind, I called Hank.

He sounded surprised when he picked up. "Hey, Brian. Everything all right?"

"Today was great," I said. "Richie and I saw a movie and went swimming."

"Cool. School field trip?"

"Nope. Just the two of us."

"What about your, uh—"

"Nope."

Long silence. "Brian, where are you now?"

"A hotel."

"What? How? With who?"

With whom, I thought, because I was a grammar nerd. "No one. We're better off alone."

Hank exhaled. I could hear him searching his brain for what a grown-up was supposed to say to a thirteen-year-old runaway.

"Just letting you know we're fine, in case you hear we're missing or anything. Good night." I hung up before he could say anything else.

This was a test. For me, and for Hank too. I needed to know what he'd do. I figured he'd freeze my account, so I'd withdrawn enough cash to last a while. Would he search for us? Make an anonymous tip to the cops? Do nothing?

My phone rang. It was an unidentified number, not Hank. I let it ring. After it stopped, a text popped up, and my heart somersaulted.

It's Dad. Calling again. Answer your phone.

Of course. Hank's first move was to call Dad. I should have seen that coming.

Even though I expected it, I jumped when my phone rang again.

"Brian," Dad said when I answered. "What do you think you're doing?"

I hadn't planned for this, but maybe I secretly wanted this test. I pushed aside my natural instincts and answered. "I'm doing what I have to do, Dad. Isn't that what you always say?"

In Dad's two seconds of silence, the universe rearranged itself.

He laughed in surprise. "OK. You're running away. What are you planning to accomplish?"

Don't think too hard. Say it. "I don't know yet. How's it working for you?"

More silence. I almost blurted "sorry," out of habit, except I wasn't sorry.

"Huh," Dad said. "I guess I deserve that."

What now? This is way off our usual script.

"Where are you?" I asked.

"Toronto. Trying to figure things out. Where are you?"

"A hotel. Trying to figure things out."

Dad laughed again.

My face tingled. "This is funny?"

"I'm surprised you're giving me lip. You never give me lip." Dad wasn't mad. He sounded almost proud.

"Things are different, Dad. You're not here. Mom's not here. Everything's different."

"I know, B-Man. I'm trying, but . . ." He changed the subject. "How are you in a hotel?"

I told him. He whistled. "Jeez. That was clever. Though

don't make a habit of skipping school. Or stealing from old ladies."

"I'll pay her back. And I'm suspended anyway."

"Suspended? *You?*"

"I punched Victor. Like you said. I don't think he'll bother me anymore."

Dad coughed. "Listen. I'm glad you're standing up for yourself. But you've gone from zero to a hundred here."

"What am I supposed to do, Dad? You're gone, Mom's in the hospital, and I can't deal with these people. They want to send me to a psychologist or something."

My face burned and my throat went tight. The ice was melting. *Keep it cool.*

"Huh," Dad said.

Huh? What does that mean?

He sighed. "You shouldn't have to deal with all this. It's too much."

I flopped on the bed. "What are you saying?"

"I'm saying take care of yourself. Forget what I said about keeping secrets. If you need to talk to somebody, do it. Look after you and Richie. That's all that matters now."

I didn't like where this was going. "Why can't you come home? Maybe you can make a deal with Sergeant States."

Long pause. "Who?"

"The police officer on your case."

"How do you know that?" Dad's voice hardened. My shoulders tensed.

"I, uh, he came to the house, when Mom . . . then he found me when I went to see her."

"This cop is stalking you?"

"No, he's OK, Dad. He actually gave me the best advice of anyone."

"You're taking advice from the guy trying to put me in jail?"

"You just told me to do what I had to do."

"So I did. You're right." Dad sighed.

I'm right? What's happening? This was the weirdest conversation we'd ever had. Before Dad could object, I found Sergeant States's card and read Dad his number. "Maybe you should call him."

"I don't know about that," Dad said.

"You have a better idea?"

Dad laughed. "Listen to that attitude. Good for you. We'll talk soon."

I had a dozen other things I wanted to say, but nothing came out before Dad hung up.

Brian versus Brian, Round 4,229
Me: Today was amazing. I pulled off things I never would have dreamed of doing before.
Also Me: You skipped school, told a dozen lies, committed at least two kinds of fraud, and stole from people who are trying to help you. Nice work.
Me: Richie and I had fun for the first time since the Incident. He's safe and happy.

Also Me: For now. How are you going to keep this up?

Me: Can we not go there yet? Focus on the positive. I called Hank without panicking. I argued with Dad, and he actually listened. He sounded proud!

Also Me: He thinks you need help.

Me: That's not—

Also Me: He said you should talk to somebody. He can tell. Everyone can tell. Even Victor. Everyone knows you're losing your mind.

Me: . . .

Also Me: You know it's happening, right?

Me: Shut up.

Also Me: You don't sleep. You barely talk. You broke a guy's nose and robbed your foster parents and ran away. Normal kids don't do these things. Troubled kids do.

Me: I'm just trying to get through this.

Also Me: Get through what? There's no end here. Your life is a disaster. Your mom had a breakdown and your dad's a fugitive. They're broken, and so are you.

Me: Shut up shut up SHUT UP.

Also Me: You're doomed.

I didn't sleep any better than I did at the Wentzells'. I barely slept at all.

14. PINK ELEPHANT

EZRA

Brian wasn't in school on Monday. I looked for him until I remembered that punching Victor was probably worth a suspension. Maybe he wasn't coming.

I was still thinking about him on Tuesday as conversation ping-ponged around me during morning break. Kevan grilled Colby on the latest developments with Jemma.

"Have you kissed her yet?"

Colby gave a sly shrug. "I kissed her on the cheek."

Ty laughed. "The cheek? What are you, European?" He adopted a terrible accent somewhere between British and French. "Thank you for a superb evening, *dah-ling*."

Colby reddened. "Her friends were around. I didn't want to . . . you know."

"A cheek kiss still counts," Kevan declared. "Right, Ezra?"

I blinked. "What? Sure."

"Really? No jokes?" Colby tilted his head. "You're so zoned out today."

"Um . . . just thinking about this riff I'm learning," I mumbled.

Colby rolled his eyes. "You're obsessed, bro." He pointed at my fingertips, moving in rhythm on the cafeteria table. I tucked my hands in my lap.

"Go with the spacey rock-star thing," Kevan told me. "It works for you. I heard Madi say you have dreamy eyes."

"You do have beautiful eyes, Ezra," Ty said. "They're ten out of ten dreamy."

Colby scowled. "Knock it off." He slugged me on the shoulder. "I told you Madi likes you. You should ask her out."

"Not right away," Kevan objected. "Pretend you're not interested. Build up the mystery."

"Mystery?" Ty laughed. "Where do you guys get this stuff?"

I tuned out as they bickered over romantic strategy. I wished we were having a different conversation.

When the bell rang, we split up, and Ty and I headed to social studies.

"What's up, E?" he asked. "You really are extra-spacey today."

I took a breath and said it. "Do you think we try enough? With Brian?"

"What do you mean?"

"I didn't know he had a beef with Victor. He never mentioned it."

"B handled Victor just fine." Ty grinned and threw a jab.

"Yeah, but . . . he's our teammate. That means something, right?"

"*Together Everyone Achieves More.*" Ty placed his hand over his heart and imitated Coach. I managed a "heh."

"He plays with us at lunch," Ty said. "He knows he's one of the team."

"I guess." I let it go. But I knew Brian hadn't played once last week.

I tried to stop thinking about him, but it was like that game where someone says, "Try not to imagine a pink elephant." Instantly, it's the only thing you can picture.

Then, at the end of the day, a police officer walked past my locker. Ms. Floriman was with him, and they went into Mrs. Clelland's classroom.

It had to be about Brian.

Why was a police officer here? That wasn't a good sign.

Whispers rippled along the hall as kids headed for the exit. I stood there, torn on what to do. But I couldn't take it anymore. I burst into Mrs. Clelland's room.

"Sorry to interrupt, I know it's not my business, but is this about Brian? Is he OK?"

The three adults stared at me. With every beat of their silence, I felt worse.

Ms. Floriman's eyes narrowed. "Do you know something we should know, Ezra? When's the last time you talked to Brian?"

My face grew hot. "Uh . . . last week? I mean, I saw him hit Victor, but—"

"You didn't talk over the weekend? Or yesterday?"

Ms. Floriman's tone made me sweat. I shook my head. "What's going on?"

They exchanged another long look. Obviously, something had happened—something so bad they didn't want to tell me. Suddenly I had to lean over with my hands on my knees.

"Oh, Ezra," Mrs. Clelland said, and led me to a desk.

Before she could speak, the door opened again, and a teenage boy stepped inside. He looked like he was in high school. He was tall, more than six feet, with light brown skin around the same shade as mine.

"Hi, Mom," he said to Mrs. Clelland. "Still need a ride home? I texted you." He noticed the police officer and broke into a grin. "Hey, Oliver! What are you doing here?"

The officer clasped the boy's hand. "Hi, Gabe. Long time no see."

The boy laughed. "Right. Thanks for lunch on Sunday." He glanced around the room. "What's up? Is this about that kid you were talking about on Sunday?"

Mrs. Clelland and the police officer stared in surprise.

"I kind of eavesdropped," Gabe admitted.

Ms. Floriman pursed her lips. Mrs. Clelland sighed.

"Well, we might as well do this all at once," she said. "Ezra, this is Sergeant Oliver States, who happens to be a family friend. And my son, Gabe."

They both waved. "Hey, man," Gabe said, and offered me a fist bump.

"So," Mrs. Clelland continued. "Brian and his younger brother are missing. They were dropped off at school yesterday but never went inside. They haven't been seen since. That's the reason for the questions, Ezra. If you know anything that might help, we'd appreciate it."

Everyone waited, as if I was the key to this mystery. I squirmed, feeling like a fraud. I couldn't believe Brian ran away. It didn't seem like something he'd do. But neither did punching Victor.

"Brian's pretty private," I said. "He doesn't say much. I wish I had something helpful to tell you. Sorry. But whatever you're doing to find him, I want to help."

"Me too," Gabe said.

The adults went silent again. Sergeant States scratched his head.

"I appreciate your concern, guys, but we don't need a search party right now." He pulled a business card out of his pocket and handed it to me. "You can help by keeping an eye on social media. If you see anything related to Brian, let us know."

I took his card and didn't mention that Brian might be the most offline kid at Halifax North. "Do you want my number in case you find anything I should know?"

He smiled. "Sure. Couldn't hurt." I gave him my number.

"Oliver and I are going to talk to Brian's mother," Mrs.

Clelland told Gabe. "So I don't need a ride, but I'll see you at dinner."

"Thanks for your cooperation, Ezra," Ms. Floriman said. "Please keep this to yourself for now. We'll see you tomorrow."

I caught the hint in her tone and said goodbye. Gabe walked out with me.

"You're friends with this kid?" he asked.

"Uh, yeah." I pushed away a surge of guilt.

"You know where he hangs out?"

I shrugged. "He likes the library."

Gabe slowed. "You have anywhere to be right now?"

"Not really."

He grinned. "Want to take a quick road trip?"

I followed Gabe to his car. A girl sat in the passenger seat, so I hopped in back.

"Ezra, this is my girlfriend, Brittany," Gabe said as he climbed in the driver's seat.

Brittany turned. Her hair was shaved on one side, and the rest swooped in front of her face like a comma. One streak at the front was dyed pink.

"Nice to meet you, Ezra. I'm also a fully functioning person on my own terms. Cool Japandroids shirt." She turned to Gabe. "What's going on? We're leaving your mom, but you found a junior high kid with impeccable taste in music and kidnapped him for me? That's sweet."

I liked Brittany already.

Gabe shook his head. "Remember I told you Mom was worried about one of her students? He's missing. Ezra's his friend. We're going to go look for him."

"Oh." Brittany glanced in the mirror. "Sorry. A kidnapping joke wasn't cool."

"It's OK." Gabe saying "friend" made me feel guilty again.

Brian was headed for the Central Library on Spring Garden the day we met on the bus, so I directed Gabe there. The library downtown was one of the coolest places in Halifax, a five-story glass building designed to look like a stack of books. Inside, the middle was wide open with crisscrossing staircases. We split up in the lobby. I described Brian to Gabe and Brittany and we exchanged numbers.

"Text me if you think you see him," I said. "He's really shy and he might get weirded out if a stranger approaches him. No offense."

Gabe laughed. "None taken."

I searched the kids and teens section on the second floor. I knew there wasn't much of a chance Brian was chilling at the library, but I still walked the whole floor and scanned the rows of kids using computers. I even looked up books on beekeeping in the nonfiction section on the fourth floor, but Brian wasn't there, and he hadn't hidden any secret messages inside *A Short History of the Honey Bee*. (Yeah, I checked.) Of course he hadn't remembered my random joke and left a clue only I would understand. I wasn't the star of a cheesy detective movie.

"What were you *thinking*, dingus?" I said out loud as a bearded man in suspenders walked past. He gave me a dirty look, but I pretended to be absorbed in bee literature.

I met up with Gabe and Brittany in the fifth-floor café. They hadn't found anything either.

I let out a breath. "I wish I knew why Brian ran away."

Gabe and Brittany went quiet in a way that told me they knew something I didn't.

"What?" I asked.

Gabe hesitated. "I'm not sure I should say." He glanced at Brittany. "I shouldn't even know. I eavesdropped on Mom and Oliver, and I told Brittany, but . . ."

I understood what he didn't say: If I was really Brian's friend, I should already know.

My frustration at my own uselessness bubbled over. "OK, I know I'm a lousy friend. We sat together on the bench all through basketball season and I still barely know him. Nobody knows him. People tease him, and I'm the only kid who knows he's missing, and it's wrong and it sucks, but I want to find him. So if you know something, you should tell me."

I slumped in my seat, sure that these two high schoolers would decide I was a fraud and take me home.

"You guys are both on the basketball team?" Gabe said. "Nice. I play for Citadel High."

Brittany jabbed his chest. "*That* is the first thing you bring up? Come on. Tell him what you heard, Gabe."

Gabe exhaled. "He's been staying in a foster home. Oliver's involved because of Brian's parents for some reason. I didn't hear the details. Mom sounded upset, like she was really worried about Brian. Now he's missing."

I remembered how miserable Brian looked the morning before we ended up on the bus together, and how hopeless he seemed the last time I saw him, right before he threw a punch. Victor was just the last straw.

What if I'd stood up for him then? What if I hadn't been such a wimp?

Maybe he wouldn't have snapped. Maybe he wouldn't be gone.

Brittany must have noticed how lousy I felt, because she gave me a kind smile. "We'll find him."

We sat, deliberating our next move. I was grateful for their company. We weren't any closer to finding Brian, but the weight in my chest didn't feel as heavy.

My phone rang. I didn't recognize the number, but it was local, so I answered.

"Ezra? This is Mrs. Clelland." She paused. "This might sound strange, but I'm at the hospital with Brian's mother. She wants to speak with you."

15. THE HAUNTED CABIN OF HORRORS

BRIAN

The cab ride to our next hideout was longer than it looked on my phone. Our driver pulled into the gravel driveway and glanced in the rearview mirror.

"This is it?" I read the suspicion in his wrinkled forehead. He was probably wondering why he drove two kids from a hotel to an empty house in the middle of nowhere.

"Yeah. Thanks." I passed him three twenties, enough to cover the fare and a decent tip. Richie and I hopped out. The cab didn't move, so I walked as confidently as I could toward the cottage, praying the key would be under the planter like the email instructions said.

Bingo. I unlocked the door and waved to the cabbie. The car slowly backed away.

I turned to check out the cottage. The owner described it as "rustic," but that turned out to mean "old and musty." The open living room/dining room/kitchen was smaller and dingier than in the photos. The furniture sagged, and the stale smell made me think of yellowing newspapers. Richie tossed his backpack onto the worn plaid couch and a cloud of dust rose in the air.

He sneezed and wiped his nose with the back of his hand. "Why didn't we stay at the hotel? This place is gross."

"It'll be fine, Rich," I said. "We'll open some windows."

Richie grumbled and headed for the bathroom. As soon as the door closed, he screamed.

"AAAGH! BRIAN!"

I dashed across the room and turned the door handle, but the door didn't budge.

"Richie? Are you all right? Unlock the door!"

"I didn't lock it! Ew ew EW!"

I jiggled the handle again. The door was stuck. I rammed it with my shoulder. On the second hit, it swung open. I stumbled into the tiny bathroom and almost collided with Richie. He was hopping up and down, trying to peel a giant spiderweb off his face.

"Oh, Rich. Let me help."

He glowered as I picked sticky strands from his eyebrows. "It was *huge!* There were *flies* in it! A mummified dead fly touched *my mouth!*"

I bit my lip. "I'm sorry, bud."

"I still have to pee! I can't pee in here now!"

"Go outside, then. We're in the woods."

With a face-melting glare, Richie elbowed past me. He threw open the patio door and did his business off the deck.

"I might get eaten by a wolf out here and it'll be all your fault!" he hollered.

"There are no wolves in Nova Scotia, Rich."

"You don't know that!"

"Actually, I do. I did a science project on local ecosystems."

I didn't tell him that there *were* coyotes with wolf DNA. And suddenly, I was thinking about coyotes with wolf DNA, and how far we were from the main road.

He came inside and flopped on the couch. "This is like a cabin in a horror movie where people get murdered. It's probably haunted."

Great. There went my chance of a better night's sleep.

The cottage closed in on me. My chest tightened. I went outside to the deck, but it didn't help. Thick woods surrounded us. A branch cracked in the distance, making me jump. Richie wasn't wrong. Anything could happen to us here, and no one would know.

Signs You're Dead Meat in a Horror Movie
1. You're fleeing a troubled past.
2. Your escape goes too smoothly.
3. You find an eerie hideout removed from
civilization.
4. No one knows where you are.
5. You're too clueless to see the foreshadowing in
steps 1–4 until it's too late.

I closed my eyes and took deep breaths. I was being silly. The woods were not full of hungry animals, or escaped killers, or vengeful spirits. I needed to keep it together for Richie.

I sat down next to him and dug a bag of Skittles out of my backpack. I'd stocked up on supplies during our Walmart stop. I popped a handful of candy in my mouth and held out the bag. Richie resisted for five seconds. Without a word, he dunked his hand in the bag.

We chewed in silence.

"We should stay with the Sidhus," Richie said eventually. "Leo told me we could have their room, and he'd sleep in his nana's room, and Kevan could sleep on the couch."

My stomach plunged. "Richie, what have you been telling people?"

"I only told Leo. He asked why I was never around after school anymore." Richie looked up. "Leo's parents are nice, and Nana Sidhu loves me. I bet they'd let us stay."

I thought about how impossibly awkward it would be to stay with the Sidhus. Kevan seemed OK—he was nice to Richie, and he never made fun of me or anything at school. I couldn't imagine camping out in his room and kicking him to the couch, though.

But I also remembered how much Richie laughed when he was with Leo. Mrs. Sidhu regularly sent him home with extra food, samosas and pakoras and the most incredible spicy chicken. She always waved hello if we passed in the street, like she knew me even if I'd never been in their house. Their family seemed warm and generous.

I swallowed, "I don't know, Rich. That's a lot to ask."

I expected him to argue, but he didn't. We ate more Skittles in silence. When Richie spoke again, his voice was small.

"I miss Mom and Dad. I want to go home."

I sighed and put an arm around him. "I know, Rich. Me too."

16. WHAT ELSE I KNEW

EZRA

Gabe found a parking spot two blocks from the hospital. I stared down the tree-lined street while he fed the meter. Questions rolled through my mind, starting with *Why me?* And *Why is Brian's mom in the hospital?*

"You OK?" Brittany asked, stirring me from my day-dreaming.

I nodded. With her ripped jeans, heavy black boots, and the prickly way she talked to Gabe sometimes, Brittany seemed tough on the outside, but she had a way about her that made me feel comfortable.

"Do you have younger brothers or sisters?" I asked.

Gabe smiled. "You've discovered her secret already. She acts tough, but Miss Punk Rock wants to take care of everybody."

Brittany shot him a mock scowl before turning to me. "I do take care of my brother and sister. Somebody has to. Dad tries, but he's clueless." She tucked her hands in her back pockets. "Our mom died in the fall. Cancer."

She offered this so matter-of-factly it caught me by surprise. "Sorry," I said.

"That's how we met," Gabe added. "My dad was in the military, and he died overseas last summer. When I heard about Brittany's mom, we formed our own Dead Parent Club, and things kind of . . . escalated. Romantic, huh?"

Brittany shook her head, laughing. "You're terrible."

She took Gabe's hand as we walked. I couldn't believe how easily they talked about serious stuff like death. One of the basic rules of junior high survival is you try not to give anyone ammunition to make fun of you.

Back in November, I was with Colby after school when he discovered his pet turtle, Rocky, had died. He'd had that turtle since he was five. When Colby cried out in shock, Jackson burst into his room to see what was up. He mocked Colby for being sad over a "stupid reptile." I've never wanted to fight someone so badly in my life, but Jackson is bigger than me. When he finally left us alone, I put a hand on Colby's shoulder and asked if he was OK, but he pulled away. He wouldn't look at me.

"*I'm fine,*" he'd snapped. "*Don't you dare tell anyone I cried over a turtle.*"

It stung that Colby could even imagine I'd use that against him.

As we neared the hospital entrance, Brittany slowed. She turned pale.

"What is it?" Gabe asked.

"I didn't think this would bother me so much. I haven't been in a hospital since . . . I can't. Sorry." The last word was a whisper.

Gabe wrapped an arm around her. "Don't be sorry. I should have thought about that."

She closed her eyes. "You guys go ahead. I'll wait here."

Gabe looked from Brittany to me, obviously torn.

"I can go by myself," I said. "I don't mind."

They promised to wait, and Gabe gave me a fist bump. Despite what I'd told them, my stomach fluttered as I walked through the automated glass doors. I was used to wandering on my own, but a solo trip to music lessons wasn't the same as visiting a stranger in the hospital.

Sergeant States met me when I got off the elevator at the psychiatric unit. A nurse watched us, and she didn't look happy. He nodded at her in a way that told me they'd talked—and maybe argued—about why I was there.

We walked until we reached Brian's mom's room near the end of the hall. Mrs. Clelland beckoned me in. Our eyes met and my brain fully connected that Gabe's dad had been her husband. She'd lost someone too.

Sergeant States waited outside as I followed Mrs. Clelland. Brian's mother sat in a chair beside the bed. She was younger than I expected, younger than my mom. She looked tired, and sad.

She waved toward the chair next to hers, and I sat down.

"Thank you for coming." Her voice was soft and

scratchy, like someone getting over laryngitis. She looked at Mrs. Clelland. "Can you give us a minute, please?"

Mrs. Clelland hesitated. I nodded. I didn't know why Brian's mom wanted to talk to me alone, but I wanted to make her happy. Maybe I could do one small thing, to make up for what I hadn't done for Brian. Mrs. Clelland relented, backing out of the room.

Brian's mom sat quietly. I swallowed, trying to soothe my dry throat. She offered a smile that didn't erase the sadness in her eyes.

"I'm sorry for the setting, but I'm glad to meet you. Brian thinks so highly of you."

This made my throat hurt more. "He does?"

"I know he's not the most expressive . . . but your kindness means more than you know." She sighed. "He'd be mortified that I told you."

I rubbed my eyes behind my glasses. "I like Brian." My own voice went scratchy. "I'm sorry I didn't always—"

"Ezra, no. Don't do that. You're in seventh grade," she interrupted, as if that explained everything. She patted my hand. Her fingers were cold.

With a glance at the door, she leaned closer. "But he might listen to you."

I sat up straighter. "You know where he is?"

She shook her head. "Hank talked to him, but Brian wouldn't say. He has a phone. If you called . . ." She tugged at her hospital bracelet. "It would be better if you didn't tell anyone. Like the social worker. Or the police."

Who was Hank? And why was Brian's mom asking me to keep this from the police?

She exhaled. "I know it's a lot to ask. Brian's father got tied up in some things. It's all so complicated . . . I'm just trying to do what's best for Brian and Richie. Brian doesn't know who to trust. He might trust you."

Her attempt at explaining left me more confused and nervous, but this last part hit me in the stomach. "What do you want me to do?"

Her eyes watered. "I'll give you his number. I wrote it down. Just try to talk to him."

She picked up a book from the bedside table and ran her hand over the cover.

"Brian brought me this. He's so thoughtful. He tries to take care of me. Of all of us." She closed her eyes. "It was his birthday, and we . . . Oh, I'm so sorry."

She covered her face. Her shoulders twitched as she cried quietly. I squirmed, wondering if I should get Mrs. Clelland. I hardly ever saw adults cry.

"Can I, um—?" I carefully took the book and found Brian's number written on the first page. I put it into my phone.

Brian's mom wiped her eyes. "You must be wondering why I don't call him myself."

Of course I wondered, but it seemed like a question I shouldn't ask.

She swallowed. "We made a mess of things. It's more

than you can fix, Ezra. But maybe Brian will talk to you, at least."

"I'll try," I said. "I promise."

She walked me across the room and stopped by the door. "Can I give you a hug?"

Her eyes were so sad it hurt to look at her. When I said yes, she wrapped her arms around me like she never wanted to let go. I knew she was thinking about Brian.

As I hugged her back, I thought about my own mom. I knew she loved me, but I couldn't remember the last time she'd hugged me like this.

"Tell Brian I miss him so much," she whispered. "Tell him I'm so, so sorry."

The weight of my mission sank in as I left the room. Brian was reachable, maybe, but he wouldn't talk to the people who knew him best.

What if he wouldn't talk to me either?

Why should he talk to me, after I stood there uselessly while Victor bullied him?

What if I screwed up, and he disappeared completely?

For a moment, I imagined a different day where I didn't barge into Mrs. Clelland's classroom and none of this had anything to do with me. I quickly shook it off. That was why Brian went so unnoticed at school. Everyone decided he wasn't our problem.

Not anymore.

I was so wrapped up in my thoughts that I forgot about Mrs. Clelland until she caught the elevator doors. I apologized as they slid shut behind her.

"Are you all right?" she asked. "I'm afraid we've dumped an awful lot on you today."

I liked Mrs. Clelland. She was a good teacher. When she looked at you, she really saw you. I wanted to tell her everything. But teachers probably had official rules on sharing information with the police, so I kept quiet. I didn't want to blow my shot at finding Brian.

"I'm all right. I hope Brian's OK." I straightened my glasses. "I wish I'd talked to him more last week. I wish I'd known something was wrong."

"Me too." Mrs. Clelland smiled a sad smile. "You're a kind soul, Ezra. A little kindness goes a long way."

I wanted to tell her Gabe had told me about her husband and I was sorry. I wanted to say her kindness went a long way too. But before I found my nerve, the doors opened, and we had to squeeze through a pack of chatty old men who started piling into the elevator before we could get out.

We met Gabe and Brittany outside, and I gave them the edited update.

Gabe turned to Mrs. Clelland. "What now?"

"There's not much we can do right now," she said. "We should drive Ezra home."

Brittany gave Mrs. Clelland the passenger seat and sat in the back with me. When we pulled up at my place,

Brittany patted my arm. "Nice sleuthing with you. I'm sure he'll turn up."

"We'll let you know if we hear anything," Mrs. Clelland said. "You should do the same."

Her look made me think she suspected Brian's mom had told me something. "Thank you," I said, trying not to sound guilty. I climbed out.

Once I was in the house, I checked the texts I'd ignored all afternoon. Kevan had asked if I wanted to hang out. I sent off an excuse for my late reply. Mom said she was leaving the office at six and meeting Dad for sushi. Want to catch a cab and join us?

I'm good. Have a romantic dinner, I replied.

I had the house to myself. I should call Brian right away. Don't overthink it.

No, I had to be prepared. How was I supposed to convince him to come home? Where even was *home* now? This was way out of my league. I needed to think. And I was hungry.

After I layered a tortilla with peppers, cheese, and leftover chicken and threw the whole thing in our sandwich grill, I picked up my phone again.

OK. Do it.

I opted for a text first. Hey Brian. This is Ezra.

Start simple, right? Don't jump straight to "So I hear you're on the run."

What if he doubted it was me? On a whim, I snapped a photo and sent it.

See? C'est moi.

Was that weird? We shared goofy pictures in the Juice all the time. A couple of weeks ago, Kevan sent a shot of his first armpit hairs. He was very proud. Naturally, Colby replied that even on full zoom he couldn't see anything. The thread got grosser from there.

I put my phone down and focused on not burning my dinner. As I lifted it from the grill, my phone lit up.

Do you have a secret girlfriend?

It was Kevan.

What are you talking about? I replied.

You keep ghosting after school and being all shady. What's the deal?

The perfect answer came to me. I've been meaning to tell you. I joined a space cult. Pledge your loyalty to Zyrgaz the Seven-Faced and you will be spared the Reaping

lol dude you're so weird. Want to play online?

Maybe later. Eating now

As I took my first gooey bite, Kevan wrote back. I tucked a loose cheese string in my mouth before I checked my phone.

How did you get my number?

It wasn't Kevan.

I swallowed wrong and had a coughing fit. Bits of half-chewed tortilla flew everywhere. For an awful moment I couldn't catch my breath. I stumbled to the sink and gulped from the tap. When I could breathe, I had to laugh at my own clumsiness.

"Boy receives text, chokes to death on burrito," I said to no one.

After pouring a glass of water, I wrote Brian back.

I found out at school that you were missing. I looked for you this afternoon. Your mom asked to see me and gave me your number.

Three long minutes passed before Brian wrote back. You saw my mom?

Yeah. Mrs. Clelland was there too. She's worried about you. I am too tbh

Two minutes this time. Did anyone tell you what happened? Did my mom?

No. I only know things aren't good. I want to help. Can I come to wherever you are?

Four minutes passed, then five. I couldn't eat; I was too nervous I'd spooked him.

Finally, he replied. I'm fine. I don't want Kate to know where I am.

Who's Kate?

Nvm. It's complicated. I can't go home and I'm not going back where I was.

I won't tell, I wrote. Only your mom knows I have your number. Tell me where you are and I won't bring any adults

How would you get here?

I'll manage. Cab if I have to

He went silent again, until he asked the question I knew was coming. Why are you doing this?

I took a breath before I replied. **Because you're my friend.**

I hoped he believed me.

Three minutes later, Brian sent an address. **Please don't tell anyone.**

I did it. I knew where he was. After a celebration dance, I texted him back.

Can I bring you anything? Pizza?

That would be great. Richie's hungry. I'll pay you back.

Don't worry about it. See you soon

I texted Mom that I was going to a friend's. Then I sucked up my nerve for one more conversation.

Gabe didn't like my plan. I guessed from his expression, but he made it clear as we drove away from my house.

"Mom should be coming. She knows this kid, and he's obviously not in a good state. What if—"

"Gabe," Brittany gently cut him off. I was glad I called her first and convinced her I knew what I was doing. Maybe.

"You have to let me try," I told Gabe. "I promised Brian I wouldn't tell any adults."

He frowned. "What did you tell your parents?"

"I texted Mom that I was going to a friend's."

"*You texted her?*"

"She and Dad met for dinner after work."

Now they were both looking at me.

"They invited me," I added.

"Are you an only child?" Brittany asked.

"Not exactly." I told them about Natalie and my older half sister, Lila, who was twenty-six, living in Ottawa, married, and pregnant.

"You'll be an uncle," Gabe said. "That's cool."

"I guess. It's strange to think about. My family's kind of weird."

"Every family's weird," Brittany said. "The people who love us the most are usually the people who mess us up the most too."

"Yup," Gabe said. "Sometimes they up and die on you too. That sucks."

Brittany met my eyes in the mirror. "We charge a premium rate for chauffeur services, but the depressing life advice is free."

I nodded. "Much appreciated."

It felt like they had let me into their club. The way Brittany talked like I was her equal and not an annoying kid reminded me so much of Nat.

"You seem more mature than a lot of seventh graders," she said. "Does that make school hard?"

I shrugged. "Not really. I have friends and stuff, and school's OK most of the time. But sometimes—"

"Sometimes you think junior high is an elaborate form of torture?" Brittany said.

"Yeah. That."

Gabe nodded. "It gets better."

"How would you know?" Brittany turned to me.

"Gabriel Clelland is one of the most popular humans at Citadel High. He and his sporty friends call each other silly nicknames and wrestle in the middle of the hall. He doesn't know what it's like to be a weirdo."

Gabe laughed. "Oh, please. You're not the only one who's misunderstood. Try being a big, athletic Black guy and see what people assume about you."

"Ugh, you had to go *there*," Brittany said, but she was laughing too. No topic seemed too sensitive.

"You know what I mean, E?" Gabe said. "You got some spice in your mayo, right?"

It took me a second to figure out what he meant. I nodded with mock seriousness. "I'm a Trini-Polish combo. My mayo is extra spicy."

"I knew it. A fellow hybrid." Gabe reached one hand back for a fist bump.

Brittany shook her head. "Don't encourage him, Ezra." She turned on the stereo, and they bickered over music choices.

"Your call," she said to me.

"No fair!" Gabe protested. "He's just going to side with you."

Brittany rolled her eyes. "*Obviously*, because my taste is so much better."

Gabe drowned her out by warbling along, loudly and off-key, to the ballad on the radio. I joined him with a high falsetto harmony. My voice cracked, and Brittany couldn't stop laughing long enough to argue. All of it was so much fun and I didn't want it to end. It was almost enough to distract me from the reason we set out in the first place.

"This is way out in the boonies," Gabe said as we headed north on the highway, away from the city. "How'd Brian end up out here?"

I wondered the same thing. I kept double-checking my phone to make sure I was directing Gabe to the right place. When we turned off the highway, Gabe announced he needed gas and pulled into a plaza near the exit ramp. I tried to give him some gas money, but he refused. While he filled the tank, I walked across the parking lot to a pizza place. Brittany came with me. I ordered a medium pepperoni for Brian and his brother, and we sat by the windows, waiting as the pizza rolled through the oven. We were the only customers in the place.

"You did good," Brittany said. "You got Brian to tell you where he is. That's huge."

I nodded. Now that we were close, reality was hitting again.

"Don't worry." She pounded a fist into her palm. "If they put up a fuss, we'll just grab them. I heard he punched a kid, but I doubt he can take all three of us."

I smiled. "Brian's not really a fighter. The Victor thing was unusual. He's quiet. But super smart. There's more going on in his head than he says out loud."

I didn't mean to say all that. My cheeks grew warm.

"Maybe most people don't see him," Brittany said. "But you do."

I traced the edge of a grease stain on the countertop. "I guess."

Here's what else I knew about Brian, the things I barely admitted to myself:

I liked how he flicked his coppery hair out of his eyes.

I liked how intently he concentrated on the bench or the court, and the way his cheeks glowed pink when he worked up a sweat.

I liked how his whole face lit up when I made him laugh.

I liked daydreaming that one day I'd know the secret world inside his head. I daydreamed about playing guitar for him and brushing the hair out of his eyes.

Brittany's voice went quiet. "Maybe there's more going on in your head than you say out loud too."

The strangest sensation swept over me, burning hot on the outside and freezing on the inside. I kept my eyes on the grease spot. It felt like Brittany was staring into my brain, right at the knot I was afraid to untangle and tried not to let anyone see.

Except maybe I wanted her to see it. Maybe I was a little relieved.

Still, answering her question that wasn't really a question felt like pushing a boulder up from my belly. My reply came out in a choked whisper.

"Maybe . . . maybe I kind of have a crush on him."

He wasn't the first boy I'd ever liked this way. Sometime in the sixth grade, I realized how I felt about Colby was definitely not how he felt about me. I never told him, because I knew how that would go.

With Brian, it was different. With Brian, I thought *maybe*.

Except I was scared.

I was scared he wouldn't like me back.

I was scared he would, and it would change everything.

I didn't say any of this, but Brittany must have read it in my face. She touched my hand. "I've only known you for about five hours, Ezra, but I think you're pretty great. Exactly as you are."

I knew this was her way of telling me it was OK. There was nothing wrong with liking a boy, but I was still scared it would make school harder. I was scared of what my friends would think, and how it might change things even more than they were already changing. Saying it out loud would make it official, so I didn't. It seemed easier that way.

But hiding all the time was hard too.

"Medium pep," the cashier called, making me jump.

"I'll get it." Brittany smiled and squeezed my shoulder before she collected the pizza. I wiped at my eyes, feeling silly for getting emotional. But I was glad I'd told her.

"Mmm, pizza," Gabe said as we slid into the car.

He'd waited outside on purpose. I saw it in the way he looked at Brittany before he glanced at me. He didn't say anything, but he nodded.

He started the car. "Let's go collect our fugitives."

17. FOUR WORDS

BRIAN

Richie sprawled on the couch, half watching a SpongeBob episode he'd seen three times already. "When's your friend coming?" he grumbled. "I'm starving."

I ignored him. He'd gotten saltier all afternoon. First his Switch died, and he realized he'd forgotten his charger, which he insisted was somehow my fault. (It wasn't.) Then he didn't want canned soup for dinner, because soup is worse than—well, take one guess. I told him I couldn't exactly pack a pizza in my backpack, so it was soup or nothing. But we couldn't even have soup, because our moldy cabin didn't have a can opener. What kind of cabin didn't have a can opener? A dusty, haunted murder cabin, that's what. This place wasn't getting a five-star review from me.

I'd started hacking at the can with a knife, but I was afraid of accidentally slicing my hand. Finally, I'd given up and taken it outside to whack the lid with a rock. But when I did, the can burst and soup spilled everywhere. I'd kicked it across the yard and swore. A lot. Loudly.

Thank goodness Ezra was bringing food instead.

I still couldn't believe he'd looked for me. I wasn't sure I'd made the right decision telling him where we were. I spent a while worrying this was a setup and Kate was using Ezra to catch me. Then I worried that paranoia was another sign I was losing my mind.

I glanced again at the four words Ezra wrote when I asked why he wanted to help.

Because you're my friend.

I couldn't help remembering the last time I saw him, when Victor cornered me and he looked the other way, just like everyone else. That hurt. But his messages seemed sincere. He wouldn't have looked for me if he didn't care, right?

Maybe it was wishful thinking. Ezra couldn't fix this mess. But I was tired of trying to wade through it by myself.

My stomach ached. I went to the bathroom—checking for spiders first—and that's where I was when someone knocked on the door.

"Finally!" Richie yelled.

"Richie, wait," I called, but he was already thumping toward the door.

18. WEIRD

EZRA

My heart beat a kick-drum rhythm when the door swung open. A boy with shaggy hair sized me up, then grabbed the pizza. I assumed this was Richie.

"Brian!" he yelled. "Your friend brought food!"

He ran off with the box, and I took a cautious step inside. Richie parked on the couch and attacked the pizza. Behind him, a door along the far wall opened, and Brian stepped out.

A bunch of feelings surged through me all at once: pride that I'd found him, relief he was safe, and the unnerving crush-flutter in my chest that had grown more intense all year.

"Hey," I said.

He leaned against the door frame, arms across his belly. "Hey."

Maybe it was my imagination, but he seemed skinnier and paler than usual. His eyelids drooped like he wanted to curl up and sleep.

I wanted so badly to rush across the room and hug him. But that would be weird.

He turned to his brother. "Richie, slow down. Did you even say thank you?"

Richie looked up, cheeks swollen with cheese. "Thmps," he mumbled.

Brian rolled his eyes. "Don't mind Richie. He has no manners. But honestly, thanks. I, uh . . ." He trailed off.

"You should eat too," I said.

He shook his head. "I'm not hungry."

"Are you OK?"

Wrong question. He dipped his head, letting his hair fall over his eyes. "Yeah. Things are just . . ."

"Weird," I finished.

"Yeah."

Tell me, I wanted to say. *Tell me everything.*

"How did you find this place?" I asked instead.

He shrugged. "I booked it online."

"Seriously?"

"He snuck us into a hotel yesterday too," Richie bragged. "Brian's a genius."

Brian smiled.

"I always suspected you were hiding your superpowers," I said.

He froze. Was that the wrong thing to say too? I was trying to lighten the mood, but what if he saw through me?

"Like being a secret jerk puncher," I added, forcing a laugh.

Brian covered his face. "Everyone's talking about that, aren't they? Now they think I'm even more of a freak."

Colby's words echoed in my head. *"Ghost has been weird all year . . . maybe he has mental issues."* It made my stomach churn.

"You're not a freak," I said.

"Can you guys talk somewhere else?" Richie called. "I'm trying to watch TV."

Brian's cheeks flushed. "Sorry, Ezra. I'm being rude. Come in."

I followed him to the bedroom. My heart kicked up the tempo. Other than those few minutes on a bus, we'd never hung out alone, just the two of us. I had imagined it plenty of times, though never in such strange circumstances.

The room was big enough for a double bed and a dresser and not much else. Brian sat at the head of the bed and I sat at the foot, so he wouldn't think I was trying to get too close.

"Sorry," he said again. "I should have illegally faked my way into something bigger. With a hot tub."

I laughed. He blinked, and the surprise on his face slowly dissolved into a smile. He never made jokes. Not around other people, anyway.

"I'm dying to know how you snuck into a hotel," I said.

He began slowly, growing more animated as he warmed up. I watched his hands, his jiggling knee, his hair drifting across his eyes. By the time he described how he nearly panicked and fled the hotel barefoot in a wet swimsuit, I was cracking up.

"That's awesome. Like a Home Alone movie."

He grinned. Did anyone else at North ever hear him talk this much?

"Your turn," he said. "How did you get here?"

I remembered Gabe and Brittany in the driveway, probably growing impatient. "Mrs. Clelland's son drove me."

Brian's eyes widened. "You told Mrs. Clelland?"

"No!" I fumbled out a version of my odd day. Brian hugged his knees to his chest when I mentioned his mom.

"Did she seem . . . OK?"

I wasn't sure how to answer. "She misses you. She wanted me to tell you—"

The door swung open. Gabe filled up most of the frame.

"We need to talk," he said, "before things get way more complicated."

We sat in a row on the couch—Brian at one end, me at the other, Richie in the middle. Gabe stood with Brittany at his side and explained his mom had called him, because Oliver States had called her, because a social worker had called him. Brian and Richie had been gone long enough that the social worker wanted to put out an official MissingKidsALERT.

"So unless you want your pictures on the internet, you need to come with us," Gabe said.

Richie perked up. "Cool! We'd be famous."

"We don't want to be famous, Rich." Brian rubbed his forehead. "Why did Sergeant States call Mrs. Clelland?"

"We've known Oliver forever," Gabe said. "He was good friends with my dad."

Brian stiffened. He sank into the couch and crossed his arms. The Brian who'd been laughing in the bedroom was gone.

He stared at the floor. "I'm not going back to the Wentzells' house."

Brittany wrinkled her nose. "Who?"

"The cranky old people we've been stuck with," Richie said. "Ever since Mom—"

"*Richie.*" Brian's tone was so sharp the room fell silent.

"I'm not taking you there," Gabe said. "You're coming home with me."

Brian stared. "To Mrs. Clelland's house?"

Gabe smiled. "I live there too."

Brian sat stunned. I wanted to tell him maybe it would be OK, but I doubted he wanted my opinion right now.

"Do you play video games?" Richie asked.

Gabe chuckled. "Yeah. I have a PlayStation 4."

"Do you have the newest *Call of Duty*? I hear it's awesome."

Gabe shook his head. "I don't do war games."

"Why not?"

"My dad was in the military. He, uh, he died. Last summer."

Brian covered his face. "Richie, oh my *God.*"

"It's OK." Gabe straightened. "Here's the deal. You don't have to tell me your business. I know sometimes life sucks and bad things happen. But Mom is worried about you, and you're making her sad. She's had enough to be sad about—"

Gabe stopped. His eyes welled up. Brittany rubbed his back. The three of us on the couch sat in silence. I risked a glance at Brian. He watched Gabe, wide-eyed.

Gabe wiped his eyes. "So you're coming with me. You'll let Mom look after you, and you won't give her any more grief. That's how it's going to be. Deal?"

"Deal," Brian whispered.

Gabe gave him time to pack his things. I offered to help, but Brian shrugged me off. "I need to talk to Richie. I'll meet you outside."

He wouldn't look at me anymore.

19. ATTACK OF THE VOID

BRIAN

The sun dipped behind the tree line as Gabe drove, casting the world in a fuzzy light that matched my fuzzy thoughts. Reality had rearranged and I struggled to catch up. My English teacher's son was taking me to my English teacher's house, where apparently Richie and I were spending the night. I got what I wanted, sort of. I wasn't going back to the Wentzells'. If I had to trust an adult, Mrs. Clelland was a good one. Still, she was my teacher. How awkward would it be to stay at her house?

I pictured her with the tall boy in the driver's seat. And I thought about what Gabe told us about his dad. Mrs. Clelland's husband was dead. This knowledge made me feel guilty.

"*She's had enough to be sad about.*" Gabe had nearly cried when he said it.

Some things in the world were scarce, but there was more than enough sadness.

Thinking about staying with Mrs. Clelland made me anxious, so I thought about Ezra, sitting on Richie's other side.

I'd made him laugh, like on the bus. Things felt so much easier when it was just us. But it was all complicated and he knew my mom was in the hospital and a cop and a social worker were chasing me. He knew my life was a smoking crater after a meteor strike. Maybe he regretted getting involved at all.

My pocket buzzed. The text was from Ezra.

Are you mad? I'm sorry. I was trying to do the right thing.

Sorry? I glanced past Richie. Ezra watched me with bunched-up eyebrows like . . .

Like he cared what I thought.

It's OK, I answered. **I'm not mad.**

He smiled and started typing. **I know it probably feels weird to stay with a teacher. But at least it's Mrs. Clelland. Imagine living with Ms. Virth.**

Our social studies teacher called us "citizens," urged us to fight apathy, and held class forums where we were supposed to "engage in passionate debate" like future UN ambassadors. She was intense.

I bet she'd wake me up with a megaphone, I wrote back. **RISE AND SHINE CITIZEN DAY. ARE YOU READY TO MAKE A DIFFERENCE TODAY?**

Ezra snickered. I'd made him laugh again.

Hey you can text or call whenever if you want to hang out, he replied.

I came up with a response less desperate than the truth. **Will you always bring pizza?**

Ezra laughed. **Yes. Now you know my secret. I'm an**

immortal pizza wizard. I can summon pepperoni and cheese from the phantom dimension

I couldn't help laughing too. **Good to know**

When we stopped at Ezra's, he leaned toward me. "See you at school tomorrow?"

"I guess," I said. "Technically I'm suspended, so I'll probably be stuck in the office."

"Maybe they'll let you out for lunch. I'll come find you."

As he got out, Brittany climbed out too and said something in his ear before she hugged him. We dropped Brittany off next, then Richie and I were alone with Gabe.

Richie adored him already. I could tell. He chatted away about video games and school, and Gabe responded with laughter in his voice. Gabe was a teenager who could be on TV, the kind with good looks and confidence and charm. The opposite of me.

I sank deeper into the seat. All of this was too strange.

The Clellands lived in a yellow house in the West End. A basketball net hung above the garage. As I retrieved my backpack from the trunk, Mrs. Clelland stepped outside. Dressed in jeans and a sweater, she'd transformed from teacher to mom. My gut tightened as Sergeant States appeared behind her. I braced for Kate to show up next, but she didn't. That was a relief.

"I had a talk with your mom and Ms. Evans," Mrs. Clelland said softly. "We're all on the same page that you two can stay here for a while. If you're OK with that."

Thinking of my mom, Kate, and Mrs. Clelland in the same room made the static in my brain grow louder. I could only nod.

She led us inside. "Are you hungry?"

Richie patted his belly. "I'm full. Ezra brought pizza. Brian didn't eat any, though."

Mrs. Clelland's house was simpler than the Wentzells' and there were no cat statues in sight. My eyes drifted to a picture of a happier Mrs. Clelland and a younger Gabe posing beneath a bright red maple tree with a girl who had to be Gabe's sister, and a man who was clearly their father. The late Mr. Clelland.

My eyes went blurry. Behind me, Mrs. Clelland asked Gabe to show Richie to his room. Richie went happily, no protesting about being separated this time. Sergeant States sat beside me on the couch, while Mrs. Clelland hovered in the doorway.

"I'll skip the lecture. I wouldn't say anything you don't already know." Sergeant States paused. "But I need to know if there's a reason you left your foster home."

I blinked. "I told you. The day I . . ." I didn't want to revisit that memory. "I hated it there."

"I understand. But did anything specific make you feel you had to leave? Any concerns about your safety or well-being? Or Richie's?"

He chose his words carefully. Mrs. Clelland watched with concern in her eyes. I realized what Sergeant States was asking. It hit me how serious this was, not only for us, but the Wentzells. Two people who only wanted to help a messed-up kid.

I tensed. "No. They didn't . . . they're not bad people. It's not their fault. I—everything is—I just had to get away."

My words wouldn't land right. A weight settled on my chest, pressing harder and harder.

Sergeant States lowered his voice. "I know it's been tough, Brian. Maybe you're feeling overwhelmed—"

He knew I was losing it too. I closed my eyes and let out a breath. "May I please go to bed?"

"Yes. That's enough for tonight, Oliver." Mrs. Clelland used the same stern tone she did when someone stepped out of line in class. Sergeant States relented.

After he left, Mrs. Clelland led me to a room with cream-yellow walls plastered with posters of singers.

"Sorry it's kind of girly," she said. "It's my daughter Lana's room. She's going to college in Montreal and staying there for the summer. For a job, officially, though I think a boy is involved."

She was making small talk, telling me about her life. I wanted to respond, but the weight on my chest grew heavier. It wasn't SAWS, exactly. SAWS made my brain go into hyperspeed. This was a sludge building up inside, making it hard to do anything.

"Richie is next door," she continued. "The bathroom is across the hall. If you decide you're hungry, help yourself to anything in the kitchen. Make yourself at home."

I thanked her, but it came out flat and mechanical, the

way you say thanks when a cashier hands back your change. I hated appearing so ungrateful when she was doing so much for me. I just couldn't pull myself together. A pulse in my head thrummed *leave me alone leave me alone*. I didn't even say good night to Richie. As soon as Mrs. Clelland left, I climbed into bed.

The Void swallowed everything and everyone: Mom, Dad, Richie, my whole school. I tried to save them—I ran and screamed—but it took them one by one until I was alone in the universe with the Void bearing down on me.

When I jolted awake, it was so dark that I couldn't remember where I was. Which bedroom? Which house? I lay still, waiting for my heart to slow. It didn't. My chest pounded like I'd run ten sprints on the basketball court. I was awake but the Void was still there, filling the room. It felt like gravity was broken and I couldn't tell up from down. The bedsheets were soaked in sweat. I kicked back the covers, and the rush of cool air helped me remember.

I was in the Clellands' house. I was safe.

But I wasn't safe. My pulse wouldn't slow, and my chest tingled, and I couldn't catch my breath. Something was horribly wrong. Maybe I was having a heart attack. Wave after wave of terrible thoughts pounded me and I couldn't break through the surface to breathe. I'd been afraid many times about many things, but this was an explosion of fear, all the worst thoughts ripping through my brain at once.

Dad is going to jail **Mom is sick**
Mom will never get better
Dad will never come back They're giving up on
you **They don't love you enough You are sick**
in your brain Richie knows you're weak
There's something WRONG with you No one **likes**
you You'll never have friends **Richie's going to leave**
you too *No one can help you* **You will end up**
alone and no one will even notice **and**
YOU ARE GOING TO DIE

I shook. I couldn't breathe. The sludge was strangling me. I felt like I was dying.

I had to get out of here.

The idea was so urgent, my body acted on reflex. Next thing I knew, I stood in the hallway. My belly quivered. I needed someone to save me before I stopped breathing and keeled over, so I stumbled toward the brightest light in the house, a blue flicker in the basement stairwell. Halfway down the steps, my eyes went starry and my stomach caught fire. I had to lean against the banister and wait for my senses to recalibrate.

"Brian? Whoa," Gabe said somewhere below me. "You look awful."

I couldn't speak. Gabe guided me to the couch. He'd paused his PlayStation in the middle of a basketball game. I hunched over my knees, trying to breathe.

"Are you sick?" Gabe asked. "Want me to get Mom?"

"Don't go," I croaked. I didn't want to be alone. I'd never felt so helpless.

He placed a hand on my shoulder. "What's going on?"

"I . . ." Squeezing out words was so hard. "I . . . can't . . . breathe."

He studied me. "Is your heart racing? You feel out of control?"

I nodded.

"Sounds like a panic attack. Try taking deep breaths and letting them out slowly."

Gabe rubbed my back. An awful eternity passed before my hammering heart slowed and my stranded-fish gasping relented. I felt the coolness of the wood floor against my bare soles. Gabe smelled faintly of sweat and Old Spice, and his hand moved in gentle circles against my ribs. Slowly, slowly, the sludge dispersed.

I wasn't going to die.

"There you go," Gabe said. "You're all right."

"I'm sorry," I said, because that's what I always said.

"Don't be sorry. It's OK."

I wanted to explain, but I didn't know how. As the panic let its claws out of my chest, I felt light and detached from my body. I watched my shoulders twitch and tears flow. I watched Gabe wrap his arms around the shuddering weepy wreck that was Brian Day.

"It's all right," he said. "I got you."

20. LITTLE BY LITTLE

EZRA

"Dude," Kevan called. "Ezra."

Colby, Ty, and Kevan slouched against the fence outside the basketball court. I almost walked past them without noticing.

"What's your deal, bro?" Colby said. "You're so zoned out lately."

"I think he's in love," Kevan said. "Is it Madi?"

It felt like a swarm of fire ants were crawling up my neck.

Colby laughed. "You are so red right now. It is Madi, isn't it?"

I swallowed. "Um."

"Grow up, you guys," Ty said. "If the man don't want to talk, that's his business. Not everybody has to brag every time a girl looks at them, Colby."

They bickered back and forth as we walked in to school. I stayed with them, but I barely heard a thing.

Brian wasn't in class. I checked before I stepped outside for the morning break. I nearly texted him a dozen times, but I didn't want to seem like a stalker. I couldn't stop thinking about him, though. But I couldn't talk to my friends about it, because I was afraid where that conversation might lead.

I had English with Mrs. Clelland after the break, so I slipped away before the bell to try to catch her before the rest of my class showed up.

She looked up from her desk and smiled when I entered. "Hi, Ezra."

"Hey." I closed the door behind me. "Is Brian here today? I didn't see him earlier."

Her eyes softened. "He's home with Gabe. We let him rest after . . . well, everything."

"Oh." I adjusted my glasses. "Do think maybe he'd want to hang out after school?"

"That might be nice. I'd offer you a ride, if that's not too strange." She wrinkled her nose. "It's all strange, isn't it? Ms. Floriman and Mr. Hartland didn't know what to think when I told them I wanted to bring Brian home. I hope I'm doing the right thing, but I don't know."

The bell rang. Mrs. Clelland looked at me like she wanted my opinion.

"I definitely think you're doing the right thing," I said.

She blinked like she was holding back tears. Before she could say anything else, the door opened, and kids started filing in. Mrs. Clelland smiled at me before she turned to greet the others. Before class started, I shot a quick text to Brian.

✩✩✩

We went to Kevan's at lunch, which was always better than lunch at school. Especially when Kevan made dessert. He set a plate on the coffee table in the Sidhus' small den. "Behold, my newest invention."

Colby snorted. "Bro. These are donuts."

"You've never had a donut like this. Try one."

I grabbed one and took a bite. Flavors exploded in my mouth, sweet and salty and doughy and spicy—extremely spicy—all swirling together.

Ty hollered for joy. "Sweet Baby Moses on a Jet Ski! It's a miracle in my mouth."

Kevan's grin widened. "Maple, bacon, chili, and a bunch of spices. I took the most Canadian food and made it more Indian, and more delicious. I call it the Reverse Colonizer."

Ty took another bite and moaned. He tackled Kevan to the couch and they landed in my lap. I barely avoided squishing maple icing in Kevan's hair.

"I love you, you spicy genius," Ty declared.

Colby shielded his eyes. "Easy, bro. Don't turn gay for a donut."

A piece of my heart turned to stone, fell out of my chest, and rolled under the couch.

I didn't want him to see how much his comment bugged me, so I did what I usually did: I made a joke. "Your donuts are magnificent, Kev. But you need a better name that doesn't include *colon*."

Ty got off Kevan and reached for seconds. "Call them whatever. I want all your Fiery Colon Donuts." He grinned through a mouthful of dough. "You should make these for my party."

Kevan perked up. "For real? Your mom said yes?"

Ty nodded. He'd been scheming for weeks to sell his parents on an end-of-school party. It would be the greatest social event any seventh grader at Halifax North had ever experienced, the party by which all other parties would be measured for the rest of our lives—or at least until high school. That's how Ty and Kevan envisioned it, anyway.

"We should plan after school," Ty said. "Ezra, you're in charge of music."

"Don't play all weird indie stuff," Kevan added. "You have to throw in some bangers."

I squirmed. "I'll make a playlist. But I can't hang out today. I, uh, have plans."

"Space-cult plans?" Kevan said sarcastically.

Ty laughed. "What?"

Kevan kept watching me. He wasn't going to let me off without answering.

I took a breath. "I told Brian I'd play ball with him."

They looked at me in surprise. Colby's expression was more *ugh, why?*

"You guys hang out now?" Kevan asked.

"I've been talking to him more since, you know."

I braced for them to grill me. Kevan shrugged. "That's decent. Sounds like his life's rough right now."

"What do you mean?" Colby said.

"Brian's brother is Leo's best friend," Kevan said. "He's usually here all the time, but he hasn't been around in weeks. He told Leo he's staying with these weird old people, but he couldn't say why."

"Like foster parents?" Ty said.

"I guess. Now Leo's worried because Richie hasn't been in school this week."

"So their parents must be screwed up," Colby said. "Maybe that's why Brian's so . . . you know."

Colby's tone bugged me. "Leave him alone," I said. "He has a lot going on. The last thing he needs is people spreading rumors."

Everyone stared at me. Ty, Colby, and Kevan bickered all the time, mostly goofing around, but I was usually the chill peacemaker who cracked jokes. I never snapped at Colby.

"Jeez, relax," he shot back. "I don't waste time gossiping about Brian. You're the one who's obsessed with him lately. What's your deal?"

That was the question I was afraid of. I swear a blazing spotlight flicked on above me, hot enough to melt me into a puddle and expose my secrets. Surely Colby was thinking it right now: *You're in love with him, aren't you? Gross.* His question hung in the air, a balloon expanding with each beat of my silence. A few comebacks came to mind, all defensive or snarky, all guaranteed to make one or both of us feel worse. So I said nothing.

"We should get back to school," Kevan said. "If I have to hear Ms. Virth's 'late for the revolution' joke again, I'll jump out the window."

Colby gave me a long stare. He was first out the door, and he talked with Kevan on the walk to school. He didn't look back at me. Not once.

I was mad at him. Mad at his *don't turn gay* crack and his *I'm so cool now* attitude. Mad that he cared more about Victor than Brian.

Mad that he cared more about Jemma than me.

Mad that after all the time we'd spent together, I couldn't tell him something big without being afraid it would change everything.

Mad at myself for being afraid.

Mad at the world for being unfair, because everything was changing whether I told him or not. Nat once told me this famous saying she'd learned in college: *No man ever steps in the same river twice.* It means life keeps moving and nothing is forever. Sometime after we started junior high, the river branched out and Colby and I started drifting apart.

Sometimes things change in one big explosion, like whatever happened to Brian. Sometimes the shift happens little by little, until it hits you hard on a Wednesday afternoon and you want to cry.

"Hey." Ty spoke so softly that Kevan and Colby didn't hear. "You should invite Brian to my party. You're right. He's a good teammate. He could hang out with us. Play ball and stuff."

I swallowed. "Yeah. That would be cool."

Ty punched my shoulder lightly. "Kevan's right about music. No sad songs. I want people to have fun, not curl up on the couch and mope."

"You mean like this?" I launched into a super-depressing breakup song.

"Ezra, no. Stop that."

"*You're a thousand miles awaaaaay, still close enough to make my heaarrrt break . . .*"

"I will fight you."

Ty tried to stay serious, but he couldn't go a minute without smiling. He nearly snagged me in a headlock, but I squirmed away. He chased me down the sidewalk, both of us laughing.

I felt better, but my belly still fluttered on the way back to school. I had told my friends I was on Team Brian, but I was afraid to let them know everything. Would they still be my friends if I did? How long before I had to make a choice?

21. H-O-R-S-E
BRIAN

A sunbeam was shining in my eye when I woke. I squinted, trying to remember where I was. More urgently, I needed to pee. I climbed out of bed and stepped over a sleeping bag, which reminded me I was in Gabe's room.

Embarrassing Memories for Permanent Storage and Frequent Recall
1. Being so scared you thought you were literally going to die
2. Crying all over a guy you'd just met, like a toddler
3. Being so tired and messed up you couldn't put a sentence together
4. Gabe practically carrying you to bed, like a toddler

After I finished in the bathroom, I found Gabe in the kitchen, cooking eggs and mumbling rap lyrics. The kitchen clock said it was almost one P.M.

Gabe popped out his earbuds. "Hey. I told Mom you weren't feeling well, and we let you sleep. It's exam week and I don't have any tests today, so I was home anyway." He pointed his spatula toward the table. "Hungry? Brunch is almost ready."

My self-consciousness came flooding back. "Sorry about last night," I said. "Sorry I stole your bed."

"Don't be sorry," Gabe said. "Has that ever happened to you before?"

I shook my head.

He slid me a plate of bacon and eggs. "Want to talk about it?"

I threw him a silent, vigorous *no way*.

He shrugged. "OK, but it's not unusual. One of my friends has panic attacks sometimes. I know a few people who do, actually. High school's like Anxiety Central."

My face must have said everything because Gabe gave a sheepish laugh. "That wasn't helpful, huh? How about I shut up now."

We ate in awkward silence.

I didn't want to be this way with Gabe. He was being so nice to me. But every time I looked at him, I remembered blubbering on his shoulder, and I felt so small. Maybe it was the penalty for Ice Mode. I had tricked myself into thinking I didn't have to feel anything, but everything I buried came bubbling up and exploded.

Gabe finished eating and wiped his mouth. "Ezra said you're on the basketball team. Want to shoot around in the driveway?"

Shooting seemed not terrifying, so I agreed. Basketball

was the one thing that slowed my brain and made me feel normal anymore. I cleaned up and met him in the driveway. After taking a few shots to get loose, I hit three in a row. Four. Five.

Gabe whistled. "I see how it is. You're a ginger Steph Curry, huh? How about a game of HORSE?"

I couldn't help smiling. "OK."

Gabe was big and quick, and he would have crushed me one-on-one, but HORSE was a shooting contest. Maybe I could hang with him.

We traded makes and misses. When we were both at H-O, Gabe said, "Let's make this interesting. I win, you tell me why you were in the middle of nowhere yesterday. You win, I'll tell you about my dad."

I froze. Had this been this Gabe's plan all along? To trick me into talking? I didn't want that.

Well, maybe I did.

I'd told the runaway story to Ezra, and it wasn't a disaster. I'd made him laugh, and it felt good.

I gulped. "OK."

"Great. My turn." He sank a turnaround fadeaway. My attempt clanked off the rim. H-O-R. Two more misses and I was done.

Then I caught fire.

Gabe matched a few of my shots, but I got him to H-O-R-S and swished a long bomb from the middle of the street. His heave fell short and thunked against the garage door. H-O-R-S-E. I won.

Gabe fell to his knees in mock despair. I threw my arms in the air. With a dramatic sigh, he picked himself up and gave me a congratulatory fist bump.

"Nice shooting," Gabe said as we sat down on the front steps. "You must light it up at school."

Winning made me feel good enough to be honest. "Not really. I get nervous in games."

"Huh. Well, I guess I owe you a story." Gabe spun the ball in his hands. "I didn't cry for a week after Dad died. I was too pissed at him for dying on me. How weird is that?"

I looked up. He was really going to do this?

"At the funeral, everyone talked like he was a hero, and I wanted to punch somebody," Gabe continued. "A couple of days later, I went for a run, trying to get this thing out of my chest. I ended up at the Stateses' house. Oliver opened the door and I started venting at him, right on his doorstep. I expected him to try to calm me down, tell me you shouldn't be mad at your dad when he dies serving the country, but he didn't. He said, 'You feel whatever you need to feel, Gabe.' I told him I didn't want to be mad anymore. That's when I fell apart."

Even as he said it, his voice cracked.

I pulled my knees to my chest. "You don't have to—you can stop."

Gabe swallowed hard. "It's all right. I used to hate crying in front of people, but I got over it. Anyway, that's it. There's no happy ending. It still hurts. Father's Day last Sunday was real hard. I hung out at Oliver's all afternoon, and it helps that I can talk to him. But sometimes it still hits me that Dad will never see me graduate or play college basketball. He's still gone."

It actually felt comforting to hear Gabe be honest. Every time an adult talked to me about the Incident, I wanted to disappear, but Gabe was different.

He fell quiet, waiting for me to talk. That's how it was supposed to go, right? He told me his tragic story, so I'd open up and do the same. The words swirled in my head, straining to come out. But they got stuck in my throat.

"Thanks for telling me," I mumbled. "I could maybe use a shower now."

He wrinkled his nose. "*Maybe?* Honestly, you are *ripe*, my dude. Did you pack deodorant on your expedition to the forest? I could lend you some body spray—"

"I'm good." I smiled.

Gabe found me a towel. Before I showered, I checked my phone. Ezra had sent a message: Hey want to hang out this afternoon? Mrs. Clelland said I could come over

Sounds great, I wrote back.

Was it really that simple? Was this how normal kids made plans?

After I showered and dressed, Gabe called to me from the kitchen. My heart locked up when I saw Kate was with him. She had our suitcases.

"I brought the rest of your things," she said. "Do you want to check and make sure we didn't miss anything? Then we need to talk."

Kate was the last person I wanted to talk to. I retreated to the yellow bedroom and took my sweet time checking my suitcase. Everything was there, so I guess we officially weren't going back to the Wentzells'. I was relieved, and grateful to be spared an awkward goodbye, but the thought of Kate and Emma gathering my stuff still bugged me.

Gabe was still in the kitchen when I returned. "Do you want me to stay, or . . . ?"

I shook my head. I didn't want him hearing whatever lecture Kate was about to give. He hovered for another moment before he retreated to the basement.

After he left, I gave Kate an envelope. "This is for the Wentzells. Don't open it."

She eyed it like I'd handed her a letter bomb. "What is it?"

"An apology."

"Oh."

She didn't need to know I had wrapped seven twenty-dollar bills inside a sheet of loose leaf with a handwritten note.

Dear Emma and Gordon,
Sorry I worried you, and sorry I borrowed your credit card. This should cover it.
P.S. I know you tried. Richie liked your cake. Thank you.

I was a mess, but I wasn't a thief. And I knew none of this was the Wentzells' fault.

With another puzzled look, Kate tucked the envelope in her bag. She pulled out another envelope, a big brown one.

"Here's the situation, Brian." She tapped the envelope. "It's unusual to place a child with their teacher. I wouldn't have considered it if your mother hadn't agreed."

It still stirred a flood in my brain to think that Mom and Mrs. Clelland had worked this out. *Mom is allowed to decide now. That means she must be doing better, right?*

Kate pressed on. "People are taking chances on you here. Especially after you ran away. If things don't work here, we'll have to consider more secure options. Like a group home."

Imagining a group home made me shudder. Being stuck with the Wentzells had been hard enough. Being surrounded by more strangers and other kids I didn't know would be worse.

"I won't run away again," I said. "I promise. I want to be here."

"Glad to hear it." Kate slid the envelope toward me. "I need you to fill this out."

Warily, I opened it. The papers inside resembled the multiple-choice bubble sheets that came with provincial exams in school.

For each statement below, choose the response that most applies to you. One = never; two = rarely; three = sometimes; four = often; five = consistently.

I feel distant from my peers.

I have trouble sleeping.

I think about harming myself or others.

I enjoy taking risks.

I have recurring headaches, stomachaches, or other physical pains.

I have persistent negative thoughts that don't go away.

A psychological assessment. Kate really did think I was losing it. I nearly threw it at her. "Forget it."

Kate slid it back. "It's not optional. Your teacher's going to bat for you, and it's my job to ensure she has the support she needs. You're a bright kid, Brian. I know you've been through a lot, but it would be nice to know you're willing to let people help."

I understood. I'd made her job miserable, but now she had something I wanted. This was blackmail.

"Fine," I said reluctantly.

Kate nodded. "I'll step outside and give you time to fill it out. We'll make an appointment for a professional to discuss it with you soon."

I didn't ask what that meant. I waited for her to leave before I looked at the sheet again. My stomach twitched. I hated multiple-choice tests. Even when I knew an answer, I second-guessed that another option might be better. This was the worst test ever. Screw up and I'd get a label. TROUBLED. DISTURBED. SICK. Kate might decide it wasn't safe for Mrs. Clelland to keep me and stick me in a group home anyway.

I tried to describe myself in the most normal terms possible. I considered shading all the *Never* bubbles, but surely they had a diagnosis for kids who pulled that stunt. After I finished, I doubted my answers. I erased a few bubbles and picked others, until I worried someone would notice and judge this too.

Evaluation: This kid is such a mess he can't even decide what kind of mess he is.

Diagnosis: Doomed.

22. ELBOWS AND PLAYLISTS

EZRA

My mom is hands-off with most things, but she has a hang-up about eyeglasses. She has this traumatic story about losing her first pair in a tropical storm, so she's weirdly intense about eyewear. She made me get a dorky set of plastic-rimmed sports glasses for gym and basketball. I was halfway to the Clellands' after school when I remembered they were still in my locker.

We walked to the court near the Clellands' and played two-on-two, Gabe and Richie against Brian and me. Gabe took it easy at first, passing to Richie most of the time. Then I made a shot, and Brian hit two in a row.

I gave him a high five. "Good shooting."

"So it's like that, huh?" Gabe grinned.

Suddenly, he was everywhere. Brian and I had to double-team him to slow him down. I tried to sneak up from behind and steal the ball—just as he pivoted, planting his elbow in my face. My eyes watered and I fell on my butt.

Gabe knelt beside me. "Shoot. Sorry. Are you all right?"

My glasses were missing. That was the first thing I noticed, because everything was blurry. Then my nose began to throb, and my cheek stung from where the frames dug into my skin before going flying.

"Here." Brian handed me my glasses. "You're bleeding."

I touched the raw spot on my cheek.

"No, your nose."

A drop slid across my lips. Then the drip became a gush.

"Oh man," Gabe moaned. He helped me to my feet. I pinched my nose with one hand and set my glasses in place with the other. They sat so lopsided that I took them off and stuck them in my pocket.

"I'm so sorry," Gabe said. "I'll pay for those."

"It's OK." I sounded like a Muppet with my nose pinched. "I have another pair at home."

Gabe sighed. "Let's go clean you up. Mom's going to freak out."

"Can you see?" Brian asked. "Do you need me to guide you?"

He was half teasing. "I'll live," I said. "Just point me toward the right fuzzy blob."

Brian put on a serious Coach voice. "That was a major Lack of Sizzle Sauce, Ezra."

I laughed, and blood shot out my nose. Brian swore in surprise, which made me laugh harder and spray more blood. I pinched my nose tighter.

"Definite sizzle deficiency," I said.

Brian's hand was on my shoulder. He stood so close I could feel the in and out of his breath, still heavy from playing ball. *Don't be weird, think about something else.*

That didn't work at all.

My nose stopped gushing before we reached the house, but Mrs. Clelland still gasped at my blood-spattered shirt. Brittany had shown up, and she and Mrs. Clelland lectured Gabe as they brought me ice and a washcloth and lemonade. Gabe apologized again. I repeated that I was OK, and I didn't need a bandage, and my nose was not broken, and Mrs. Clelland didn't have to call my mom. It was all pretty embarrassing.

"That was so much blood," Richie said cheerfully.

"We should do something about your shirt, before it stains," Mrs. Clelland said.

"Cold water and peroxide will get out blood," Brittany offered.

Gabe raised an eyebrow. "Should I be impressed or disturbed that you know that?" She stuck her tongue out at him.

"I can lend you another shirt," Brian said.

I followed him to a bedroom that belonged to someone who loved male pop stars.

"Nice, huh?" Brian joked. "I decorated myself, obviously."

I looked away from a poster of a dark-haired guy in a tank top. I didn't love his music, but I thought he was cute.

It was only a joke, right? Unless it was Brian's way of

saying, "Ha, those posters obviously aren't mine because I'd never want to look at boys." What if he was a total homophobe? What if he'd think it was gross that I liked him?

My chest ached. It wasn't fair that this was so hard.

"Are you OK?" Brian asked. I must have been quiet for too long.

I touched my nose. "Sorry. Zoned out for a second. My head still hurts."

It was a rotten lie and I hated it.

He rooted through a suitcase, then brought me a T-shirt. "Hopefully this fits. I should have packed more the day I, uh, left home." He looked away. "Do you want me to go out?"

"It's OK." I wasn't going to be weird about changing in front of him. I'd done it in the locker room plenty of times. I pulled off my bloody T-shirt and slipped his clean one over my head. Brian was taller and slimmer than me, but it fit.

"Thanks," I said. "I'll bring it back tomorrow. And I'll try not to bleed on it."

"Stay away from Gabe's elbows."

"Poor Gabe. He feels so bad." I laughed. "He's really nice."

"Yeah. He's been good to me." Brian ran a hand through his hair. "I wasn't sure at first, but I'm glad I'm here. I mean, I'd rather be home, but—you know."

"Do you know when your mom will get out of the hospital?" I asked.

"No." He paused. "Yesterday . . . you were going to tell me what she said."

"Oh, right." I thought back to the hospital. "She wanted me to tell you she was sorry. And she gave me a hug. She definitely misses you a lot."

Brian went quiet. He sat with his chin on his hands.

I shuffled my feet. "I can leave, if you want a minute."

"I haven't even visited. Not since . . ." He trailed off.

"Do you want to go?" I said. "I can go with you, if you want."

He stared at me in disbelief. *Was that too much to offer?* I went sweaty. "I mean, if it would help. I could bring my guitar and play 'Eye of the Tiger' like you're in a movie montage."

Brian laughed. My whole body tingled.

"I should probably just go," he said. "But thanks for the offer."

"Sure."

"I mean it. Thank you."

He was so sincere as he looked into my eyes. In a movie, this was the moment I would summon my courage and kiss him, even just on the cheek. But if I tried in real life, he might freak out and I'd ruin everything.

I cleared my throat. "I should do something about my shirt."

"You'll have a good story at school about how Mrs. Clelland's son beat you up." Brian paused. "Or you could say I did it. Might as well build my reputation as a total psycho."

It was a joke, but I caught the edge in his voice.

"Don't say that. Anyone who talks about you like that is a jerk. Forget them," I said. "Oh, Ty said to tell you that you're invited to his party on Friday."

Brian looked up. "What?"

"You should come. It'll be fun."

He went quiet. "I'll think about it."

Mom got dramatic when she saw me. "Ezra? What happened to your face? Where are your glasses?" Once I assured her I was fine, she immediately drove me to the optician. The store was closing up, but Mom convinced the man locking the door that it was an emergency.

He straightened my mangled frames and nodded in satisfaction as I set them on my face. "Almost good as new," he said.

"Check his eyes," Mom insisted. "Make sure he's not injured."

The man frowned. "Ma'am, I'm an optician, not an ophthalmologist."

"You look at eyes all day," Mom countered. "Surely you can tell if he's got a scratch."

Sometimes Mom's lawyer side kicked in and she got intense. The optician sighed and motioned for me to take off my glasses. He pressed his eye-measuring thingy to my nose and told me to stare straight ahead. The metal nose-piece stung against my scratched face.

"All clear," he declared.

Mom smiled sweetly. "Thank you."

"You should carry your sports glasses in your backpack," she insisted on the way home. "Don't leave them in your locker. And be more careful, honey. You only get one set of eyes."

She brushed my cheek with her fingertips. Maybe she was overreacting, but as I thought about Brian and his mom, I didn't mind my mom fussing over me.

I was lounging on my bed, practicing a guitar riff, when my phone played a familiar song that meant Nat was video-calling.

"Ouch," she greeted as she popped into view. "What happened to your face?"

"I took an elbow playing basketball."

"I like that you have a sporty side. You're very well-rounded, Ezra."

I grinned. It was good to see her. She gave me some new music recommendations and asked what I was learning on guitar lately. I played a little for her.

Eventually, she said, "So? What is it?"

"What is what?" I asked.

"You tell me."

"Tell you what? I'm confused."

"You're fidgety. Like something's on your mind."

"What makes you say that?"

"Big-sister radar. Am I wrong?"

I tugged at the neck of Brian's T-shirt. "Uh, not really. I guess I could use your advice."

"Of course." She leaned closer to her camera.

I wiped my palms on my shorts. "Well . . . what's the best way to tell someone that you, um, you like them?"

Nat broke out in a smile. "I had a suspicion it was crush related. That's easy. Be honest. Honesty is everything in relationships."

"But what if—" Ugh. Why was this so hard, even with the person who knew me best? I knew Nat wouldn't judge me. She had gay and bi friends in school. But I still struggled to tell her. "What if they don't like you back, and it changes things? How do you stay friends?"

"Oh, Ezra. I can't promise that won't happen, or that it won't hurt. But if they're decent, they'll appreciate your honesty and won't let it ruin your friendship."

"What if it's more complicated?" Deep breaths. "Say, if the person I like is . . . a boy."

Nat didn't look surprised. She didn't even pause. "Is it Colby?"

"What? No. I mean, I used to . . . But I'm over it."

"Good. You deserve better."

I grinned, mostly out of relief. I'd told my sister, and it didn't faze her at all.

"So, who is this mysterious crush?" she asked.

Everything poured out. I barely stopped for breath as I told her about Brian.

Her eyebrows bunched together. "Wow. That is complicated. He sounds sweet, and sad, and like he could use somebody to talk to."

"Yeah. But it's not like I feel sorry for him. I really like him, Nat. I have for months. I was just afraid to admit it."

Saying it out loud felt incredible. For a second, I wanted to run around the house, my neighborhood, all of Halifax, yelling at the top of my lungs. *I like Brian Day.*

Nat smiled. "I can tell. Don't rush, though. I know I told you to be honest, but sometimes timing is everything. Sounds like he needs a friend first."

"I know. Thanks, Nat. This helped a lot."

Her eyes went misty. "Thanks for telling me. Miss you, Ezzy. I wish I was close enough to give you a big hug."

A lump clogged my throat. "Me too."

After I said good night to Nat, I started a playlist for Ty's party. I'd gone to school dances, and I knew which songs got people moving. But I also sprinkled in some personal touches to make people go "Hey, what's that?" As I picked those songs, I imagined another playlist. One for Brian.

Everybody had a soundtrack in my head. Nat was a Yeah Yeah Yeahs song she'd played on repeat for a solid month in high school. Ty was a Drake track that he sang all the time just because it drove Colby bananas. I hadn't settled on Brian's yet, but maybe his would be somewhere on the playlist I started crafting for him after I finished the party playlist. I picked songs that cheered me up, and mopey tracks for wallowing in a mood. Songs I bellowed when no one was home, and quiet songs that were so gorgeous I listened to them on headphones while lying perfectly still, so I didn't miss a note.

After I arranged them in the right order, embarrassment washed over me. It was way too personal. These songs were *me*. Maybe he'd think it was too weird. My finger hovered over the Delete button.

Instead, I swallowed and sent him a link.

Yeah, it was personal. But maybe it would cheer him up, or at least distract him from the stuff he was dealing with. I had to take a chance. Be honest, like Nat said. This was step one.

23. PERFECT STORM

BRIAN

Richie's voice carried down the hall, growing more heated with every word. My worst-case-scenario instincts flared as I rushed to the kitchen. What if he was throwing a massive tantrum and the Clellands couldn't deal? I had to calm him down.

He stood toe-to-toe with Gabe, staring up. "You are *so wrong,*" Richie insisted. "Hulk is the *worst!*"

"He's unstoppable when he's mad," Gabe shot back. "Who can beat that?"

"Richie's right," Brittany weighed in as she pulled a lasagna from the oven. "Unchecked male rage is a terrible superpower."

Richie poked Gabe in the stomach. "See? Brittany's smarter than you."

"Listen. I'll show you Hulk." Gabe tried to grab him, but Richie slipped away, giggling. Gabe chased him around the table.

I stood in the doorway, watching Richie wheeze with laughter. He was barefoot and loud, the way he acted at home. He had survived at the Wentzells, but now he was fully himself again.

We were safe here.

The High Alert beacon in my brain finally switched off, and a giant weight fell from my shoulders. As we dug into Brittany's delicious dinner, Gabe and Richie joked around and Brittany and Mrs. Clelland talked like old friends. The coziness of it all dragged up another thought I couldn't keep buried anymore.

I miss home. I miss Mom and Dad.

Somehow, I kept from bursting into tears, but it was close. After dinner, Gabe quietly shooed his mom out of the kitchen so he and Brittany could clean up. Gabe and I had at least one thing in common: We both tried to take care of our moms as much as they took care of us.

I still felt close to crying, so I retreated to the yellow bedroom. I didn't just miss my parents; I missed *before.* Before Dad left. Before Mom fell apart. Before I knew how it felt to be sad and angry with someone you loved but still miss them so much it hurt.

Mrs. Clelland knocked on the door. She came in and sat beside me.

"I'm sorry Ms. Evans visited without me. I asked her to wait, but she felt it was important to talk to you as soon as she could." Her forehead wrinkled. I suspected she disagreed with Kate on that, and maybe on other things too. "I know she gave you an assessment to fill out. I want you to know that's not unusual. Lots of students do them."

Mrs. Clelland knows about Kate's test? Yuck.

Then a worse thought struck me. "Did she ask you to fill out something about me too?"

"She did. But that's common. I do a lot of student assessments."

Sure. For kids who swore at teachers or got suspended for throwing chairs.

Who was I kidding? I swore at the principal and got suspended for punching a guy. I forced a grin, like we were joking around. "There must be at least one kid in school more disturbed than me, right?"

She blinked in surprise. "You're not disturbed, Brian. You're a thoughtful, intelligent boy going through a hard time, through no fault of your own. There's no shame in that."

I tugged on my ninja dog tag.

She folded her hands in her lap. "I spoke with your mom again today. She'd really like to see you. When you're ready."

I scratched an ache on my chest. "Is she . . . getting better? Be honest."

Mrs. Clelland smoothed the bedspread. "She told me about your last visit. I think she's much better than you might be imagining. She's worried about you and Richie, of course." She paused. "Your mom knows she hurt you, and she's worried about how that's affecting you. I think she's afraid you won't be able to forgive her."

I focused on one breath at a time, to keep from falling apart.

Talking was so hard. But I made myself do it. "I'm afraid too."

"Oh?"

Say it.

"I know it's weird, but I have this fear that maybe she doesn't want to be my mom anymore. Maybe she gave up on us."

I was scared that saying it out loud would make it more real, or make me sound so messed up Mrs. Clelland wouldn't know what to do with me. But neither of those things happened.

She slid closer. "Mental illness can be awfully hard on people, and on those who love them too. But your mom loves you and Richie so much."

I swallowed. "Did she tell you that?"

"She did. But I didn't need her to tell me. In twenty years of parent-teacher meetings, you learn things about parents. I notice the questions they ask, how they talk about their kids. It was obvious from the moment I met your mom that she's your biggest fan."

I hunched with my elbows on my knees. I wasn't sure I was ready to see Mom, but imagining the worst wasn't helping. Better to face it head-on again. Maybe. "We should go tomorrow. I think Richie needs it too."

"We can go after school," Mrs. Clelland said. "Speaking of . . . I know it might feel strange showing up with me. I can drop you off along the way, if you'd prefer."

I hadn't thought about that. Obviously, more rumors

would spread if kids saw me in Mrs. Clelland's car. I didn't want to make her feel bad after all she had done. I wanted to say it didn't matter. But we both knew how junior high worked.

"I'll text Ezra," I said. "Maybe you could drop me at his house, and we could walk together."

"That's a good idea." Mrs. Clelland stood. "I know this is unusual, and we're all figuring it out as we go. But I'm glad you and Richie are here." She paused. "If it's OK, I'd like to give you a hug."

Is that OK? I decided it was.

I found two messages already waiting from Ezra.

Hey music is my thing so if you need a distraction maybe this will help

But DO NOT listen to Track 7 after you've chugged a mocha frappucino or you might get hyper and jump off your bed and dragon uppercut the ceiling (or so i've heard)

Ezra was the best. He included a link to a playlist. I stuck in my earbuds and pressed Play.

The first song was familiar, something from an ad or movie trailer, one of those epic songs that makes everything seem dramatic. It made me smile. I scrolled through the rest of the list. I only recognized a few songs. Ezra knew way more about music than I did. I was halfway through the second song before I remembered to text back and ask if I could walk with him.

For sure, he answered. **See you tomorrow.**

Tomorrow. The word rumbled in my belly, a train gathering speed. By the time I said good night to Richie and got ready for bed, tomorrow barreled toward me in a steady rhythm.

Tomorrow
Tomorrow, everyone's going to stare at you, the weirdo who punched Victor.
Tomorrow, Victor might seek revenge.
Tomorrow, Kate will tell you her test proves you're broken.
Tomorrow, you'll go to the hospital, and you're scared, you're scared, you're scared.

Ezra's music helped, but it wasn't enough. Dread blanketed my chest, bringing back memories of the night before. I had to cut it off before it grabbed me. I headed for the basement, where I could hear Gabe and Brittany talking. I felt bad about intruding, and I made lots of noise on the way downstairs so I wouldn't walk in on them kissing or anything.

They sat on the couch, playing a video game. "Hey," Gabe called. "Grab a seat."

"Sorry for busting in," I said.

"Don't be. You say sorry a lot, you know."

My cheeks flushed. "I know. S—"

I caught myself before I apologized for apologizing,

but they still laughed. I managed a sheepish grin as I took a corner of the couch.

"Want to play?" Brittany asked.

I shook my head. "You don't have to talk to me. I can listen to music. I just . . ."

"Didn't want to be alone?" Brittany finished.

"Yeah."

They don't think this is weird. My shoulders eased back into the couch.

"What are you listening to?" Gabe asked.

"Ezra sent me a playlist."

Brittany smiled. "I bet it's perfect. Ezra has good taste."

I nodded and settled in to watch them play. Even at home, I watched video games more than I played them. I'd burrow with a book while Dad and Richie raced cars or rescued princesses or fought evil empires. I joined sometimes, but I was happy just listening to them. They had an easy way with each other. Dad didn't need to work as hard as he did with me.

Though I was bad at conversation, I liked listening to other people. Sitting with Gabe and Brittany, I felt less anxious than I did alone. They bantered as they played a fantasy game with swords and magic. Brittany was way better than Gabe.

"I didn't know I *had* a rune sword," Gabe grumbled as Brittany explained how to defeat the giant that had squashed him flat. "There's too much to remember in this game."

"Oh, please," Brittany shot back. "You can identify

a hundred NBA players by their sneakers. There's lots of room in your head for useless information."

I popped in my earbuds and returned to Ezra's playlist. He'd included all kinds of music, hip-hop and big pop songs and loud rockers. As promised, track 7 was a total ripper— a song about turning into a werewolf. Brittany caught me grinning and glanced at my phone.

"Ugh, I want to keep Ezra. How does a seventh grader have better taste than every boy I know?"

"I'm going to pretend I didn't hear that," Gabe said.

I texted Ezra. Brittany is raving about your playlist. I really like it too. Thanks!

Oh good, he answered. I was worried you'd think it was weird lol

Me: You were right about the wolf song. It's my favorite so far

Ezra: Isn't it amazing? Maybe the best werewolf song ever. Top 3 for sure

Me: How many werewolf songs do you know?

Ezra: Many. The werewolf is a majestic beast, worthy of musical tribute

Next time I'll send you an all-werewolf playlist

Me: I didn't know you were so into lycanthropy

Ezra: OK genius. I had to look up what that means

But in case you heard rumors, I do NOT transform under a full moon

Well except that one time but that was a fluke

I laughed. Ezra was good at making me laugh.

I wanted to ask about Ty's party. I still couldn't believe he'd invited me. I wanted to say yes, but I pictured a noisy crowd and I wasn't sure I could handle it. I didn't know how to say that to Ezra. Not without sounding pathetic, anyway.

My chest fluttered again. Every time I felt better for a minute, my brain found something else to be anxious about.

I was lost in thought again until Gabe and Brittany stood up.

"Curfew time," Brittany said.

"Thanks for dinner," I told her. "It was so good. And thanks for letting me hang out."

"Anytime." She surprised me with a hug. It turned out I didn't mind all these hugs at the Clelland house.

I waited downstairs while Gabe walked Brittany out. When he returned, I fidgeted with my dog tag as I forced out my sad little question. "Would it bother you if I slept here on the couch?"

I knew it was silly, but I couldn't face the yellow room right now. Not alone. It turned out I needed Richie all those nights at the Wentzells' as much as he needed me. Down here, at least Gabe would be close if I had another meltdown.

He yawned. "You can sleep in my room. I'll set up our air mattress."

He offered so casually, as if it was normal that I couldn't handle the night anymore.

"You sure?"

Gabe shrugged. "I understand, man. I don't know your whole story, but I know what rough nights are like."

In minutes, he'd inflated a camping mattress and topped it with a sleeping bag and pillow for me. We got ready for bed and Gabe flicked off his lamp.

Bedrooms were different in the dark. A mask came off when the light went out. In the dark, the Wentzells' bedroom whispered *you have no place* and the hotel room said *it's all too much* and the yellow room said *you'll never make it*. But this room was homier, with sneakers lined up under the bed and basketball shorts tossed over a chair and the warm smell of Gabe in the air. All this was a layer of insulation, keeping the worst thoughts at bay. I only heard the same thing I'd heard all day, whenever Gabe or Ezra or Brittany or Mrs. Clelland looked at me.

Try.

"Gabe?"

"Yeah?"

"Do you ever worry about your mom?"

Gabe rolled over. "For sure. I still do, but the worst was right after Dad died. I was paranoid something would happen to her too. I kept googling the symptoms of depression."

I closed my eyes. "When Dad left, Mom took a lot of

pills. She nearly died. That's why she's in the hospital. That's why we're here."

"Brian, whoa." Gabe leaned over the side of the bed. "That's like my worst nightmare."

"It's why I can't sleep."

I said it, and it didn't kill me. Gabe slipped down onto the floor beside my mattress. I sat up beside him, both of us leaning against his bed. For once, the darkness helped. It was easier to talk without looking at him. And I talked. A lot. I told him about Mom, and Dad, and how I always froze at school. I said things I'd never said out loud. Gabe asked a few questions, but mostly he listened while all the junk in the ugliest corners of my brain came flooding out.

"Kids with as many problems as me don't make it," I finally said. "I might be doomed."

Gabe put an arm around me. "I'm not sure you can be doomed when you're only thirteen. You're not Hamlet, my dude."

I pulled my knees to my chest. "My social worker thinks I'm troubled. She's going to make me see a psychologist."

"I saw a counselor after Dad died," Gabe said. "It was Mom's idea."

"Did it help?"

"Yeah. I only went twice, but she helped me understand it was OK to be a mess. There's no perfect way to deal when life punches you in the nuts."

I laughed. "You sound like Dad. He told me life would kick me in the junk someday. He's always telling me to be tougher, but that doesn't really work when you're the shyest kid in your class."

"Hey, you drilled a dude in the face," Gabe said. "That's a G move."

"Yeah, Dad was proud of that."

We both laughed. *Am I allowed to joke about this kind of stuff?* But Gabe was laughing, and it felt good.

Eventually, he yawned. My self-consciousness came flooding back.

"Sorry. It's late. I should shut up now."

Gabe ruffled my hair. "You are officially banned from saying sorry to me anymore. I'm enjoying Chatty Brian. You been saving those words up for a while, huh?" He yawned again. "We can resume your entire life history tomorrow."

He climbed back in bed. I had never talked to anyone so easily, except Mom. I'd told Gabe my worst fears, and he didn't treat me like I was weird or broken. Already I wondered if it was some magic of the moment, a perfect storm in the dark. What were the chances I'd ever be able to do it again?

24. OUR REAL SELVES

EZRA

Four shirts lay spread across my bed. Two had logos of bands I'd included on Brian's playlist, so I took them off because wearing them might seem corny. Now I was torn between a bright blue polo and a plain black V-neck. Maybe the polo was too fancy. But maybe black was too gloomy for a warm day in June.

I probably worried about what I wore more than a lot of seventh-grade boys, but most mornings weren't this bad.

Most mornings I wasn't walking to school with Brian.

"Ezra, you have company," Mom called down the stairs.

I pulled on the V-neck. Brian wore V-necks sometimes and looked good in them. (Yeah, I noticed.) After a quick mirror check to make sure my hair hadn't sprung off in too many directions, I grabbed my backpack and bounded upstairs.

"Sorry to keep you waiting—" I rounded the corner and stopped. Ty stood in the doorway, talking to my mom.

"Whoa," he said. "You get punched in the face?"

Mom frowned, puzzled. "He was playing basketball. I thought he was with you."

"I didn't do that." Ty grinned. "Was it Brian? Dude's turning out to be dangerous."

I touched the scrape near my nose. "It wasn't Brian. I was with Brian, but . . . it was an accident."

"Brian?" Mom said. "Do I know Brian?"

"He's on the basketball team." I tried to stop my cheeks from going red, but I think I failed. "He'll be here soon. We're walking to school together."

"I thought he lived by Kevan?" A look of recognition crossed Ty's face. "Oh, right. He's not at home."

Mrs. Clelland's car pulled up. Gabe was driving, with Mrs. Clelland in the passenger seat. Brian climbed out of the back seat. Gabe honked goodbye, which made Ty turn and look.

"We should go," I blurted. "Bye, Mom."

"I'm about to leave too," she said. "Do you boys want—"

"We're good, thanks." I practically dragged Ty out the door.

Brian waited at the end of the driveway with his hands in his pockets. I wanted to tell him Ty just showed up, but that would sound insulting to Ty.

"Hey, Brian," Ty greeted. "Was that Mrs. Clelland?"

Brian dipped his head. "Yeah," he practically whispered.

Great. My hope that Brian would be relaxed like when we were texting about werewolves last night evaporated. This was going to be awkward. We started walking.

"Did she pick you up from your foster place?" Ty asked.

Brian's eyes widened. He stared at me hard.

"I didn't say anything," I blurted. "It was Kevan. Richie told his brother."

I wondered if Kevan felt a random jab ten blocks away as I threw him under a bus.

Brian ducked his head and his hair fell over his face. "Actually, um. I'm staying at her house."

"Really?" Ty bounced on his toes. "That must be weird, huh? Gabe's cool, anyway."

"You know Gabe?" I said.

"Of course." Ty counted connections on his fingers. "He's one of the best high school players in the city. I see him at the Y, and we go to the same church. We know a lot of the same people." He nudged me, grinning. "You know the Black Network is strong."

Ty's ancestors had been in Nova Scotia since the Black Loyalists arrived in the 1780s. He had a history here that went deeper than mine, as a biracial kid with immigrant parents. Ty never treated me like the difference mattered, though.

"Do you have a lot of relatives?" Brian asked me.

I shook my head. "Not here. My sisters are in Ontario, and most of Mom's family is in Trinidad. I only see them every year or two. How about you?"

Brian went quiet. I immediately regretted asking, because—

"I guess if you had relatives around, you'd be staying with them and not Mrs. Clelland," Ty said.

Brian's shoulders drooped.

Ty meant well. He was naturally friendly. But Brian didn't seem in the mood for the full Ty Marsman experience. I had to change the subject.

"Gabe's the one who elbowed me in the face," I said.

Ty winced. "Ouch."

"It looks worse than it was."

"Not like when you punched Victor, right Brian?" Ty threw a one-two combo. "I'm dying to know. What made you do it?"

Brian reddened.

"Ty, come on," I pleaded.

"Just curious." Ty hopped ahead and turned so he was facing us, walking backward. "Anyway, I don't think he'll bug you again. Victor acts tough, but he's all talk."

Ty did most of the talking the rest of the way. When we reached school, he headed for the basketball court. He invited us to join, but Brian hesitated.

"I'm still suspended. I should go to the office. I'm not sure I'm allowed to have fun."

Ty grinned. "You're a bad man, B. Did Ezra tell you about my party? You coming?"

Brian nodded. "I guess. If I'm still invited."

"Of course! I have a pool, so bring a swimsuit if you want." Ty dashed off to play ball.

"Sorry, Ty's basically pure energy," I said. "I didn't know he was coming today."

"It's fine. I like Ty." Brian exhaled. "If you want to play ball—"

"Nah. My sports glasses are in my locker, and Mom lectured me about playing without them. I'll walk you in."

We shuffled toward the entrance. Brian's shoulders tensed as we passed through the main doors, but I didn't want him to disappear on me yet.

"I'm glad you're coming to Ty's," I said. "We can go together, if you want."

Wait. Did that sound like I was asking to go together? Heat rippled through my body as I backtracked. "I mean, he lives a few blocks from me, if you want to get dropped off again—"

"Yeah. OK." Brian paused outside the office door. I had to lean in to hear him over the noise of the hall. "I want to go. But I don't know . . . in crowds, like *here* . . ." His eyes darted to a group of eighth-grade girls walking past. "I freeze. I can't help it. I hate it."

His face went red, as if saying that much in the school hall took enormous effort.

"It's OK," I said. "You don't have to talk a lot."

He sighed. "It's easier around fewer people. I talked to Gabe a lot yesterday." He met my eyes. "And I like hanging out with you."

A burst of warmth shot through my chest and ran all the way to my fingertips. I wanted to take his hand and lead him somewhere quieter, somewhere we could listen to music and tell each other everything and be our real selves, just Brian and me.

I cleared my throat. "After Ty's party, you could spend the night at my house, if you want."

Brian lit up. "That would be fun. I'll ask Mrs. Clelland."

Cue fireworks and a triumphant orchestra and—

Ms. Floriman stepped out of the office. "Well hello, Brian. Nice of you to join us today."

He blushed. "Hi."

"Ms. Floriman?" I said, before she could lead him away. "Can I eat lunch with Brian? He doesn't have to be alone all day, does he?"

Her eyebrows furrowed. I stood my ground.

"I suppose that would be all right," she said.

"Great," I said. "Thanks."

"Yeah. Thanks." Brian smiled at her. And at me.

25. TERRAFORM

BRIAN

An in-school suspension hardly felt like punishment. Isolated in a closet-size room beside Mr. Hartland's office, I didn't have to think about Ms. Virth calling on me in social studies, or Victor and his sidekicks laughing when I sputtered some two-word answer. I worried that Kate might show up to grill me about my mental state, but other than Ms. Floriman checking on me, I had the morning to myself. I dove into the work my teachers left me as a distraction from the thing looming after school—our visit with Mom. I'd conjugated a bunch of French verbs and nearly caught up on three days of math when the bell rang for morning break.

Small Victory #1: Ty had talked to me. Ty was one of the most popular kids in seventh grade. He was a great teammate who gave me a high five when I scored or made a good pass. He was like that with everyone, so I assumed he didn't ever think about me off the court. But he seemed genuinely interested in what I had to say. He didn't think living with Mrs. Clelland made me a freak. He personally invited me to his party. That was a step beyond "nice shot."

Small Victory #2: I told Ezra about SAWS, sort of, and he didn't think I was weird. He even asked me to sleep over.

I couldn't remember the last time I'd been invited to a party or a sleepover. I wasn't sure I could handle either without a SAWS attack, but that was tomorrow's problem. For now, I was happy anyone cared I existed.

Ezra came back at lunch, as promised. I got him talking about his playlist and his favorite bands. He burst out singing at one point, then he blushed.

He had a great voice. "You sound like a rock star," I said.

His cheeks went pinker, but he got even more into talking about music. His hands came alive, as if he couldn't think about a song without feeling it in his fingers. He kept picking up half his sandwich and setting it down without taking a bite. Bits of lettuce fell out every time. I tried not to laugh, because I didn't want him to think I was mocking him.

Suddenly he stopped. "Sorry. You're probably bored by now."

"No way," I said. "I like how much you love music. It's obviously your thing. Like you have life figured out already."

"Well, not everything." He focused on his sandwich. "What about you? What's your thing?"

My thing was not talking about myself. But I talked to Gabe and it wasn't terrible. I wanted to talk to Ezra too.

Try.

"I, uh, I like basketball, obviously. And I read a lot." I toyed with the snap on my lunch bag. "I like writing too. I'm good with words." Pause. "Well, not saying them out loud."

Ezra grinned. "We could write songs together. I love making up music, but I'm not great at lyrics."

"As long as you do the singing. Public performance is definitely not my thing," I admitted. "I literally have nightmares about it."

"Really?" Ezra smiled, but it was the opposite of the leer Victor wore when he watched me suffer. Ezra looked sympathetic.

"Yeah. I wake up sweaty and everything."

"Huh." He leaned closer. "I'm scared of frogs."

"Frogs?"

"I have frog-monster dreams sometimes." Ezra laughed. "I know it's silly. But they move so quick, it freaks me out. Colby caught one when we were eight, and it jumped out of his hands and nearly went down my shirt. Scarred me for life."

I drew back. "Right. I forgot you're friends with Colby."

Colby swaggered around our class like he ran the place, flirting with girls and teasing teachers. He was Victor's friend. His laugh was familiar, and it never made me feel good.

Ezra hesitated. "Yeah. Well, we were best friends in elementary. Now . . . I don't know. Things are changing." He collected his stray shreds of lettuce.

"He seems kind of in love with his own awesomeness," I said.

Ezra snickered. "Yeah, that's Colby." His smile faded. "Hey, um, I know he and Victor are mean to you. I saw— well, you know. And I'm really sorry."

I stared at the table. "It's OK," I mumbled.

"No, it's not."

I looked up. Ezra took a shaky breath.

"I should have said something, but I wimped out. I promise it won't happen again." He pointed to himself with both thumbs. "Next time, this immortal pizza wizard has your back."

I couldn't help smiling. "Do you magically appear and start throwing slices?"

Ezra stretched out his arms. *"Pepperoni smash,"* he intoned in his deepest wizard voice. We both laughed.

Ms. Floriman peeked in the half-open door. I thought she might lecture us about having too much fun while I was suspended, but she just gave us a tiny smile and kept walking. A minute later, the bell rang.

"See you after school?" Ezra asked.

I wanted to tell him about visiting Mom, but the words got stuck in my throat.

"I have something after," I said. "But I'll text you later."

Unless you're meeting a newborn baby, most people only visit hospitals when something's wrong. Hospitals are a collection of tragedies. My body buzzed as I crossed the lobby, a step behind Kate, Richie, and Mrs. Clelland. Kate insisted on coming even though I didn't want her involved. Her presence made me feel worse.

As the elevator doors closed, an alarm in my brain flashed *stuckstuckstuckstuckstuck*. The elevator crept upward and Kate talked and Richie ignored her and I bit my lip and pleaded with my body not to revolt, but it was too late.

KABOOM 2: THE SEQUEL

This visit will be a *disaster* They'll never let you go home with your mom **She doesn't want to be your mom anymore anyway** *Dad ran away for good* Kate's going to separate you and Richie **You'll end up in a group home** Your brain is broken *You're going to have a* TOTAL PERMANENT MELTDOWN

My heart went double-speed, my stomach churned, and I couldn't breathe. I understood what was happening this time, but that didn't make it less terrifying. When the elevator finally stopped, I pushed out and took three steps before my vision narrowed to a starry point. I listed sideways and slumped against the wall.

"Brian?" Mrs. Clelland said. "Are you all right?"

I couldn't answer. Sweat gathered on my forehead and under my arms.

She rested a hand on my back. "Can you move? Do you want to sit down?"

"Let me find a nurse," Kate said.

I waved her off and shuffled to a chair in the waiting area. I hunched over my knees, fighting for breath.

Richie leaned in beside me. "What's happening? What's wrong?"

I didn't have the wind to reply. I strained to hear Kate and Mrs. Clelland talking.

"He never mentioned panic attacks," Kate said. "He doesn't seem ready for this."

"That needs to be his choice," Mrs. Clelland said. "Give him time."

Richie hopped up. "We're not leaving until we see Mom. I want to see Mom."

Heat rolled upward from my stomach. I was sweating rivers. I was maybe going to barf. I was probably going to barf. I wobbled over to the single bathroom and locked the door.

Kate followed me. "Brian?" she said at the door. "What's going on?"

What, she wants a play-by-play? The room tilted sideways while I huddled over the toilet, trapped in that horrible moment of anticipation when I was sure I was going to barf and I really didn't want to barf but I was equally desperate for it to be over.

I wanted it all to be over.

I didn't barf. The worst wave passed, and I slumped against the wall, waiting for the misery to end. I pressed my ninja tag hard against my chest, to focus on feeling something different.

A new voice appeared at the door. "Hey. You OK?"
Gabe.

I slid over to let him in. He closed the door behind him.

"Sorry, parking took forever." He looked me over. "Another panic attack?"

I nodded.

"As bad as the other night?"

Talking was hard, but I tried. "Almost. I hate this."

He sat beside me on the bathroom floor. "Can I do anything?"

"I don't know. What you did the other night . . . maybe it helped."

Gabe began massaging my shoulders. I felt pathetic, a baby seeking comfort for a boo-boo, but Gabe's steady rhythm helped me settle. I tried to breathe, in and out. Gradually the panic faded.

He helped me up, and I washed my sweaty face in the sink.

"Do you want to go home?" Gabe said.

I shook my head. "I want to see Mom."

He nodded. "You're tough, Brian."

Tough? Me? "Ha."

"I'm serious."

"We just sat on a bathroom floor while I had a panic attack."

"Give yourself some credit," Gabe said. "You've had a terrible month, you've looked after Richie the whole time, and you're still going. You're stronger than you think."

Strong wasn't a word I'd use to describe myself, but Gabe's pep talk did make me feel a little better.

He squeezed my shoulders again and unlocked the door. I checked my reflection. I looked as empty as I felt, but I'd stopped sweating and I didn't puke or faint or cry, so that was a plus. In the aftermath of the attack, I'd gone a little spacey and numb. But maybe that was OK.

As I stepped out of the bathroom, I nearly bumped into Richie, who must have been waiting outside the door. I summoned a nod to let him know I was OK. Kate looked relieved too. She probably would have faced a lot of paperwork if I blacked out in a bathroom on her watch.

"I'm ready to see Mom now," I said.

She blinked. "Are you sure? We could reschedule."

"I'm sure."

Mrs. Clelland and Gabe waited behind. As we followed Kate down the hall, Richie slid his hand in mine. I gave it a squeeze.

Kate led us to a small lounge. There was no mechanical bed or beeping machines this time, just two couches and a coffee table. Perched on the couch facing the door was a woman dressed in a sweater and jeans, with her dark hair neatly brushed. Mom.

She stood. Richie released my hand and ran to her, nearly bowling her backward as he wrapped his arms around her. She kissed the top of his head. I joined the embrace, with one arm around Mom and one around Richie. Mom was quiet, but her shoulders trembled. She was crying.

I'd imagined this moment a hundred times since my birthday. Now that it was here, I felt oddly hollow. I ran a mental checklist on Mom. She squeezed us tightly, so no Zombie Mode. When she pulled back, her eyes were red, but happy-sad. She smiled as she brushed tears away.

"Look at you two," she said in a scratchy voice. "Have a seat and catch me up."

We sat on either side of Mom. Richie leaned against her and launched into an account of our lives since my birthday.

"First we stayed with these creepy old people. The lady never listened to us, and she bugged Brian all the time, so we ran away."

"So I heard." Mom stared across the room at Kate hovering in the doorway.

Richie talked and talked. Mom said "mmm" and ran her fingers through his thick hair.

"Your hair's so long," she murmured absently. "You need a haircut."

Her eyes kept drifting to Kate, and I realized this was part of the official checklist: a supervised visit to make sure we could be in the same room without any disasters. We still had to prove ourselves.

I was lost in thought when Mom touched my shoulder and I twitched. I caught her wounded look. When had I ever flinched under her touch?

But she forced a smile. "I hear you've had some adventures. Seeing the town and taking out bullies."

I examined my fingernails. "Something like that."

Something had changed. Usually, I talked to Mom more than I talked to anyone. Even on her bad days, we read in silence and it never felt this awkward. Part of the problem was the setting, this fake living room where we pretended everything was peachy while a social worker watched. But it was deeper than that. Even if we'd been alone, I didn't want to tell her anything. Not about Victor, or Gabe, or running away. Definitely not the panic attacks. Nothing.

Mom turned to Richie. "Sweetie, can you give me a minute to talk to Brian?"

Richie scrunched up his face. "We just got here!"

"You can come right back. I need a minute with your brother." Mom stared at Kate. She wasn't asking. Her glare said, *You're giving me this, like it or not.*

Kate frowned, but she gave in. "Come on, Richie. Let your mom and brother talk."

Richie sighed and followed Kate into the hall. She left the door open. Mom and I were alone.

I fiddled with my dog tag. "Sorry we didn't come earlier. I wanted to, but . . ."

"But I hurt you last time and you were afraid to try again." Mom's eyes went misty. "I'm so sorry, Brian."

I didn't know what to say. I hunched forward. Mom touched my shoulder. I didn't flinch this time. I forced out the question playing on repeat in my head.

"Do you even want to be here?"

She rubbed my back. "I can't wait to get out of here,

Brian. I needed the help, but I'm ready to be home with you and Richie." She smiled. "It's looking like I'll be discharged on Monday. We'll all go home."

Monday. Home. My stomach flipped as the words sank in. Monday was four days away. Four days and everything would go back to—

Not normal. Normal was gone.

"That's not what I meant." I pressed my elbows into my knees. "I mean, do you want to be here at all. Alive."

Mom dropped her hands to her lap. "Are you asking if I'd rather be dead?"

"Well, you did almost kill yourself. On my birthday."

The last part slipped out, but I wasn't sorry I said it.

Mom sighed. "Brian, I'll regret that morning for the rest of my life. I don't blame you if it's hard to trust me right now." She closed her eyes for a moment. "But I love you so much, and I want to be here for you and Richie for a very long time."

I hugged her. It was what she needed, so I did it. Even with my arms around her, I knew our relationship had changed. The world I knew ended on June 7. I was still terraforming a new one, and I didn't know where my parents fit yet.

"I love you too," I said. "But I can't ever do this again."

"Brian—"

"I just can't go through this again." My voice cracked at the end. I hated that.

Mom nodded, eyes reddening. "We need to do some

things differently. All of us." She paused. "I talked to your father. I told him you and Richie were safe. And I told him he needs to come back. Whatever happens, there are things we can't avoid forever."

I didn't know what to say, except "oh." Mom waited, but I couldn't find words for my jumble of feelings about Dad. I was angry, I missed him, and I was afraid of what might happen to him all at the same time. It was too much to say out loud.

She put an arm around me. "When Kate and Richie come back, we can talk about what comes next for us. We're going to be OK. Do you believe that?"

I wanted to believe it. But I still wasn't sure.

Richie literally skipped back to the waiting room after our visit. "Mom's coming home next week!" he yelled to Gabe. The woman at the reception desk looked up, but Richie was so happy, she didn't have the heart to shush him.

Kate matched my slower pace. "How are you?" she asked. "Probably a lot to process, huh?"

I didn't answer. She pressed on, her voice softer than usual. "I hope it's all right I waited and let your mom tell you. It felt like the right call. I'm rooting for you, Brian. Keeping families together is always my favorite outcome."

This was Kate trying to make peace. I wasn't angry with her anymore, but I couldn't manage more than a tight nod. Even her attempt to boost my spirits pricked a raw spot.

We wouldn't all be together. Not without Dad.

Kate left us with Gabe while she and Mrs. Clelland stayed to talk with Mom. As we walked to the car, Richie declared we should celebrate with ice cream.

"Deal," Gabe said. "As long as it's reasonably priced ice cream. I have ten bucks on me."

"Brian can pay," Richie said. "He's loaded."

"Richie," I cautioned.

Gabe raised an eyebrow. "How loaded?"

"It's an emergency fund. From Dad. It's supposed to be secret," I added, glaring at Richie.

"How big is this secret emergency fund?"

Richie ignored my *shut up or I'll kill you* stare. "Ten grand!"

Gabe stopped. "Richie's joking, right?"

I tucked my hands in my pockets. "Close. I spent some when we ran away."

Gabe cackled. "Are you *serious*? We're definitely celebrating."

I sighed. "I'm tired, Gabe. I just want to go home."

The last word slipped out and startled me so badly I froze. *Home.* It lingered on my tongue, sour and raw.

Home was my boxy house on Albert Street, and that wasn't the place I'd meant at all.

My eyes grew hot, and wet. "Hey," Gabe said. I let him wrap me in a hug. It was what I needed, but I felt even guiltier as I burrowed against his shoulder.

Mom was coming home in four days. Two weeks ago, I'd never wanted anything so badly in my life.

But now . . .

Our conversation in the hospital replayed in my head. Mom told me she loved me, and I knew it was true, but she didn't promise things would never be this bad again. Because she couldn't. I knew that too.

I felt protected with Gabe and Mrs. Clelland. They were a safe moon in the dark expanse of the Void, and I didn't feel ready to face a new world. What did that say about me?

Gabe patted my back and led me to the car. "New plan," he announced as he drove. We stopped at the grocery store, and I gave Richie twenty bucks and waited in the car. A few minutes later, Gabe and Richie returned with peanut butter fudge crunch ice cream, caramel sauce, marshmallows, Skittles, and M&M's.

"We've got all the major candy categories covered," Gabe said. "Time to create some art."

Not long after we got back to the Clellands', Brittany arrived, carrying a black box. Ezra was with her.

"Gabe texted," Ezra told me. "He said we should come over."

I looked at Gabe. He shrugged.

"What's in the box?" Richie asked.

"Brittany is an excellent barber," Gabe said. "First sundaes, then haircuts. Nothing lifts your spirits like a fresh cut."

Richie groaned. "I shouldn't have told you what Mom said. I hate haircuts."

Gabe ruffled his hair. "I can tell. But Brittany will just freshen you up."

She bowed. "Satisfaction guaranteed, or your money back."

I didn't want any of this. I wanted a nap. But Ezra was here, and Gabe pushed a bowl into my hands. I made a sundae, minus the marshmallows, because cold marshmallows are rubbery and weird.

Brittany told Ezra to pick some music. I kind of knew what he would choose. As soon as the song started, Brittany high-fived him and they bopped around the kitchen, playing air guitar and singing about turning into a werewolf.

It's hard to stay mopey when you're eating ice cream and watching people you like play air guitar.

Brittany cut Gabe's hair first, to prove she could be trusted. She used clippers to trim his edges and touch up his fade.

"That looks good," Ezra said as he switched spots with Gabe. Brittany buzzed down the sides and back of his head next.

"I'm not touching the top," she said. "Your curls are fantastic."

When she finished with Ezra, I pushed Richie toward the stool. He protested, and we argued, and Gabe bribed him with more ice cream, and finally he said *fine*, but Brittany had to promise not to cut too much. She trimmed just enough that he didn't look like he'd been living in a forest anymore.

When she held up a mirror, Richie shrugged.

"It's not bad," he admitted.

Then it was my turn. Brittany showed me a picture on her phone. "I think this would look great on you. What do you think?"

I hesitated. It was way shorter than I usually wore my hair. Gabe gave me an encouraging nod. I trusted them both, so I took a deep breath and said OK. Brittany went to work. The warm clippers tickled against my head. An unnerving amount of red hair fluttered onto the cloth around my neck. When she handed me the mirror, I hardly recognized myself. She'd buzzed my sides like Ezra's and Gabe's, cut back the top and slicked it away from my face. The hair I hid behind was gone.

Gabe grinned. "That's perfect on you."

"Yeah, you look amazing," Ezra said. He coughed. "Your hair, I mean. It's great. I like it."

"My head feels naked," I said.

Brittany brushed loose hairs off my neck. "You'll get used to it. It suits you."

She and Gabe kicked us out of the kitchen to clean up and start dinner before Mrs. Clelland came home. Richie went downstairs to play PlayStation, and Ezra and I took Gabe's basketball out to the driveway. I beat him in a game of Twenty-one.

"You're cheating," Ezra said. "You keep making funny faces to distract me."

I brushed at my nose. "I can't help it. I have a hair stuck to my face. It keeps tickling me."

Ezra took a step closer. "Here. Do you want me to . . . ?"

"Please."

Ezra carefully wiped the hair off my nose. He brushed another from my cheek.

"That feels much better. Thanks."

"You're welcome," he said, except his voice creaked. His cheeks turned pink.

I patted his shoulder in sympathy. "Don't you hate when that happens?" I made my voice go high and squeaky. Ezra giggled.

"Let's play one more," he said. "No cheating this time."

"I don't cheat. I'm just *good*." I picked up the basketball and casually flicked it one-handed at the net. It dropped through with a perfect *swish*. I couldn't have done that again if I tried. Ezra and I looked at each other and burst out laughing.

"Now you're showing off," he said. He shoulder-bumped me. I bumped him back.

He tried to shove me again, but I dodged, and he tripped over my foot. He crashed into me and we fell on the lawn.

Ezra reddened. "Sorry, I didn't mean to—"

I grinned and dug an elbow into his ribs.

We were tumbling breathless on the lawn when a shadow fell over us. Mrs. Clelland stood on the walkway.

"It constantly amazes me how much boys love wrestling each other," she said. Her eyes widened. "Brian, your hair! Did Brittany do that? It looks very handsome."

"Um. Thanks." I might have blushed, except I was already pink from play-fighting.

"Well, don't let me interrupt. I'll call you when dinner's ready." Mrs. Clelland smiled and went inside.

I watched her go. For the first time in a while, I remembered she had spent the afternoon talking with Kate and Mom. I'd stopped thinking about the hospital during sundaes and air guitar and haircuts and Twenty-one. I guess Gabe knew what he was doing.

Ezra brushed grass off his shirt. "I should probably head home."

"I'm really glad you came over," I said.

"Anytime. This was fun. I, uh . . ." He trailed off, like he'd forgotten what he was going to say. He cleared his throat and straightened his glasses. "I really like your haircut. And you're kind of sneaky-strong, you know. You have exceptionally pointy elbows."

"Why, thank you. I'm very proud of them." I jabbed him again.

He laughed and tackled me.

26. THINGS I COULDN'T SAY

EZRA

Kevan and Ty both showed up at my house before school to walk with Brian and me. Kevan came even though it was out of his way. This was Ty's doing. He had decided Brian was in, and now he was making him feel welcome. Ty was great like that. But . . .

"Whoa, your hair!" Kevan exclaimed when Brian showed up. "You look so different!"

Brian touched his hairline. "I'm still not used to it."

"It's fresh. I dig it," Ty said. He turned to me. "Yours looks good too. You guys go to the barber together?"

"Sort of," I said. We started walking.

"How's Richie?" Kevan asked Brian. "I honestly miss that little turd. He's the least annoying of Leo's friends."

"Richie's fine," Brian said. "He's basically invincible."

"No kidding," Kevan said. "He's the only kid who eats my spiciest food. Even Leo won't."

Brian's eyes lit up. "Rich brought home chicken once from your place. It was *so* hot, and *so amazing*—"

"My Chicken 65. You like that? You'll have to come for dinner sometime."

Brian didn't just look different. He was talking more, walking taller, acting like the guy who beat me at Twenty-one yesterday and wrestled on the Clellands' lawn. It was good, but . . .

"Kevan's food is pure fire," Ty said. "How did you end up at Mrs. Clelland's, anyway?"

"Yeah, I thought you were staying with foster parents," Kevan said.

Brian reddened. "Uh . . . we kind of ran away."

Kevan stopped so fast I nearly stepped on his heels. "Get out. Really?"

He and Ty were in awe as Brian told them about the hotel and the cottage. Kevan kept yelling "You did what?!" Brian cringed the first time, but he relaxed as he realized how much they loved his story.

"That's literally the coolest thing I've ever heard," Kevan declared. "First you punch Victor, then you're like, *Peace out, losers, I'm in charge now?* I had no idea you were so gangster."

"For real, B," Ty said. "You're a boss."

Brian grinned. Watching him figure out my friends liked him was amazing, except . . .

Yesterday had been perfect. Brian seemed sad at first,

but soon he was making impossible shots and letting me brush hair off his cheek and wrestling and laughing. It was perfect.

I kind of wished it could stay that way. Just us.

How selfish and awful was that?

"So why'd you come back?" Kevan asked. "Did the cops find you?"

Brian glanced at me in surprise. "You didn't tell them?"

Kevan and Ty stared at me, and I had no choice but to tell my part. But I kept it short.

Kevan elbowed me. "That's why you were sneaking around? You could have told us."

I looked at my shoes. "Ms. Floriman told me to keep it quiet. There were already rumors going around about Victor and stuff."

Sometimes you can say something that's technically true and it still leaves a queasy feeling in your stomach.

Kevan accepted my excuse. "Hey, we should all pull that sometime. We could say we were sleeping at Ty's, then disappear to a cottage. That would be awesome."

He spent the rest of the walk describing a perfect parent-free getaway. Brian went quiet. I wondered if he was thinking about what he'd give to have his own parents back. Ty humored Kevan's rambling, but he kept glancing at me.

I replayed for the millionth time how I went tingly all over when we were wrestling and Brian pressed his elbows into my chest with a big grin.

I wondered if he'd felt what I'd felt.

I almost told him, right on the Clellands' lawn. *I like you.* But I chickened out.

Was it wrong that I didn't tell him? Maybe he wouldn't have wrestled with me if he knew the truth. Maybe he wouldn't want to be friends at all.

It wasn't fair how something that felt so good could be confusing and scary too. What a rotten combo meal.

As we reached school, Ty gave us fist bumps and wandered off to remind people about his party. Kevan and I said goodbye to Brian by the office and headed to our lockers.

To my surprise, Colby was leaning against mine, arms folded across his chest.

"I guess I've been replaced," he said. A flash of guilt ran through me.

"What are you talking about?" I said, even though I knew what he meant.

"I saw you guys. Traded me for Brian and didn't even tell me."

He flashed a casual grin. And in that moment, I saw what Brian saw.

He seems like he's kind of in love with his own awesomeness.

"I promised to walk with Brian, and Kevan and Ty just showed up," I said. "Besides, you usually walk with Jemma now."

"I was kidding, Ezra. Jeez." The hall began to fill. Colby pushed off my locker. "Anyway, you should ask Ty to invite Victor tonight. It's not cool he's being left out."

A dozen questions popped into my head. I focused on opening my locker until I settled on the right one to ask first. "Why are you asking me? It's Ty's party."

"You know why," Colby said.

I kept twisting the dial on my combination lock. "Actually, I don't."

"Come on, bro. You invited Brian, so Ty didn't invite Victor. You guys are taking Brian's side and you don't know the whole story. He jumped Victor, you know."

It was driving me nuts how my temperature rose so easily at Brian's name. It distracted me enough that I screwed up my combination again. "I'm glad Brian's coming, but Ty asked him. I didn't invite anybody or take sides."

Colby scoffed. "Seriously? You're Brian's bestie after a week, and now you talk trash about Victor, same as everyone else. There's more to him than you think." He hesitated. "You have to turn it all the way to the right—"

"I know how my lock works!" I thunked it against my locker in frustration, sending an echo of metal on metal down the hall. "I played basketball with Brian all winter. There's more to him than you think too. And all I ever said about Victor is I don't think Brian would punch anyone for no reason. If you want Victor to come and he can show up without being a jerk, you can ask Ty yourself."

Half a dozen people were looking at us now. One of them was Victor. His nose was still swollen, and maybe more crooked than usual. He raised one eyebrow at Colby before he disappeared into Mrs. Clelland's homeroom.

Colby dropped his voice to an annoyed whisper. "What's your deal, bro? You're so pissy lately. It this about Victor? Or—Jemma? Are you jealous I have a girlfriend?"

"I couldn't care less if you have a girlfriend. Not everything is always about you, Colby."

It came out harsher than I intended. Colby recoiled like I'd spit at him.

Sorry. That was mean.

Honestly, maybe I'm a little jealous. I know it's silly, but . . .

It's not even Jemma. It's everything. We're both changing and I wish we knew how to talk about it. I miss how we used to be.

All those thoughts flickered like sparks and faded without crossing my lips.

The bell rang. Kids hurried to homeroom. With a wounded glare, Colby joined the crowd, letting it carry him to Mrs. Clelland's room. Away from me.

27. LEGEND OF THE NOBODY

BRIAN

Party Preparation Tips for Super Awkward Weirdos
1. Apply fresh deodorant so you don't stink when you inevitably start to sweat.
2. But not too much deodorant. Don't be That Guy who smothers people.
3. Rehearse safe topics to thwart SAWS. ("Any plans for summer?" "Did you see [insert popular movie here]?")
4. Try not to feel ridiculous talking to yourself in the bathroom mirror.
5. Try to forget normal kids don't work this hard to be around people.
6. Try not to imagine a dozen ways you could make a fool of yourself.
7. Fail badly at step 6 and start picturing worst-case scenarios.
8a. Admit you're hopeless. Text your friend that you're not feeling well, and spend the night alone, hating yourself.

Or...

8b. Take a chance and trust your friends.

Gabe dropped me at Ezra's, yelled, "You look great! Have fun!" and peeled away before I could change my mind.

Ezra must have been watching for me, because he pulled the door open as I approached and we set out for Ty's. It was only a few blocks' walk. Ezra talked the whole way. He seemed extra hyped for the party, or maybe he was filling the silence because he could tell I was nervous. His steady chatter distracted me from thinking about potential party disasters. Still, my throat felt tight by the time we reached Ty's.

If Ezra was hyped, Ty was practically radioactive. He greeted us with a holler and an elaborate hand-slap/fist-bump/shoulder-check combo.

"Ezra! Music Man! Sound system's on the deck! Ooh, nice jersey, B!"

I let out a sigh of relief. I'd worn my new jersey that I got for my birthday over a white T-shirt, but I worried it was too much. That was one of a dozen choices I'd second-guessed before Gabe told me to chill and dragged me to the car.

Ty led us inside. We were the first to arrive besides Kevan, who was unwrapping a tray of cookies in the dining room. He waved, then frowned.

"Brian, you OK? You're really pale."

Ty peered at me. "Yeah, you look terrified. Relax, I promise my house isn't haunted."

If there was any blood left in my face, it drained away as they studied me. Ezra looked worried.

"Uh . . ." My voice shook. I hated this, but there was no point pretending. "I'm glad to be here, but . . . sometimes in crowds . . . well, most of the time . . . I kind of struggle with anxiety."

I stared at the floor, feeling pathetic.

"We know," Ty said. "Come see the chill zone."

I looked up. "The what?"

"Come on."

We followed him to the deck, which wrapped around a circular above-ground pool that had a beach ball and two pool noodles floating on the water's surface. Ty led us to a patio table beneath a canopy. A string of blue and green lights wove between the poles. A beanbag chair rested in the corner against the deck railing.

"Welcome to the DJ booth–slash–chill zone," Ty said. "Ezra's setting up here, and you can hang out if you need a break. There's water and stuff in the cooler under the table."

"I stashed some cookies in there too," Kevan said. "They're homemade."

Ezra gave me a shy smile. Obviously, this was his idea, but they'd all helped.

I swallowed hard. "This is great. Thank you."

"We got you covered, B," Ty said. "We know your vibe is quiet and mysterious."

I fiddled with my dog tag. "I thought my vibe was Super Awkward Weirdo, but that sounds cooler."

They laughed.

"Trust me," Ty said. "Tonight's going to be legendary."

Ty's party wasn't like the parties in movies. No one was chugging beer or grinding to slow jams. I guess that stuff didn't happen when you were finishing the seventh grade and the host's mother kept asking if anyone needed more snacks.

"We're fine, Mom," Ty insisted. "You said you'd leave us alone."

A crowd gradually filled the house and spilled onto the deck. As Ezra started some music, I hung in the chill zone and watched Ty zing around like an electron, giving out fist bumps and cracking jokes, making everyone feel welcome. Watching him was inspiring—and exhausting. I'd probably collapse if I talked to that many people in a row.

"I'm going to go say hi to people," Ezra said. "Want to come?"

I shook my head. "You go ahead." I appreciated the offer, but I didn't want to stay glued to his side like a cling-on all night. I waited a bit, then braced myself and wandered into the house.

The air inside had grown thick with noise and heat. Four girls talked while they poured pop at the kitchen counter. I hung back, waiting for them to finish. They weren't in a hurry.

Brian versus Brian, Round 4,246
Me: I'll say, "Excuse me," pour a drink, move on. It'll take thirty seconds.

Also Me: What if they start talking to you?
*Me: Nobody talks to me. And I could probably manage
to say "Hi."*
*Also Me: You're notorious now. What if they bring
up Victor?*
Me: . . .
*Also Me: What if you get nervous and spill everywhere,
and they laugh?*
*Me: You know, I'm not that thirsty. I should pace myself
so I don't have to pee.*

I wandered through the dining room, trying to look
casual. Kevan was with Miranda Wong from our class.
She bit into a cookie and gasped. "You made this? It's
amazing."

Kevan grinned. "My own secret recipe." He caught my
eye and nodded, but his expression said, *I am with a girl, so
please don't interrupt.* I kept moving.

"Russell Westbrook, huh?"

I turned. Jayden Grouse and half the basketball team
were looking at me.

"What?" I said, cluelessly.

Jayden pointed at my chest. "He's your favorite player?"
"Yeah."

Jayden waited, expecting me to say more than one
word, as people usually do.

Come on, brain. Engage social skills.

"How about you?" I managed.

He shrugged. "Russ'll probably win MVP, but I'd still take Kevin Durant."

Andre Upshaw weighed in, then everyone was talking about their favorite players. I only said one more sentence, but I didn't do anything awkward and nobody said *Why are you still here?* Technically, this counted as successful participation in a conversation. I eventually excused myself. Better to quit while I was ahead.

The girls had moved, so I filled a plastic cup and turned toward the deck. At the door, I nearly dropped my drink.

Victor was out there.

I hadn't seen him come in. I hadn't even thought to worry he'd be here. Ty had been so nice to me, I assumed he wouldn't invite my mortal enemy. But Victor stood by the pool, flanked by Colby and Scott, as usual. Three girls were with them: Alicia, Jemma, and Madi. The casual swagger on the boys' faces said, *The party can start now—we're here.*

I froze. My skin tingled and I did this gulp-swallow thing and my brain sounded an alarm to flee, but my feet didn't follow. Colby whispered in Jemma's ear, making her giggle. A few people greeted Victor with an enthusiasm that made my stomach clench.

The bleakest thought lodged in my brain: *No one actually likes you. This was all a setup to help Victor get revenge in the most publicly humiliating way possible.*

I knew it wasn't true. *Ezra and Ty are better than that. Right?*

When you come equipped with an Anxiety Hyperdrive,

the worst thoughts are like weeds. They spring up quickly and they're hard to kill.

Ezra moved toward Colby and Victor. His back was to me, so I couldn't tell if he was glad to see them or not. I wasn't sure I wanted to know.

Victor glanced over Ezra's shoulder. Right at me.

My stasis broke. I turned so fast I sloshed Sprite on my hand and nearly bumped into Kevan.

"Hey, Brian." He tilted his head. "You OK? You've gone pale again."

My ears began to ring. I managed to nod, but my brain raced at light speed.

How to Escape Without Victor Destroying Me Completely
1. Fake a heart attack. (Shouldn't be hard, since panic feels like it's thirty seconds away.)
2. Set something on fire as a distraction.
3. Go to the bathroom and climb out the window, like a fugitive.
4. Keep it simple: run.

Before I could put any of those plans in motion, Kevan's face clouded. I sensed Victor's joy-sucking vampire shadow looming before his hand gripped my shoulder.

"Look at this." The sarcasm in his voice was so thick I swear it made my drink go flat. "No more Ghost, huh? Can't believe you're actually at a party. You even cut that mop you always hid behind. It's a good look on you. Honestly. I guess that cheap shot helped you find some self-esteem."

Scott snickered. Scott was always snickering.

I couldn't speak. I felt light-headed.

"Get lost, Victor," Kevan muttered.

Before Victor could respond, Ty appeared out of nowhere.

"Yo, get your hands off B. *Now.*"

The kitchen rearranged in a whirlwind. Victor and Scott stood by the refrigerator, facing Ty, Kevan, and me.

Ty stared at Victor. "What are you doing here, man?"

He didn't raise his voice, but everyone in earshot stopped talking. An electric jolt coursed through the party, like everyone could sense the oncoming drama.

It was barely noticeable, but for the first time I saw Victor flinch.

He buried it quickly under his usual smirk. "Relax, Ty. I didn't do anything."

Colby stepped inside and slowed as he surveyed the kitchen. He managed to appear fascinated by something on the fridge as he shuffled ever so slightly toward Victor.

Ezra came in a second later. He stood beside Kevan and me.

Ty stayed fixed on Victor. "You don't come to my house and lay hands on my friends."

"Seriously," Ezra said. "Leave Brian alone. All of you." He glared at Colby as he said it. Colby's jaw tightened, and he looked away.

I glanced around. A crowd was growing behind us.

Victor raised his hands in innocence. "I was just try-ing to be friendly. I keep trying, but Brian never talks to me."

Ty pointed toward the door. "Man, you need to go—"

"It's OK," I said.

Everyone stared at me, the nobody who never talked. The kid who froze in crowds.

I wasn't in Ice Mode, because I didn't go numb. My pulse thumped in my ears as I remembered how many people were watching. But my brain slowed enough that I thought about everything I'd been through, and everything Gabe and Brittany told me, and Ezra and Ty and Kevan standing with me. The room was shifting away from Victor, and he knew it. Everyone waited for me to speak. My SAWS wrestled for control, but it lost.

"It's your call, Ty, since it's your party." My voice trem-bled at first, then grew stronger. "But it doesn't matter to me if Victor stays. He can do what he wants."

I hadn't been able to look Victor in the eye all year, but now I locked eyes with him and didn't look away.

"I'm sorry I hit you," I said. "I wasn't really myself that day. I shouldn't have let you bother me that much. But it won't happen again. I'm not worried about you anymore."

Someone went "*Ooooh.*" Victor lowered his eyes. It was over.

Ty threw an arm around my shoulders. "Way to be the bigger man, B." He stared at Victor and raised his eyebrows before turning back to the group around us. "Now let's go swimming!"

Kids whooped and flocked outside. The pool filled as guys pulled off their shirts and cannonballed into the chest-deep water. Girls followed more cautiously, protesting as boys splashed them. I had to navigate through the crowd; I was no longer invisible. Andre and Jayden gave me fist bumps. Miranda told me she loved my haircut, which was the first time a girl ever used the word *love* in a sentence directed at me.

Kevan grabbed my shoulders, cackling with glee. "Brian, that was *ice cold*."

The attention was a lot—not bad, but still a *lot*. I started to feel shaky, so I headed to the kitchen for snacks. As I was stocking up, I saw Victor and his buddies slip out the door and disappear.

28. THIS IS HOW WE DO IT

EZRA

One upside of being the DJ at a party is the built-in excuse to be alone in a corner. Usually I didn't need that, but after Colby bailed with Victor, I didn't feel like talking for a while.

I hadn't expected him to say goodbye to me, but Colby didn't even say goodbye to Ty.

Nah. I wasn't going to mope. I was still at a party, and my DJ booth also provided the perfect cover to keep an eye on Brian.

No one was going to call him Ghost again. Everyone buzzed about how he'd dunked on Victor. Eventually, he staggered out of the crowd toward me. His cheeks were flushed pink and he had a giant dopey grin on his face.

"Had to fight through your fans, huh?" I said. "How does it feel to be the hero?"

He pulled up the hem of his jersey and wiped sweat from his forehead. "Honestly? Overwhelming. I'm so hot right now."

Mmhmm. "You should jump in the pool."

We both looked toward the splashing mass of bodies in the water. "It looks kind of dangerous in there," Brian said. "I think I'll stay in the chill zone for a while."

He leaned against the fence and played with his necklace. He did that when he was stressed, I noticed.

"You all right?" I asked. "That was crappy of Victor to crash the party."

"I'm good." Brian exhaled. "How about you? Everything OK with you and Colby?"

I flashed back to the confrontation I wanted to forget: Colby by the pool with arms folded, eyes and shoulders angled away from me.

"Seriously?" I'd asked. "Showing up with Victor? What were you thinking?"

It felt like an invisible wall went up between us. "There's stuff you don't understand," he said.

Quit acting like a dink and tell me the truth, *I wanted to say. But I didn't. A tug in my chest reminded me I wasn't telling him the whole truth either. I assumed he wouldn't understand how I felt about Brian. I didn't have the courage to explain.*

Before I could respond, Ty called out Victor, things got wild, and Colby was gone.

I didn't answer Brian's question. "Watch this," I said.

I queued up a different section of my playlist and cranked the volume. Across the deck, Ty's head shot up as he recognized the Montell Jordan classic, "This is How We Do It."

"Aw yessss." He pointed at me. "This is my *jam*."

Ty was the sun, drawing everyone into his orbit. Once he started dancing, a crowd followed—first girls, then confident guys like Andre, then shy kids who realized this was a chance to let loose. By the chorus, the deck was a dance floor.

"Come on," I said to Brian.

He shrank back. "Uh . . . I don't . . . I've never . . ."

"This'll be fun, I promise." I took him by the elbow, and he let me lead him into the crowd.

Another benefit of being the DJ is you know what's coming. I didn't have to worry about getting Brian out there right as a slow song kicked in and made things awkward. I'd lined up three straight jams. Everyone would be moving, and I would convince the adorable Super Awkward Weirdo I liked to lighten up and dance.

Some things in life were confusing, but I knew music.

Brian started slowly. By the time we transitioned from Montell to Beyoncé and Jay-Z, his limbs swung more loosely, and he even had some hip action going on.

We danced in a soggy mess as people climbed out of the pool and packed into the crowd. When Jay-Z's verse started, Brian's eyes lit up. He quietly rapped along. I couldn't help staring.

Ty noticed Brian mouthing the words and laughed maniacally. "B, *what?* How are you so secretly hardcore?"

Brian's dopey grin came back. By the hook we were all shouting along. Brian was laughing. It was perfect. I now knew my mental soundtrack for him would be Jay-Z, because the moment he grinned at me, my crush-flutter swirled into a tornado of color and light, thrilling and terrifying all at once. I was hopelessly into him.

"Ezra!" Madi clamped onto my arm. Startled, I turned. "Isn't this such a great party?" she yelled over the bass. "Did you pick all the music?"

"Yeah." I pried my arm free. "You're still here?"

She stared like I'd asked if she had dog poop on her shoe.

"I thought you were with Victor and those guys," I clarified.

Madi rolled her eyes. "Ugh. I knew that would be a disaster, and I *told* Jemma, but she literally does whatever Colby wants—"

Madi launched into way more detail than I wanted about the inner dynamics of Jemma and Colby. She called them "Jolby," which made me want to plunge my head in the pool and scream forever. I nodded and tried to back away, but the crowd was too tight. Finally I blurted, "Sorry, time to load up more music," and turned back to Brian.

But he was gone.

29. LIFE AS A DUMPSTER FIRE

BRIAN

I was dancing. With other people. At a party. This was the strangest, most epic night.

I almost didn't notice my phone vibrating in my pocket.

I ducked into the kitchen to check who was calling. Hank? At 9:40 on Friday night? That couldn't be good. Maybe something had happened to Mom or Dad. My stomach went hollow.

"Hello? Hank?"

"B-Man. Where are you?"

It wasn't Hank. I leaned against the counter. "*Dad?* Why are you on Hank's phone?"

"I'm at Hank's apartment. Where are you? It sounds loud."

"You're in Halifax?" Dad was here. He came back. What did that mean?

"Yeah. So if you can tell me where you are . . ."

"I'm at a party." I gave him Ty's address.

"A party? Well. I hate to ruin your fun, but we need to talk. Pick you up in ten minutes?"

"Uh . . . give me twenty?"

He paused. "Sure. See you soon."

I hung up and leaned over with my hands on my knees. I'd held together through the Victor showdown and everything else, but Dad's unexpected return tipped me off the cliff. An emergency alarm sounded in my gut. I raced to the bathroom. When I finished, I cracked open the window. This would be my final impression: After a fleeting moment in the spotlight, the awkward quiet kid would go weird again and flee the party early after fouling up the bathroom. Universal balance restored.

I hurried down the hall, thankful not to find anyone waiting for the bathroom. A group of kids had filed inside to refresh on snacks, filling the house with a muddy torrent of noise that made my head go dull. My chest tightened.

I couldn't have a panic attack now. I needed out.

I swerved toward the front door and nearly ran into Ezra.

"I have to leave early," I blurted. "I'm sorry, I can't stay over. Maybe another time?"

Ezra blinked. "Uh, Sure."

"Great. Sorry. Bye."

I pulled back from the tipping point once I was outside, away from the crowd. I sat on the step to focus on breathing and wait for Dad.

What happened now? My feelings about Dad kept tumbling around in a confusing swirl, so I'd tried not to think about him at all. But now—

Ezra stepped out behind me. "Brian? Are you OK? What's going on?"

I took a breath. I trusted Ezra, and I wanted to tell him, but it still wasn't easy.

"My dad called. He's picking me up. I haven't seen him since—" I caught myself. "It's been a few weeks."

"Oh." Ezra lingered. "Want me to wait with you?"

"Uh . . . you don't need to leave the party."

"I could use a break too." He sat beside me.

Silence.

Ezra hunched closer. "Your mom hinted that something bad happened on your birthday. You can tell me, if you want."

I took one more deep breath. "That's when Dad left. The police are after him. I think he might go to jail."

It felt good and awful to say it out loud.

"Oh." Ezra fell silent. I waited for him to ask why Dad was in trouble, but he didn't.

"Your dad seems cool," he said. "He comes to most of our games, right?"

"Yeah, he's . . ." Pause. Regroup. "It feels weird to say he's a criminal because he's not how that sounds. Not around us, anyway. He plays basketball and video games with us. We have the strangest conversations, though. Sometimes he's all, *Here's how life works, son.* And by the end

I'm half-terrified. Like, Dad, I don't want to know this yet. It's too much sometimes. And he . . ."

He left us.

I stopped before I said that out loud. This was already the most personal collection of sentences I'd ever said to anyone my age. I risked peeking at Ezra. He didn't look freaked out. He was listening.

"My dad and I barely talk about anything," he said after a moment. "We get along fine, but he's real old-school. Mostly he leaves me to figure stuff out for myself." Ezra's knee bounced at jackhammer speed. He'd been less chill than usual all night. "Anyway. I'm sorry about your dad. It's bad timing that he's in trouble while your mom's in the hospital."

I touched my ninja tag. "That's why Mom's in the hospital."

I told him about the letters, and the pills, and calling 911.

Ezra's jaw dropped. "Brian, wow. I'm so sorry. That must have been awful."

"It was awful." I retied my shoelaces to distract me from reliving the Incident in too much detail. "She's doing better, though. She comes home on Monday. But I nearly watched her die. How do we go back to normal after that?"

"No kidding." He leaned closer. "How are you even OK?"

The thump of bass and muted sounds of laughter floated from the backyard. My heart fluttered as I summoned the nerve to tell Ezra the scariest part.

"I'm not OK." My voice shook. "I started having panic attacks. There might be something wrong with me. Maybe there was already something wrong with me. But this made it worse."

Ezra looked at me gravely. "It's not your fault. There's nothing wrong with you. Your life just sucks." He turned pink. "That came out wrong. I didn't mean—"

I snickered. "No, you're right. My life is a flaming dumpster fire of suckage."

Ezra giggled, and we both lost it. We fell into each other, weak with laughter.

"There's our first song title," he gasped. "'A Dumpster Fire of Suckage.'"

As we caught our breath, he put his arm around my shoulders, like he was saying *you can count on me.* It felt nice.

"Thanks for being such a good friend," I told him. "It really means a lot."

Suddenly he pulled away. His knee bounced again.

"Ezra? What's up?"

"I . . ." He rubbed his eyes under his glasses. "I'm sorry, this is the worst timing. But I need to be honest. I don't want to be weird, or fake, or . . ." He exhaled hard. He turned so pale and shaky I worried he might faint.

"I like you, Brian," he whispered. "I like you a lot."

At first, I didn't know why he was so rattled. I almost said, "I like you too."

But then I understood.

30. IF THIS WERE A MOVIE

EZRA

This was a mistake.

A terrible, horrible, desperately-wish-I-could-take-it-back mistake.

Brian's mouth hung open. He was shocked, and freaked out, and I never should have touched him, and I never should have said anything, because it was all an enormous mistake.

I was doing a killer job of ruining all my friendships in one night.

I jumped up so fast my eyes blurred. Brian rose slowly, still watching me, still not talking.

"Never mind," I blurted. "I shouldn't have brought this up now. Forget it. Your dad's coming, and you have enough to think about, and . . ."

A storm of words kept flying from my mouth. My head spun. I needed to disappear. I thought about sprinting all the way home, but I wasn't sure I'd make it without collapsing. Maybe I could get to Ty's room? I backed toward the house.

"Ezra," Brian said. "Wait."

He hugged me.

A tidal wave of feelings swallowed me. Brian wasn't mad or grossed out. I didn't have to be afraid. His arms were around me and his cheek was touching mine and I could smell his hair gel. I could have stayed there forever.

But a tug right below my heart reminded me that if this were a movie and the boy I liked truly liked me back, he probably would have kissed me by now.

It was all so much. I thought my chest might explode. Instead, I started to cry.

I felt silly about it, but Brian squeezed me tighter. I hugged him back, until a flash of fear struck that someone might look out Ty's window and see us.

I let go and wiped my eyes. "I'm so sorry. I shouldn't have—"

"Ezra, don't," Brian said. "I'm glad you told me."

He sat on the step and wiped his cheeks. My chest ached. Brian was dealing with impossible, terrible things, and here I was sweating whether kids from school would care if I was gay. I used to think Brian could use my help, but he was braver than me.

I sat beside him and pressed my palms flat against the cool stone.

He fiddled with his necklace. "Sorry I froze. I was just surprised. I didn't know what to say, because . . . I'm not sure . . . I mean, I don't know—"

"That's OK," I interrupted. I didn't need to hear him say the words. "I'm mostly glad you're not weirded out."

"Ezra, of course not! You're my friend."

He rested his hand on mine. His long, thin fingers were sweaty and pulsing with energy. His eyes went wide and his Adam's apple bobbed nervously, but he didn't let go.

I fought past a hitch in my voice. "You don't have to do that."

"I know." He inched closer. "I want to."

I squeezed his hand. We didn't talk much after that. We just held hands on Ty's front step. All I could think was, *I told him, and he still likes me, and he's holding my hand.*

A silver Honda crept down the street. Brian let go of my hand and took a steadying breath as the car pulled up to the curb. Other questions sprang to my mind.

"Is this a good idea?" I asked. "I mean, if your dad's in trouble, will you be safe?"

Brian blinked, as if he hadn't thought about this. "I have to see him. It'll be OK. I think."

"OK. Text me later?" I said.

"I will. Thank Ty for me, please. Tonight was fun." He put a hand on my shoulder and pushed himself to his feet. I could still feel the warm imprint of his fingers as he walked toward his dad.

31. READY TO FIGHT

BRIAN

Walking down Ty's driveway was like crossing a bridge between galaxies. My mind bounced between replaying my wild night and imagining what might happen with Dad.

Ezra has a crush on me. That is . . . something.

I wasn't sure what it meant, exactly. I wasn't sure about a lot of things.

I liked when Ezra put his arm around me, the same way I liked when Gabe did it. I hugged him and held his hand because he was scared, but those things felt good too. I wanted to make him feel safe the way he made me feel safe. But I didn't want to kiss him or anything.

I didn't have *those* kinds of feelings for anyone else either. Not yet, anyway. Talking to people was tricky enough. If junior high were a video game, *liking* and *crushes* and *kissing* were mega boss battles and I'd barely cleared level two.

Everything about being thirteen was complicated. But some complications were better than others. Having a friend like Ezra was a good complication.

Thinking about him was more fun than thinking about whatever was about to happen as I reached our car. A car I hadn't seen in nearly three weeks.

I opened the passenger door. Dad smiled, and for a moment my heart leaped. For weeks I'd been hoping he'd show up and fix everything somehow. But as I watched him, my hope faded. A scruff of red stubble dotted his normally bare cheeks, and his shoulders slumped as he sat with one hand on the steering wheel. He didn't look like he was bursting with good news.

He pulled away from the curb before he spoke. "Was that Ezra? You guys hang out now?"

"Yeah." I stared out the window. Ezra waved and ducked back inside.

"Huh. Look at you. New haircut, making friends, partying on Friday night. I'm impressed. That jersey looks great on you." Dad made a left turn. "So . . . how are you?"

"That's a complicated question."

"Fair enough. You hungry? Want to grab burgers from Ace?"

He was acting so casual, like he'd picked me up from basketball practice instead of appearing out of nowhere after three weeks. The faint strains of a hip-hop beat leaked from the speakers. I thought about other drives in this car, when Dad would crank the volume until the bass rattled my chest and we'd shout along together. Would we ever be that carefree again? What happened after tonight? How could he pretend everything was normal?

A different feeling started to stir inside me. Anger.

"No, I don't want a burger, Dad." I turned toward him. "What are we doing?"

"What do you mean?"

The coal in my chest grew hotter. "You know what I mean. Are you only here because Mom called you?"

He raised an eyebrow. "She told you about that, huh?"

"Yeah. So what happened to your plan to fix everything? What have you been doing all this time while we were trying to manage on our own?"

Dad smiled. "OK, let's get right to it. I missed you."

I folded my arms. "I didn't go anywhere."

"And I love this assertiveness. You're mad, I get it. You're allowed to be mad at me."

"Of course I'm allowed. You don't get to tell me how to feel."

So much for staying cool. Screw it. I had survived crying and panic attacks and heartfelt talks, and suddenly I was ready to fight. I wanted to fight.

"All right, sorry," Dad said. "God knows I don't want to lecture you."

"Are you kidding?" I snapped. "You lecture me all the time. You think you're this Cool Dad because you're super honest or whatever, but all your talks boil down to *Toughen up, you wuss*. And none of your garbage speeches prepared me for how awful it was when you left me alone to watch Mom almost die. Whatever advice you have planned tonight, you can shove it."

I was flushed and breathing hard. But Dad barely flinched.

"I get it," he said. "I screwed up, big-time."

I felt small, burning with such fury while he sat so calmly, but I couldn't help myself.

"You don't get it at all! I hate you, Dad. I hope you go to jail."

The acid words scalded as they left my mouth. All I wanted was to make him hurt, to pierce the ice that would always be harder and thicker than my own. Just once.

Dad blinked. He slowed and pulled into a pharmacy parking lot, then parked with the engine running. He stared straight ahead.

Is he furious? Is he going to kick me out? I waited, barely breathing.

Slowly, he turned to me. "I don't think you're a wuss," he said.

It took all I had, but I met his eyes. "I've heard you talking to Mom. You think there's something wrong with me."

For the first time, Dad faltered. "Brian, what?"

"You think I'm scared of everything and not strong enough—"

"Wait. Listen—"

"No, you listen for once! I know I'm sensitive and anxious and kind of a mess, but that doesn't mean I'm not trying. It just means I'm not like you."

"Brian—"

"But that's fine, because I *shouldn't* be like you. You

put all this weight on me, and then you ran away. You. Ran. Away."

I poked him in the shoulder with each word. Dad's eyes widened.

I could feel tears coming. I dug my fingernails into my palms to fight them off. The last thing I wanted to do was cry.

Dad broke first.

He undid his seat belt, leaned over, and pulled me to his shoulder. One hand rested on the back of my head. His voice was so close it tickled my ear. "You're right. I'm sorry, Brian. I'm sorry."

Dad was crying. I'd never seen him cry. I burst into tears too, but it didn't matter. For the first time in ages I wasn't embarrassed about losing it in front of Dad. I wriggled my arms free and wrapped them around his back.

"I didn't mean it," I breathed into the space beneath his collarbone. "I don't want you to go."

After Dad and I stopped crying in the car, he drove home and we sat at the kitchen table while he explained what would happen next. Hank had helped him hire a lawyer, and they had talked to Sergeant States. Dad was going to turn himself in by the end of the weekend. He came home to tell me in person. His lawyer was confident he could make a deal to serve a reduced sentence, maybe eighteen months or less.

But eighteen months was still a long time.

I cried again. Dad squeezed my arm.

"It's OK, B-Man," he said. "Your mom will be OK. Hank'll be around to help. You don't have to carry it all." He squeezed my shoulder. "You should get some sleep."

My room was airless and hot. A thin coat of dust had settled on my desk. The room somehow felt both smaller and emptier, as if some invisible piece had been carved out in my absence.

I was home, with Dad, and I still felt homesick. The whole universe had shifted.

When I entered my parents' room, I had a brief flashback to the last time I stood there, the pills and the panic.

"Dad?" I scratched my chest. "I, uh, I kind of can't sleep alone right now. It's just . . . hard."

I worried he'd think this was silly, but he didn't.

"I haven't had a good sleep in weeks," he admitted. "Come on."

Burrowing in Mom's side of the bed felt backward. I sometimes crawled into Dad's side on nights he was out and Mom silently disappeared. After I put Richie to bed, I brought my homework or a book and stayed till she was asleep. Sometimes I fell asleep too and woke to Dad shaking my shoulder. But that night, I lay next to him with the sheet pulled up to my chin.

"Dad?" I asked after a moment. "If I ask you something, will you tell me the truth?"

"Of course."

"OK. Um. Have you ever killed anyone?"

Dad laughed. "Wow. Don't start with a softball. No, Brian. I've never killed anyone."

That was a relief, one of those worst-case things I'd always feared. I kept going.

"Do you carry a gun?"

He stopped laughing. "No. I used to, but I never kept it in the house. Your mom hates them."

I asked about him and Mom and why things were the way they were. Dad told me about his own parents: His dad got hurt at work, then his mom left, and his dad stopped doing anything except drinking and watching TV. Dad told me he had to fend for himself and started finding creative ways to make money when he was fifteen.

"Once you start down some roads," he said, "it's easier to keep going. One day, you look around and regret ending up where you are, but you don't know how to turn around." He sighed. "I need to do better for you and Richie and your mom. And I will. I promise."

My chest ached and I didn't know what to say.

"My turn," Dad said. "Are you scared of what happens next?"

I told him the truth. "Of course I'm scared. It's going to be so different without . . ." I couldn't bring myself to say *without you.* "But it helps that I have Gabe now, and Mrs. Clelland, and Ezra. I feel . . . less alone."

Dad sighed again.

"What about you?" I asked. "Are you scared?"

He smiled. "Honestly, B-Man, what scares me most is trying to be your dad."

That was the last answer I expected. "What do you mean?"

He rolled on his side, toward me. "Don't get me wrong, it's my *favorite* thing too. But I was still a kid when you were born. I didn't have two sweet clues what I was doing, and my role models weren't great. They mostly taught me you can love someone an awful lot and hurt them all the same." He tapped my chest. "It's the last thing I wanted to do to you. But here we are."

It had been a long time since I looked at Dad from so close. He looked a lot like me: penny-colored hair and freckled cheeks.

"You were right in the car, kiddo," he said. "I put too much on you. I wanted you to be strong because I was trying to protect you from *me*. I knew I'd let you down, and I did. But I'm sorry I got it twisted. I just want you and Richie to be better than me."

I swallowed hard. My throat was raw, and I didn't want to start crying again.

"You're not *that* bad," I said.

Dad laughed. "Oh, B-Man."

I rolled toward him and lay on my belly with my head on my arms. He rested a hand on my back, and I drifted off to sleep.

32. MANGO

EZRA

After the last guest said good night and there was no one left at Ty's but Kevan and me, Ty's mom handed him a broom and a garbage bag.

Ty groaned. "Can't it wait till morning?"

Mrs. Marsman raised one eyebrow. She had the deadliest raised-eyebrow stare in the history of moms. Ty sighed. He and Kevan collected garbage while I swept up chip crumbs in the kitchen.

"Thank you, boys," Mrs. Marsman said. "Lights out afterward. You have to be in the gym by ten tomorrow, Ty. And I'm not going to drag you out of bed."

"I'll be up, Mom." Ty summoned his most winning smile, which faded to a scowl as she left the room. He muttered under his breath.

"Don't trash-talk your mom," Kevan said. "My mom would never let me throw a party this awesome."

"True." Ty's grin returned. He and Kevan relived their highlights of the night as we cleaned up. When we finished, we headed up to his bedroom and Ty unrolled a sleeping bag for me. Kevan had planned ahead to stay. I texted Mom to tell her Brian couldn't come over and I was staying at Ty's instead. She sent back a thumbs-up.

"I can't believe Colby went to the dark side," Kevan grumbled as Ty switched off his light. "He's a different person lately. I think Jemma's corrupting his brain."

I guess I wasn't the only one who noticed things had changed.

"I'm not sure Colby thinks with his brain," Ty cracked. "Don't blame Jemma. She's OK. Colby's just *going through a phase*." He said this in a perfect Professional Adult voice. Kevan and I laughed.

"When I get a girlfriend, I won't forget who my real friends are," Kevan announced. "We should make a pact."

Ty snickered. "Sure. A pact."

"I'm serious," Kevan said. "Are you with me, Ezra? If you ever date Madi, you won't bail on us, right?"

Thankfully the lights were out and Kevan couldn't see my face change color.

"That's not going to happen," I mumbled.

"Good," Kevan said. "Because the way you killed it with the music tonight, all kinds of girls were—"

"Kevan," Ty interrupted. "Chill."

Ty's room was boiling hot. I unzipped the sleeping bag.

"I, um." A sudden urgency gripped me, like I had to be honest *right now*, or else I'd keep hiding forever. "The thing is, what I meant is, it won't happen because, well, I'm not . . ."

The hardest part was remembering how to breathe.

Ty sat up. "It's cool, Ezra," he said quietly. "You can say it. It's OK."

Ty knew.

"Say what?" Kevan's sleeping bag rustled. "Wait. Are you—"

The strange hot-and-cold feeling washed over me again. "Yeah," I whispered. "I'm gay."

I hugged the sleeping bag to my chest, waiting for them to react. But nobody freaked out.

Gradually my heart slowed. "You knew?" I asked Ty.

"Not for sure," he said. "But I noticed how much you hated Ezra-and-Madi talk."

Kevan sighed. "I noticed too, but I didn't think . . . I was just messing around. Sorry for being an idiot."

"It's OK," I said.

"I also wondered about you and Brian," Ty said. "You've been *so* nervous around him lately. It's honestly the cutest thing I've ever seen." In the dim moonlight I could tell he was grinning. "I saw you follow him out tonight. I figured something was up."

Kevan lurched forward. "You're into Brian? Did you kiss him?"

"No." I swallowed. "I told him, though. He was cool about it, but I don't think he feels the same way."

"Oh. Bummer. Well, for you." Kevan coughed. "You know what I mean. Anyway, thanks for telling us. I hope it's not weird to talk about."

"It shouldn't be weird," Ty said. "One of my older cousins came out two years ago, and at first everyone was like *whoa*, but now she brings her girlfriend to family dinners and it's all good. Even my grandma likes her." He nudged my sleeping bag with his foot. "You seemed stressed lately. I hope you feel better now."

Ty was right. Whenever I told someone, the rock in my belly felt smaller. But I couldn't help wondering how many more times I'd have to do this in my life. I still had to tell my parents. I thought about other relatives, kids at school, all the people I'd ever meet and wonder if or when I should say anything. It made me tired, and a little bummed.

"I'm scared to tell Colby." My voice cracked as I said it.

No one said anything, which said everything.

After a miserable silence, Ty stretched. "Kevan was right about tonight. Your music made the party way better. You make everything more fun, Ezra. If anyone can't see that, it's their loss. Who you like is no one's business, anyway."

"Except ours," Kevan said. "Because we're your friends. Is there anyone you're into besides Brian?"

The hot-cold feeling came back. "You really want to talk about this?"

"Only if you want to," Ty jumped in. "But for real, you can tell us. It won't be any worse than listening to Kevan."

"Ha ha," Kevan shot back. "Hey, we could have a code word. If you see a cute guy, say *mango*. We'll know what you mean."

Ty snorted. "Are you saying mangoes are gay, Kevan? That's racist."

I laughed. "Listen. Potatoes are the most heterosexual food. *He's straight as a potato* should be a thing people say."

"And mayonnaise is the whitest food."

"Mayonnaise isn't a food."

"How is it not a food?"

"No one eats *just* mayo straight from the jar. It's a sauce."

"Weak sauce."

"So that's your definition of food? What about peanut butter?"

"Of course peanut butter's a food. Don't you ever eat it straight from the jar?"

"Well, yeah."

"What if something's gross unless you put other stuff on it? Like, no one eats plain oatmeal, right? Is it a food?"

"Plain oatmeal is communist."

"Pickled eggs are for serial killers."

"Nasty. Who'd eat a pickled egg?"

"Exactly! It's like eating a giant eyeball."

"Pickled eggs dipped in mayo. Yum."

"If you ever open a fridge and there's nothing but pickled eggs and mayo, run for your life. Hundred percent chance you're at a serial killer's house."

We were back to being ridiculous, like at most of our sleepovers. Every time I laughed, the rock grew smaller.

But when we settled, and air whistled through Kevan's left nostril in a steady rhythm, my thoughts ping-ponged between Brian and Colby. Brian was a whole complicated tangle of relief and heartbreak I didn't want to dwell on yet. And Colby . . . I was mad at him, but he was still one of my best friends. I kept thinking of the Halloween he had the genius idea to double up on costumes so we could hit the best houses twice. Or the time in fourth grade an older kid tripped me and Colby called him a buttwad and chased him off. Or the way we could still crack each other up over silly memories, like fridge magnets.

We had a history I didn't want to forget. I didn't know if we had a future, but I wasn't ready to give up without one more try.

33. HERE, NOW

BRIAN

Voices in the kitchen woke me on Saturday morning. I was in my parents' room, sprawled on Mom's side of the bed. Sun streamed in the window. I focused on the kitchen, trying to sort out the voices.

"Oooof. Hey, Richie. I missed you, buddy. And I missed you too, beautiful. Come here."

Laughter. "Everett, stop that. Where's Brian?"

Mom. That was Mom's voice. My whole family is here. How?

I hopped out of bed and started down the hall. They stood in a huddle, Dad with one arm around Mom and the other holding up Richie, who was hanging off his neck. Sunlight filled the kitchen. Maybe I was still dreaming, or the world had ended and this was the afterlife. All forgiven and forgotten, all our failures erased.

Mom opened her arms and I went to her. No Ice Mode this time. It was morning in my own kitchen and Dad squeezed us with Richie squashed in the middle, his back pressed against my ear. Nobody moved for a long time.

When we finally pulled apart, I noticed Hank in the doorway. He must have picked up Mom and Richie.

"How is this possible?" I said.

"I'm out for the day," Mom said. "I've been out more this week, going for walks, readjusting to life outside." She stroked my hair. "Getting ready to come home."

"So we all get to come home now?" Richie said.

Mom and Dad looked at each other. "Just for today, Rich," Dad said. "You guys can come home for good soon. I have to go away for a while."

Richie's eyes fell. "Are you going to jail?"

"Yeah."

Quiet. Dad reached for Richie's shoulder. Richie resisted at first, but eventually, he let Dad pull him in. "We don't need to think about that now," Dad said. "We're going to the beach."

I'd never been so happy to spend forty-five minutes in the car with my family. Dad drove us to Bayswater, and we talked about normal things like normal people. Mom said she'd heard a wild rumor that I'd gone to a party. I grinned.

My phone buzzed. A text from Ezra: **Everything good?**

Yeah, we're going to the beach I wrote back.

Cool where

Bayswater

Sweet cya later

Mom glanced in the mirror. "Are you texting? Seriously? We're together for the first time in weeks and you're talking to someone else on your phone? This is why I hate those things."

"Relax, Julia," Dad said. "He's old enough to have a phone."

"Besides, you should be happy for me," I said. "I finally have a social life."

Dad chuckled. Mom rolled her eyes.

"Do I get a phone for my birthday?" Richie asked. "I have more friends than Brian does."

"Wow, Rich. That's cold." I poked his leg. He batted my hand away.

Mom turned. "You are absolutely not getting a phone for your tenth birthday." She raised a hand to cut off his protest. "Save your breath, kiddo. The *All my friends* card is no good here."

Richie huffed and crossed his arms. Dad and I grinned. Mom was back in full Mom Mode, and I didn't mind at all.

We all loved the beach. Something about the rhythm of the ocean made it easier to stop thinking. The tide went in and out. Some days the surf swelled higher than others, sometimes the shore was blanketed in fog, but the ocean was always the ocean. I relaxed with warm sand between my toes and the steady tumble of waves in my ears.

The day was perfect, warm and sunny. It was the first official weekend of summer, but too early for swimming in the cold Atlantic, so the beach wasn't crowded. I let Mom rub sunscreen onto my shoulders. I couldn't entirely shake the thought we might not have another day like this for a long time, but I didn't dwell on it. We were here, now.

"Time to go in," Dad declared. The Day men had a rule about dunking ourselves no matter what. Dad, Richie, and I lined up on the shore, counted to three, and ran. We screamed as the freezing ocean shocked us. We dove in, letting the cold sting our entire bodies, then we surfaced and screamed again. Dad and Richie played in the waves, but shivers racked my skinny limbs and I had to retreat. I stretched on my belly on our beach blanket. Mom covered my back with a towel. I closed my eyes and listened to Richie shouting "Mom! Watch this, Mom!" over the rhythm of the waves.

After I was warm and dry, I walked along the shore with Mom. We talked about school, Ezra, the Clellands. The Incident didn't hang over every sentence. Mom said there was no point pretending it never happened, but it didn't have to define the rest of our lives.

"I started an art therapy group this week," she said. "It's less painful than the usual *sit in a circle and talk about your feelings* deal. I think it'll help."

"That's good, Mom." I took four steps. "You'll keep doing other stuff too, right? After you're home?"

Mom gave me the side-eye, but she answered. "I'll have regular appointments with my psychiatrist. We've adjusted my medication." She rubbed her arms as a breeze stirred off the water. "We'll have check-ins with the social worker for a while. Make sure we're . . . you know."

"Yeah." Five more steps. "Kate made an appointment for me too. At the children's hospital on Thursday. With a psychologist."

Mom slowed for a half step. "How do you feel about that?"

"I don't know. She made me take this test." I kept my eyes on the waves rolling over my toes. "You know I get anxious, but it's way worse lately. Like . . . sometimes it's *awful*, and sometimes I stop feeling anything at all. Like when I hit Victor. I wasn't even mad, I just did it. That's weird, right?"

"You've been through a major trauma, Brian. People react to stress in different ways." Mom's voice went flat, like she was reciting from a textbook.

"How old were you when you first thought something was . . . not right?"

She fell quiet so long I thought she wasn't going to answer. Then she exhaled.

"I was a little older than you. Just starting high school." She reached for my hand. "We'll talk more once I'm home, OK? You can ask whatever you want. It'll be good for you to talk to a professional too. But I want you to know I'm so proud of you. If we need to get you some help, that doesn't make you weaker or less than anyone else."

"Gabe gave me that pep talk too."

Mom smiled. "Jackie said you and Richie have been good for Gabe."

It was weird to hear Mom use Mrs. Clelland's first name. "Gabe's helped me a lot. I don't think I've done anything for him."

"Don't be so sure, honey. It often goes both ways."

Mom held my hand as we walked. I felt self-conscious holding hands with her on the beach, but she was happy, so I didn't want to let go.

Later, Dad and I sat on the boulders at the far end of the beach. He rattled off a list of things to do around the house.

"Mow the lawn every couple of weeks. You remember how to start the mower, right?"

"Mmm," I said absently.

"And help your mom with groceries. You know she finds stores overwhelming sometimes."

"Mmm."

"Hank will help with bills, but check the mail . . ." Dad trailed off. He chuckled. "I'm doing it again."

I turned. "What?"

"Lecturing you. I'll stop now." He rested his hand on the base of my neck. "You're a good kid, B-Man. You know, the way you and your mom get along, I never had that. I know it's been rough, but she loves you more than anything. Always has and always will."

I leaned my head on Dad's shoulder.

The drive home was quiet. Richie's yawns grew bigger as we wound along the coast of the Aspotogan Peninsula.

I slid into the middle seat so he could rest against me. By the time we reached the highway, he was asleep with his face buried in my T-shirt. I closed my eyes.

"What are you thinking about?" Mom asked.

I kept my eyes closed. "Nothing."

"I doubt that."

"OK. Everything."

"Did you have a good time?"

"It was perfect."

So why did my voice crack and my eyes well up? Mom and Dad knew. They didn't need to ask.

"We could keep going," Dad said wistfully. "The four of us. See where we end up."

Mom touched his arm. "You know none of us are enough for each other."

Dad sighed. "I know."

The kitchen smelled delicious when we got home. I recognized that aroma: Hot Numbing Chicken from the Hungry Chili. Hank was unpacking takeout containers. My stomach growled as we dug in. I loved the feeling of fire in my mouth, the way it made my head go tingly. Dad and I egged each other on and teased Hank, who stuck to the mildest dishes. Richie guzzled root beer and let out a massive burp. Mom burped louder, and Richie collapsed in laughter.

Mom and Dad slipped into the kitchen and talked in whispers. Then suddenly they were singing.

"Happy birthday to youuuu . . ."

Dad set an ice-cream cake in front of me, lit up with thirteen candles.

I blinked back tears.

"Happy birthday, sweetie," Mom said softly. "I'm sorry we messed up so badly the first time around. We love you."

I had to swallow hard before I could draw a breath deep enough to blow out my candles. My wish was optimistic, but hopefully not impossible. I wished that next year, on my actual fourteenth birthday, we could all do this together.

After cake, Mom and Dad retreated to the deck. I watched through the glass door as Dad wrapped Mom in his arms. This was their goodbye. Dad hunched over the railing with his back to the house as Mom came inside, wiping her eyes.

"I'll see you on Monday," she told Richie and me. "We'll come home together. Enjoy tonight with your father."

As Mom stepped outside, Hank turned to me. "I'll be around to help. Sorry I couldn't do more before, but now that your dad . . ." He scratched his neck. "Once you're all home, it's different. You need anything, day or night, you call me. You guys are like family."

Hank patted my shoulder and followed Mom out the door. I turned to the living room as Dad stepped inside from the deck. His smile was too wide, like he was afraid to stop.

"All right, boys. Last night together for a while. Let's make it count."

Our night was epic: video game battles and wrestling matches and Richie laughing so hard he almost threw up. Eventually, Dad carried Richie to bed, tucked surfboard-style under his arm. He stayed in Richie's room a long time. When he came out, he sat on the couch next to me.

"So, B-Man. We need to have one more talk. You're a teenager now . . ."

Some conversations are only meant for a guy and his dad. Especially conversations about your body. Thirty seconds in, my ears were hot enough to pop popcorn.

But it wasn't as horrible as I expected. Dad didn't lecture me. He told jokes and made me laugh. I fumbled through a few questions. I even fought past the tingling in my cheeks and told him what Ezra told me.

Dad asked what I knew he'd ask. "Do you feel the same way about him?"

This conversation would have been easier with Mom. It would have been a month ago, anyway. But as Dad leaned on one elbow, waiting, I didn't tense up like I used to.

"I don't know. Being with Ezra makes me happy. I like that he likes me. But I'm not sure if it's . . . more. I guess I don't know who I like yet. Is that normal?"

Dad stretched. "Know what, B-Man? You've heard enough advice from me. You'll figure it out when you're ready to figure it out. And whatever you decide is OK with me."

That wasn't one of Dad's usual answers. He smiled, and it made me feel lighter.

Dad wasn't perfect, not by a long shot, but he was trying in all the ways he knew how.

We were beginning to understand each other, just as he was leaving me.

He patted my knee. "We should get you to bed."

"I'm going to sleep in my room."

"You sure?"

I wasn't sure at all. But I would be home for good in two nights, and I couldn't crawl in with Mom every night. *I can do this*, I told myself. *It's only night.*

I prepared for a struggle, but as I lay in bed, with my face still warm from a day full of sun and my family's laughter echoing in my ears, only the good moments came back as I fell asleep.

In the morning, Hank returned with Dad's lawyer, a man named Jason Beals. Mr. Beals explained that once Dad turned himself in, the police would probably hold him until his first court appearance early in the week. Dad would plead guilty. They were trying to fast-track the process rather than drag it out. Dad said Mr. Beals would drive him to the police station, while Hank took Richie and me back to the Clellands'.

"No way," I said. "I'm going with you."

Dad's forehead scrunched. "Brian—"

"I'm not letting you go alone."

The adults fell quiet.

"OK," Dad said. "If you insist."

I thought Richie might insist too, but he didn't. He stared at the kitchen table, in his rarest state: silent. Dad ruffled his hair. Richie buried his face in his arms and burst into tears.

I couldn't watch. I was already teetering on the edge. I waited on the front step until Dad and Mr. Beals emerged from the house. We drove down Gottingen Street in silence.

My heart raced as we climbed the steps of the police station. I couldn't panic, not now. I reached for Dad's hand. He glanced at me in surprise, but he didn't say anything. He held on.

Sergeant States was waiting in the brick-lined foyer with a young-looking officer in uniform. "Mr. Day," he said. "Nice to meet you in person."

"Wish I could say the same," Dad joked weakly. He turned to me. "I got it from here, B-Man. This is where we say goodbye, for now."

I hugged him tight. "I love you, Dad."

He squeezed me back. "I love you too, Brian."

This was all I wanted: for Sergeant States to see my dad was more than his mistakes.

Sergeant States told the other officer to take Dad inside. He turned to me. "Where do you need to go? Can I give you a ride someplace?"

Dad stared at us. I nodded. Dad hesitated, but he nodded back.

I waved to him one last time and bit my lip as I walked out of the police station. I tried not to think about when and where I might see him next.

"Am I taking you to the Clellands'?" Sergeant States asked after I climbed into his car.

"Yeah. Gabe told me you kind of convinced Mrs. Clelland to take us in, so . . . thank you. I appreciate it."

"Didn't take much convincing." He smiled. "I'm just glad I don't have to keep chasing you all over town."

I managed a tiny grin back. I didn't say anything else until we pulled into the Clellands' driveway. "Thanks for the ride. Remember, my dad's not a lost cause. I need him back."

He stuck out his hand. "I don't believe in lost causes. Take care, Brian."

I shook his hand.

Mrs. Clelland told me Hank had taken Richie out for breakfast, and Gabe was with friends. She made us tea and we sat at the table. I stirred a spoonful of honey into my tea and watched the brown liquid swirl in the mug.

"I have a favor to ask," I said. "If you're not busy. On Thursday after school."

"Your appointment?"

I nodded without looking up. "Mom doesn't drive, and I don't want Kate to take me. I could take the bus—"

"I'd be happy to take you, Brian."

"Thanks. I'm nervous," I admitted. "It turns out I don't like hospitals."

Mrs. Clelland smiled, though she looked sad. "I'm not sure anyone likes hospitals."

She sipped her tea. "Before I forget, I have something for you." She slipped down the hall and returned with a stack of books. "Don't worry. These aren't homework, I promise. Lana asked me to ship her some things, and as I was going through, I found some books she loved at your age. I thought you might enjoy them."

I looked through the pile. I'd already read two of the five, but the others looked interesting. "Thanks. I'll get them back to you."

"No rush. You can always drop them by over the summer." She paused. "I hope you'll visit sometimes. I'm going to miss having you here."

I blinked. "I'm going to miss it here too."

Mrs. Clelland patted my hand. My throat was too heavy to say anything else. I flipped through one of the books as we sat at the table, drinking tea together. And it was enough.

34. THE HARDEST PART

EZRA

If there was ever a weekend I needed to be around friends and stay out of my own head, this was it. But Ty had a tournament, Kevan had relatives visiting, and I couldn't even call Nat because she was at a conference on how to organize and save the world. (She would have been tight with Ms. Virth.) I was almost desperate enough to join Dad at a charity golf tournament, except golf took four hours. Nothing as dull as golf should take four hours.

I kept worrying Brian would rethink Friday night and decide it was too awkward to stay friends. But I couldn't bother him with questions like you don't hate me right? He had enough to deal with.

I started and deleted a dozen texts to Colby. Finally I sent this: Can we talk? Soon? It's important.

Then I did whatever I could to distract myself. I played guitar. I binge-watched a high school mystery series where the plot was ridiculous but the sidekick guy was cute.

Colby never replied.

On Sunday morning, I waited till a reasonable hour

and walked to his house. If our friendship was over, we were going to end it face-to-face. My fingers hammered a riff on my thigh as I rang the doorbell. I was halfway into chickening out when the door opened.

Mrs. Newcombe's eyes lit up. "Ezra! It's been ages." Her smile tightened into a grimace. "I think Colby's still asleep. I haven't heard a peep from those boys yet."

"That's OK, Mrs. Newcombe. I'll make it quick. It's important." I slipped inside before I could back out of this half-cooked idea. She gave me a bewildered look, but she didn't stop me.

Colby's mom was an interior designer, so their house always looked catalog perfect. Colby's room was the exception. I knocked once and opened the door to familiar chaos: clothes everywhere, skateboard against a wall, Skittles wrappers and energy-drink cans scattered on the dresser. He thought the mess helped keep his mom out.

Colby grunted and stretched. His covers slipped past his bare shoulders. I remembered how cute he was when he first woke up, moving in slow motion with his voice all raspy and his hair a wild thicket of sunshine.

It's cruel how feelings you don't want can come rushing back at the worst possible time.

He rubbed his eyes. "Ezra? What are you doing here?"

"We need to talk . . ." I trailed off as a pile on the floor shifted. A head poked out from a sleeping bag.

When Colby's mom said "*those boys,*" I assumed she was including Jackson down the hall. Nope. She meant Victor.

He yawned and staggered to his feet. "I guess that's my cue to go pee." I looked away as he brushed past. He wasn't wearing a shirt either. If this was a terrible time to have *certain feelings* for Colby, it was a worse time to discover Victor had perfect abs.

He was comfortable enough in Colby's house to walk around shirtless. I guess he'd slept over more than I had lately.

Two steps down the hall, he looked back and nodded at me. "Nice job DJing at Ty's. You're pretty talented when it comes to music." Then he disappeared into the bathroom.

Did Victor just compliment me? He seemed sincere. I had no idea how to figure him out.

"What is your *deal*, bro?" Colby's *wide awake and annoyed* tone brought me back to earth. He'd sat up in bed, blankets bunched around his waist.

"My deal is you're avoiding me," I said. "And you're acting like an—"

"We were out. My phone died." He cut me off without a hint of apology. I started to respond, but he kept going. "Jackson's at Victor's house. You know how much Jackson sucks, right? Victor's brothers are worse. Together they're, like, Evil Voltron. So Victor stays over here." His eyes narrowed. "Are you happy now?"

"That's it?" I said. "You and Victor hang out to avoid your brothers?"

Colby hesitated. He smoothed his bed head. "He saved me from flunking math and science," he mumbled.

I frowned. "You said Jemma helped you."

"Well, yeah, but I could only focus so much with Jemma. Victor *actually* helped me." Colby stared at me. "Victor's smart. He's a good tutor, and a good friend. He never makes me feel dumb. Or like I'm a bad person because I'm not perfect or whatever."

His expression lodged like a dart in my stomach.

"Wait, *what?* What's that supposed to mean?"

Colby folded his arms. "You and Ty and Kevan are good at everything and super nice and . . . you judge me sometimes. It's annoying."

My body flushed with heat. "I don't *judge* you, Colby. I just wish you wouldn't . . ." I sighed. "When you make fun of Brian, or make jokes about my skin color—"

"Oh, come on," he interrupted. "You know I'm only—"

"Teasing, right? But that's not how it feels to me. Especially . . ." I took a deep breath, straightened my glasses, and jumped right to the hardest part. "Your jokes about things being 'gay' hurt the most, because I'm gay. And I've been afraid to tell you."

Colby's eyes widened.

I swallowed and kept going. "I have a crush on Brian. I don't think he feels the same way, but—this is who I am, Colby. I came here to tell you the truth, and I hope you can be cool with that. And if you'd rather hang around Jemma and Victor, that's fine. Honestly. I just don't want things to be weird and tense anymore. It sucks."

Ugh. Wrap it up before the tears start. "Anyway, I'll stop bugging you now. Text me whenever, if you want. You know how to find me."

I turned to race out of there before I fell apart.

But Victor was in the doorway.

He'd heard everything.

Great. Perfect. Awesome.

I put my head down and tried to leave. He stood in my way.

"I won't say anything."

I looked up. "What?"

Victor leaned against the door frame. "That look you gave me. You're afraid I'll tell people. Or make fun of you. Or whatever. But I won't."

I'd never been so close to Victor. Even from two feet away he was difficult to read, and I suspected he liked it that way. But I couldn't sense any mocking in his eyes, nothing to make me doubt he was serious.

Colby cleared his throat. "Uh, same, obviously. I won't say anything, bro. And, you know, be yourself." He coughed. "Not like you can help it, right?"

I bit back a sigh. That was a long way from Kevan and Ty making up code words to help me talk about boys, but at least it wasn't *get lost forever, creep*.

Except he'd pulled his blanket up to his armpits.

Colby went shirtless all the time. Swimming, sleep-overs, the skate park, wherever. He wasn't the least bit shy, even around girls. But suddenly he was modest now that he knew I was gay.

"Right," I whispered as my throat locked up. "See you at school."

I made it home before I started to cry. I felt better afterward, like the messy end of a stomach bug when all the grossness is finally purged. I was losing something with Colby, and it would sting for a while, but I'd gained something else. I didn't have to be so cautious around my friends anymore. I didn't have to hide.

I was so drained that I fell asleep. I woke at noon to a text thread from Kevan.

Perry Molecular in gr 8 french immersion has a rainbow pin on his backpack. Definite mango potential

*Molyneux ha autocorrect. But Perry Molecular would be a wicked superhero name

If you're into older guys

Older french guys

Bet he'd help you learn "french" lolololol

I'll run some intel on him, find out if he's cool

I'll be screening all potential mangoes btw. Not letting you date any skeezeballs

I wrote him back. Slow your roll K. But I'm glad you're so into this

I really am lol. My chances with girls improve if you're using your dreamy rock star hotness on boys

You're the best Kev

Kevan and Ty were my people. I knew that now. They'd stepped up when I showed them who I really was.

But I needed other people too. So I sent another text, to Brittany.

Hey maybe this is weird but do you have a minute to give advice to a seventh grader?

She replied in thirty seconds. You noticed I live to boss boys around, right? What's up?

I came out to my friends this weekend

Brittany didn't text back. She called. "How'd it go? Are you all right?"

"Yeah. Sort of."

"Just sort of?" She paused. "My family's at the movies and Gabe's off sportsing. I have a feeling you'd make the perfect kitchen partner for homemade pizza, loud music, and air guitar."

I smiled. "That sounds perfect."

35. THROAT-PUNCH YOUR SADNESS

BRIAN

Monday was the Mondayest Monday in the history of Mondays.

Last week of school before summer vacation. My suspension was over, so I had to go back to class. I figured Victor wouldn't mess with me, but I still expected whispers and people hoping for a scene.

In a few hours, Dad was making his first court appearance. I half wanted to go, but Mr. Beals said it would be a lot of waiting for a plea that would barely take a minute. Mrs. Clelland gently suggested it might not be good for me. Maybe she was right.

After school, I was going home. To my house. With Mom.

This was the first day of Life Part II.

I didn't feel ready. I wasn't sure Mom was ready. She seemed really healthy on Saturday, but I didn't think I'd ever be able to wipe the morning of my birthday from my mind. Would changing her meds help? How would she cope without Dad? What would happen next time she had a bad day?

The thing about surviving the end of the world is you still have to crawl out of the rubble and learn how to rebuild.

I pulled up the covers in the yellow bedroom. I had slept on my own without nightmares or panic attacks. That was accomplishment enough for Day 1.

Ten minutes after I should have been eating breakfast, Gabe barged in.

"Getting up anytime soon?"

I burrowed in the bed. "No, actually."

He flopped beside me. "Not feeling today, huh?"

I shook my head.

"You want to wallow here being all mopey and whatnot."

I shrugged.

"I get it," Gabe said. "But sometimes wallowing is unacceptable. Sometimes you need to punch your sadness in the throat."

"Is that your official life advice? Punch sadness in the throat?"

"Yes. I'm going to write a book for guys like us. You're the words guy, so you can help me. I'm going to call it *When Life Serves You a Turd Sandwich.* Don't laugh. I'm serious."

I didn't want to laugh, but I couldn't help smiling.

"All the chapters will have super-intense titles," Gabe continued. "Throat-Punch Your Sadness. Choke-Slam Your Anger."

"Kick Your Anxiety in the Junk," I added.

"That's the spirit." He reached across my chest. "Nipple-Twist Your Fears."

"Ow!" I shoved him away. "All right, already. I'll get up if you'll leave me alone."

"See? My advice works. Sometimes you have to pretend you're in a cage match with your feelings." He stood up. "We're going camping this summer. You, me, Richie, and Ezra if he wants to come. It will be a perfect ten on the scale of awesomeness. That is a Gabe Clelland Guarantee."

I rubbed my sore nipple. "Saturday was a perfect ten. Yesterday hurt like hell."

Gabe nodded. "That's how it goes sometimes. But the *hurts like hell* days remind you how sweet the perfect tens can be. You and me are alive, and it's our job to live big while we can."

"You and I."

"What?"

"You and I are alive, not you and me. Grammar."

"You're the biggest nerd, you know that? No wonder Mom loves you. Get up already." He gave me a playful shove and ran out of the room.

I sat up. I could do this. Maybe.

When Mrs. Clelland stopped to drop Richie off at school, I put an arm around him and told him I loved him. He looked at me sideways like I'd said I was joining an expedition to Mars. He poked my ribs.

"Have a good day, Bri," he said, which meant *I love you too.*

Mrs. Clelland let me out at Ezra's. He was waiting outside, alone. He walked to the curb slowly with his arms folded across his belly.

"Hey," he said.

"Hey," I said. "How was your weekend?"

"Uh . . ." Ezra adjusted his glasses. "I told the guys I'm gay, so that was interesting."

"Oh!" I took a step closer to him. "I hope it went OK?"

Ezra nodded. "Kevan and Ty have been great. Colby was . . . not terrible. Not great, but it could've been worse, I guess."

He stared at his shoes. I didn't know what to say, so I put a hand on his shoulder.

"Thanks," he said quietly. "But what about you? How'd it go with your dad?"

"It was . . . a lot. Mostly good."

Ezra gave me his look that meant *You can tell me, I'm here for you.* I knew that look now. I liked it. I told him about the beach, and Dad going to jail.

"That must have been hard," he said.

"Yeah." I swallowed. "I'm going to miss him a lot. And I'm scared of what comes next."

Ezra inched closer. "Would it be weird if I hugged you?"

"I'd like that," I said. "You're not weird, Ezra. Well, you're a little weird." I grinned. "But I'm a Super Awkward Weirdo, so we make a good team."

His eyes lit up. He put on a serious face and stuck out his hand. "Indeed. Let us form an Alliance of Weirdos."

"I concur." We shook hands, and he pulled me into a hug, both of us laughing.

"I want Brian," Ty declared on the basketball court at lunch. "He's not a ball hog like y'all are."

Andre tucked the ball under his arm and scoffed. "Look who's talking."

"Exactly. B knows how to keep me fed." Ty held up a fist in my direction. After an awkward beat, he laughed. "You going to leave me hanging?"

"Right. Sorry." My face reddened as I bumped his knuckles.

He nodded. "Let's do this, B. You, me, and Ezra. Sizzle Squad represent."

We were a squad now? I couldn't help smiling.

We played to fifteen, with regular baskets worth one point and shots behind the three-point line worth two. The great thing about basketball is nothing else matters on the court. No one thought about how Ty's father was an accountant and Ezra's was an orthodontist and mine was going to jail. Basketball was basketball. I didn't have to say more than two words at a time. Ty and Andre tossed friendly trash talk back and forth. I didn't think about Mom coming home, or how weird it would be to visit Dad. I just played.

I set Ty up for a couple baskets, earning another fist

bump. After a while, Jayden assumed I was going to pass and slacked off me, so I shot. Swish.

Next time I had the ball, he rushed out. I faked, took one sideways dribble as he flew past me, and shot again. Bank swish.

"Sizzle sauce, baby," Ezra yelled.

"Man, guard him," Andre grumbled at Jayden.

Lunch was almost over and we were tied at thirteen when Ezra collected a loose ball and passed to me behind the arc. Jayden scrambled to cover, but I didn't hesitate. I shot my shot.

As soon as it left my hand, I knew it was good. Sometimes you know.

In a second, the ball would drop through the net with a crisp snap of mesh and we would win, 15–13. Ty would whoop and slap me on the back. Ezra would give me a high five. We'd head back to class, sweaty and satisfied. After school, I'd walk to my own house, where Mom and Richie and Hank would be waiting. The Clellands said they'd bring dinner. In the evening, when I was alone in my room, I'd put on Ezra's playlist, and I'd text or call him if I wanted to talk.

But all of that was in the future. For now, the universe paused as the ball flew from my hand, spinning on a smooth arc, a planet in perfect orbit. I watched it fall.

ACKNOWLEDGMENTS

A long time ago, a shy kid named Brian Day showed up in my imagination and wouldn't leave. It took years, dozens of drafts, and plenty of help to figure out how to do his story justice. A huge thank-you to my agent, Christa Heschke, and her assistant, Daniele Hunter, for their passion for this story and guidance in making this a better book. I'm fortunate to have you both on my team.

My gratitude to everyone at Abrams Kids for believing in Brian and Ezra. Thanks to Alexander Daibes and Jenn Jimenez; Shasta Clinch, Regina Castillo, and Margo Winton Parodi for their attention to detail; Marcie Lawrence for making the book look so good; and Nick Blanchard for the fantastic cover. Thanks to the marketing and publicity teams for all their hard work. Special thanks to my editor, Emily Daluga, for her enthusiasm and keen insight in taking this book to another level. You really brought the sizzle sauce!

Rebecca Petruck has been an incredible support, on this project and on the roller coaster that is writing and publishing in general. I appreciate you so much.

I was lucky enough to be part of the Pitch Wars class of 2018, and even luckier to be mentored by Eric Bell, who guided me through multiple revisions with great advice and even better humor.

Thanks to Brenda Drake, Kellye Garrett, and the whole Pitch Wars team for the incredible work you do. Thanks to fellow mentees W. T. Brown, Emily Howard, and Jeanne Becijos for reading drafts and offering feedback. I'm tremendously grateful to Christiana Doucette, Dan Berberich, Travis Galloway, and Elizabeth Van Tassel for helping me sharpen this story along the way. I'm rooting for all of you.

I can't say enough about the Slackers crew: Alexis, Eagan, Elvin, Jacki, Jessica, Leslie, Lyssa, Marisa, Mary, Meg, Meryl, Nanci, Rachel, Rochelle, Rosie, Rowyn, Ruby, and Susan. Thanks for so many things: feedback and accountability; expert advice; shared celebrations and commiserations; GIF skills; impassioned debates over mayo, horses, and other topics I won't mention in the acknowledgments of a middle grade book; and especially the laughs. I'm so glad we found each other.

My thanks to Isaac Munday for graciously reading and providing insights into the junior high experience. Bigger and better things await you!

Thanks to my friends in the Generous Space and DCC communities for being a safe place to keep figuring things out, a process than never seems to stop.

Shout-out to Gordon Korman—like plenty of Canadian kids, I read and reread your books voraciously and was inspired enough to think, *If he could write a book when he was twelve, maybe I can too.* Took me longer, but here I am.

Love to my parents, especially my mom, who also believed that twelve-year-old me could be an author, and always encouraged me to keep at it.

To my beloved Shawna, my sympathies for discovering late in the game that you were marrying a writer, and my endless thanks for your encouragement, support, and sense of adventure. I definitely couldn't have done any of this without you.

And to April, Oscar, Maliah, and Gideon: You're the best. I probably owe you credit for inspiring most of the funniest lines in this book. But I've also spent a fortune feeding you, so let's call it even.

Read on for a look
at Chad Lucas's
new story, about learning
to face and accept your fears
—before it's too late . . .

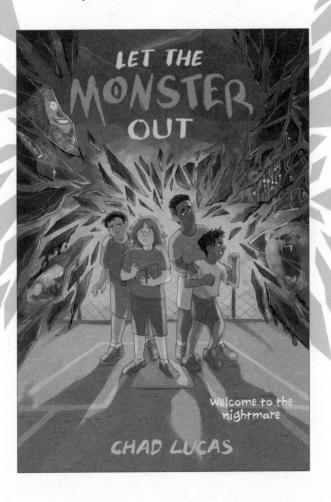

PROLOGUE
The Crows Laughed

Branches lashed Wade Elliott's face as he hurtled through the forest. Thick clouds hid the moon. He'd already lost his bearings in the dark, but he didn't slow down. He skidded down a bank, scrambled to his feet, and kept moving. He had to get as far as possible from that room. The room he'd helped build.

No. *No.* He was only trying to fix things, to help people. But they'd turned it upside down.

Pain stabbed his side. His throat burned with the metallic taste of blood. He fell at the base of a pine tree, panting.

Gradually, his pulse stopped pounding in his ears. He heard the trickle of a brook, the rustle of wind tickling the treetops. He rested his head against the tree trunk. He could hear, taste, touch. This was the real world.

Exhaustion set in, but when his eyelids drooped, the things he'd seen in that room came back.

No. He had escaped. He had to fight it. He couldn't let—

A crow's caw stirred him. He gathered his bearings: He was outdoors, in a forest, under a misty gray sky at the break of dawn. He shivered. Had he slept? Was this real?

He stood and paced, shaking stiffness from his limbs. He had to know for sure he was here—and that *here* wasn't all in his head. Balling his fist, he punched the trunk of the pine. His knuckles split and pain pulsed through his hand.

It hurt. He felt it. He smiled.

He punched the tree again. Again. Again. He stepped back and stared at his hand. The flesh swelled and reddened. He savored the steady ache. This had to be real. He threw back his head and laughed and laughed.

The crows laughed too.

Wade looked up. A dozen of them sat in the trees, mocking him.

"No!" he shouted at the birds. "You can't do that! Shut up!"

"Ha ha ha," they cackled. "Isn't this fun? Let's all go into town and watch it burn."

"Shut up!" he shrieked.

"Come with us, Wade. It's such a fun game. A murder of crows, a-murdering we go."

They rose from the branches and circled the clearing, above his head. *A murder of crows, a-murdering we go.* Soon there were two dozen, forty, fifty, a hundred. The sky darkened under a vortex of swirling black birds.

Wade wept. It wasn't over. It would never be over. Not for him.

He brought his aching, trembling fingers to the inside pocket of his jacket. Good. His journal was still there. He had to deliver it, show them the proof, before everyone saw the things he'd seen. If that happened, it would be too late.

So he ran.

1.
TRYING

Bones Malone didn't punch Tony Spezio in the face.

Not after he found Tony picking on his little brothers. Not even after he told Tony to knock it off, and Tony responded by saying something unrepeatably gross about his mother.

Sure, he did shove Tony against the basement wall and yell, "Talk about my mom again and I will *end you*." But that was better than throwing fists, right?

He was trying. That counted for something, right?

Not in Eileen Spezio's book. She thumped downstairs just in time to hear the *end you* part and blamed everything on Bones, as usual.

"You will not behave like a thug in my home!" she screeched.

Bones saw red. A white lady calling him a thug was not OK, but he held his tongue. Well, almost.

"Teach your kid some manners, before he gets himself beat," he shot back.

Mrs. Spezio's eyes bulged and spit gathered at the corners of her mouth as she lost her mind. Tony smirked over her shoulder the whole time, while heat built in Bones's chest. He couldn't stop picturing how satisfying it would feel to shove past Mrs. Spezio and knock that smug grin off Tony's extremely punchable face.

But he didn't. Not this time. He was trying, for his mom's sake.

But that didn't count in her book either. She got an earful from Eileen when she picked up the boys after work. Bones could hear every word with his ear to the door of the spare room where Mrs. Spezio had banished all three Malone boys, even though Raury and Dillon hadn't done anything wrong.

"I know you're new in town, and I was happy to open my home to your boys, but that oldest of yours is so *disrespectful,* so *aggressive* . . ."

Bones couldn't hear his mom's reply, but he recognized its tone: weary. It wasn't the first time she'd apologized on his behalf. When she opened the bedroom door, all she said was, "Let's go." The boys hurried to catch up as she marched out of the Spezios' house and down the sidewalk, each step radiating fury.

"Is the car still broken?" Dillon asked.

"Yep." She practically hurled the word to the sidewalk.

"Bones was only—"

"We are *not* discussing this now."

She met Bones's eyes for half a second. "If I have to give that woman a raise to let you stay," she murmured, "you best believe it's coming from your allowance."

Bones waited as long as he could stand it. He made his brothers wash up and set the table before he approached his mother. She didn't lift her eyes from the pot of spaghetti boiling on the stove, but her shoulders rose.

"Not now, Quentin."

Ugh. He hated his real name. She usually reserved it for formal situations, like the first time they met with a lawyer. When she used it at home, it was a warning.

He swallowed all the things he wanted to say: He was only defending Raury, *again*; the Spezios had been awful since day one; he'd be thirteen in September and he was perfectly capable of watching his brothers, so she should stop paying a useless babysitter anyway.

All of it was true, but he held his tongue. Adults weren't always ready for the truth.

"I only want to say sorry," he said instead. "No excuses. But you won't make me stay home tonight, will you?"

She froze. Bones realized she'd forgotten he had a baseball game. He was surprised how much that stung.

"You definitely have a punishment coming," she said. "Maybe if you missed a game, you'd actually get the message."

"Mom, please! It's my night to pitch. Everyone's counting on me. Ground me, take away my phone, make me sleep in the shed if you want. Just let me have baseball."

His mother gasped. "Quentin Malone."

Two Quentins in one conversation was bad news. He forced a fake laugh. "I was joking about the shed."

"Not funny." She turned back toward the stove. "Go to your game. But I want you home straight after. You are *not* off the hook."

"Thank you!" Bones paused. "You're not coming?"

His mother loved baseball. She was the one who taught him how to throw a slider. They watched Blue Jays games together, and she yelled at the TV when Toronto's manager made bad decisions. She'd only missed one of Bones's games last year, when Dillon had to go to the walk-in clinic with a raisin stuck in his nose.

She exhaled. "Not tonight. I'm still waiting for the mechanic to call about the car. And I just don't have the energy."

"Oh. OK." He tried to sound like it was no big deal that she was staying home.

She carried the pot of boiled spaghetti to the sink. "Watch your release point. Remember, you were missing high last weekend because you were letting the ball go too early."

"Right. Thanks."

He lingered in the doorway. She still wouldn't look at him.

Even as he opened his mouth, he knew he should accept the small victory and walk away.

"I didn't even hit him," he muttered.

As she drained the hot water from the pasta into the sink, his mom released the kind of sigh only a mother can make, a sustained breath declaring, *Boy, you don't even know.* From Bones's viewpoint, the cloud of steam rising toward the ceiling appeared to pour directly from his mom's head.

"You shoved him into a wall, Bones. You threatened him."

"Threatened?" Bones scoffed. "I'm half his size." Tony was three years older, a head taller, broad across the chest where

Bones was still, well, bones. He had a sacred rule about never fighting anyone smaller. But he was short for his age, so that left lots of leeway.

His mother sighed again. "Like that has ever stopped you. We've only been here for two months, and I feel like I've apologized to half the parents in town."

That was a *huge* exaggeration. He'd only been in two real fights in Langille—Tony didn't count—and Bones hadn't started either one. He also had a rule about not starting fights. They just found him, the way some people attracted mosquitoes. Or lightning.

His first fight after the move was a matter of establishing order. He was new, he was small, and this big kid cornered him after gym and said, *"I forgot my lunch money. You need to make a donation."* Bones suggested something he could eat instead, and the kid pushed Bones into the lockers. Two quick jabs made it clear Bones Malone was not bully fodder.

The second fight, he was cutting across the soccer field when he saw a group of ninth graders yelling crude stuff at a girl. He told them to grow up and leave her alone, they told him to get lost, and things escalated. OK, he might have thrown the first punch, and he'd wound up with a black eye and a split lip to show for it. But that hardly made him the bad guy, right?

He didn't rehash this with his mother, though. Open that door and she would bring up other fights before the move. Once she started on the brawl with the Volkering brothers, he was doomed.

"It wasn't a fight," he said. "Only one little shove. And Tony's the worst. I should get credit for not punching him already!"

His mom's eyes narrowed. "You think this is funny?"

"Mom—"

"When are you going to learn? I swear, if you don't come to your senses and control that temper, you'll end up—"

She stopped.

"End up like what?" Bones asked, his voice suddenly husky.

"Never mind."

"You were going to say—"

"You don't know what I was going to say." She looked away. "Call your brothers for dinner. You need to get moving if you're going to make your game."

He left the kitchen without another word.

Read on in

LET THE
MONSTER
OUT

CHAD LUCAS has been in love with words since he attempted his first novel on a typewriter in the sixth grade. He has worked as a newspaper reporter, communications advisor, freelance writer, part-time journalism instructor, and parenting columnist. Chad's debut novel, *Thanks a Lot, Universe*, was a Junior Library Guild Selection, received two starred reviews, including one from *Kirkus Reviews*, who called it "tenderhearted and bold." A proud descendant of the historic African Nova Scotian community of Lucasville, he lives with his family near Halifax, Nova Scotia. He enjoys coaching basketball and is rarely far from a cup of tea.